"RAW YOUTH"

by Tim O'Neil

First printing, 2007
http://www.lulu.com

Copyright © 2007 Tim O'Neil

All characters and situations are fictional. Any similarities to persons living or dead are entirely coincidental.

ISBN 978-0-6151-7794-6

You know who.

1

I was born dead, dead and dying as I fell from the sack of the womb dripping filth.

The doctor put me down and tried to kill me but my mother stopped him, reaching up from the stirrups and clawing at the doctor's face as he held the anesthesia mask over my mouth. Whatever red madness possessed him was gone in a moment and his rage subsided. I was alive.

When I was three I was gripped by a terrible fever, pulled across the world and near to death's door by an incipient grief of future tragedies. I lay at my mother's side for four days while my eyes remained cold and hot, focused on phantoms that lay beyond my years. After I awoke from this delirium my mother would forever regard me as a stranger.

I was in the living room when the towers fell. I remember seeing the smoke and ashes, thinking to myself that nothing would ever be the same again. Somehow I knew in my heart that what was happening across the world was just a taste, just a foreshadowing of something big and dangerous, something that would rise up and destroy us all. I wanted to know, I wanted to understand what it was, I needed to know that it wasn't just me, that it wasn't my fault. I don't think I've ever been able to satisfy myself on this point. I don't think I've ever been quite comfortable with myself since.

My mother came up behind me and together we watched the footage on the television screen as it unfolded. The TV was on mute and the only sound we heard was the dog barking outside. She set her hand on my shoulder and for a moment we were apart, together.

2

As a child I remember running. It seemed as if the terrain was made of sticky taffy and every movement was caught on the trees or the streets or the grass. I couldn't move without trapping myself, suffocating at the heart of the world.

I ran through the fields and valleys of an idyllic childhood, pages flipped across the lens of my memory. I can't see the details because the edges are blurry and the light is soft and bleeds through the cracks, but I was young and alive.

There were abandoned industrial pipes set down in a lot near our home. I pushed through the long tubes like a worm, struggling and straining to reach the light. There was fear, naked crazy fear and a nascent claustrophobia. There were no words for these things in my mind but I had known dread long before I understood restraint.

The mountain vales were green and the waters that trickled across the rounded algae-green rocks were quiet and peaceful. It was a simple and unaffected childhood in many respects, marked in part by my clean determination to learn and to understand, a determination that marked me beyond my years.

But aside from these scattered scenes of idyllic youth, the dominant note sounding through my childhood was panic, a sheer and vertiginous lust for stability and control that belied my age. Ever since the fever had taken me at such an early date I had been unable to dream. As I slept I drowned in sweat, soaking my sheets, starting bolt upright and sober as the clock struck three throughout an empty house. There was, from very early in my perceptions, an acknowledgment that something was wrong with me. Something was missing and I had no idea what it was.

So I reached further into solitude and parsed my own way through the mysteries of existence. The primal fears were unassailable, but I could at least try to come to grips with the daily agonies. The spectral images of my fever had been seared onto my brain, and I had to be ready in case they ever returned.

After graduating college I returned home and resumed tenancy under my mother's roof. It was time for the wedding preparations to begin. My wedding to Connie had been in the stages of perpetual planning for years, since before college. I entered into the theoretical compact with great trepidation and an inhuman dread. I had simply erred on the side of caution, unwilling to hurt Constance and, as a result, unable to make my feelings known at any juncture.

So we had left for college and I placed the matter on the back burner. It made perfect sense to imagine that in the course of four years the engagement would be forgotten and nullified by the passage of time. How often do these things last? What are the statistics?

Of course I lacked the strength of convictions necessary to break the engagement myself. Constance dutifully sent letters on a weekly basis, letters I rarely read. Constance visited my school and made the acquaintance of my friends and peers – they all commented on how lucky I was to have found such a beautiful and intelligent companion.

I couldn't tell them, of course, how much I truly loathed her - and how much I loathe her still, if the truth be told. My animosity had been precipitated by nothing specific she had ever done or not done, but simply by virtue of her copious virtuosity. She was very beautiful - intelligent and compassionate. She thought I was joking when I told her how much I wanted to kill her, to do anything necessary to take her out of my life and absolve myself of this persistent responsibility. She would laugh and giggle and hug me, pulling me closer to her in the bed.

In light of this approaching cataclysm the final months of school took the character of a long, anxious wait for the governor's repreive. So I took to walking the campus in the middle of the night, navigating by the light of the moon. Sometimes I carried an air rifle under my coat. There were a lot of rats in the neighborhood of the college and I enjoyed trying to kill them – but, in my defense I will also say that I was a horrible shot and they usually got away.

One night - it would have been a few months distant of graduation - as I was stalking through the darkness on the periphery of the Life Sciences building I overheard a whispered conversation around the corner of a concrete abutment. There were two figures standing in the shadows across the stairway.

The first of the shadows was taller and seemed to be angry at the second shadow. They were arguing and were having a hard time keeping their voices down – words echoed swiftly through the crannies of the hollow concrete architecture.

"Jean's got these," were the first words I heard from the taller shadow.

"I don't care what Jean has, Axel asked for these," the second retorted.

"Jean's got these," the first shadow repeated. "And you don't seem to understand that Jean doesn't want any more of these. Jean is very unhappy with these."

"Yeah, well, you tell Jean its not my fault, she needs to talk to Axel – or better yet, tell her to talk to Carter and see how she handles that."

The first man stiffened visibly. I could see how angry he was even from the safe distance of my dark corner.

"Jean is not going to talk to Carter. Ever. You'd be good to think twice before you speak like that. You could get yourself killed. That name does not belong on your lips."

"Shut up," the second shadow said. "You just shut the fuck up, no one's gonna get killed."

"Wait a minute," the first shadow stopped and put his hand on the second shadows arm to still him. "I think I heard something."

"What? Where?"

I froze in my tracks and tried my level best to turn invisible. I had no idea what was happening but I knew that I wanted no part of it.

There was a moment of tension before I saw what happened next. A policeman stepped from the fog on the opposite end of the square and started yelling at the two shadows standing in front of the Life Sciences building. They turned their heads and in that moment I saw disgust, fear and anger on both of their obscured faces. The cop was already climbing the stairs towards the two men by the time they reached into their coats and pulled out two large handguns. They were firing their weapons at the officer before I had a chance to register what was happening – I saw the policeman fall as the two men fled into the night.

I fled too. I had no idea what had just happened and I had no intention of finding out. However, it was not to be. The night failed to swallow me as assiduously as I had wished. There were sirens and lights everywhere across the campus and I hadn't made it home before the police spotted me skulking through the underbrush.

"What are you doing, boy?" the policeman called out to me.

"Nothing, sir, just going home."

"What the hell are you doing out here at this time of night?"

"Nothing, sir, as I said."

The cop grunted. "Put your hands on the wall," he said. I did so and he began to pat me down.

"What's this?" he said after a moment. He reached into my coat and found my air rifle. "What the hell is this, boy?"

"Its an air rifle, sir."

"Well, so it is . . ." the cop replied, surprised. He fingered the bolt and a handful of BB's fell out of the gun and onto the ground below, landing with a dry flat crack. "I'm not even going to ask why the hell you had this on you at this time of night."

The cop pulled my hands down from the wall and slapped handcuffs around my wrists. They were tight and sharp and I began to feel very claustrophobic. He opened the back door of his cruiser and pushed me inside. He threw my gun on the passenger seat and sat down behind the steering wheel.

There was someone in the back of the cruiser with me. I turned and saw a dark-haired boy, probably my age or a little younger, slumped over unconscious with a little bit of vomit on his shirt. He came awake with a jerk and opened his eyes wide to see me.

"Duuuuuude . . ." he began, slowly and cautiously. A stupid grin spread across his blotched face.

The policeman was quietly talking to his dispatcher on the radio. It occurred to me that I had seen my new companion somewhere before in my life.

"Duuuuuude," he repeated, more forcefully now.

"Do I know you?" I finally asked. It was really

beginning to bug me.

"Shut up," the cop said from the front seat. I gave the officer a mildly forlorn look before my new companion and I settled into our seats, him again blissfully unconscious and myself deliriously unperturbed. I had been through worse in my day, it was merely a matter of not letting the walls get to me.

And so it then occurred to me with the help of my inebriated companion that my generation lacks any sense of purpose or destiny. For the first time in forever the sense of history had been lost. History was in the past, a finite process that had somehow stopped completely in the last decade or so. Everything, or so the assumption went, was going to continue pretty much exactly as it has been for the rest of our natural lives with no real noticeable alterations in the fabric. This is how Francis Fukayama described it, and until that moment I do not believe I truly understood what he meant.

So when the towers fell there was a long fugue, a state of shock that gradually melted into brittle denial.

And I wonder just how much suffering the average person experiences in the course of their lifetime. Has my drunken friend ever had to experience the death of a sibling or a parent, madness or imprisonment, been the victim of a violent crime or a horrible life-threatening illness? I don't know. Somehow as much as I would like to tell myself otherwise I can't seem to decide whether or not that would impart any deeper meaning to the act of being piss-sloppy drunk.

I've been young and it feels like I've been old but at the moment I'm riding in the back of the police cruiser with my drunken friend and the surly cop I feel of a strangely indeterminate age, as if the future and the past had failed to crystallize in that one magic moment, leaving me adrift and alone on the shores of an eternal opaque now. I wished with a sudden and painful wistfulness that I had remembered to bring a blotter of acid with me.

When we reached the police station my friend and I were led through the most intimate corridors of the building until reaching the jail. Our pockets had been emptied and our photos taken and our names recorded and we were ready to be forgotten until the proper authorities could be notified as to the nature of our heinous crimes. I gave my name as Randall McMurphy (I don't believe the duty serganet got the joke), and my drunken friend slurred something incoherent from between his foaming lips. Undoubtedly he would have given them his actual name if he had had the wherewithal to form syllables.

But I was Randall McMurphy, at least in my mind, for the duration of the stay. I had developed the habit of hiding my real identification whenever I left my dorm or, later on, my apartment, on the principle of protecting my anonymity in the event of sudden and violent death.

My drunken companion stumbled the three feet to the hard bunk and passed out immediately. He was in rough shape and looked as if he was going to have a severe hangover in the morning. Periodically he moaned or mumbled something, which would be just barely audible out of the corner of my ear. He was tormented by something, conscious of blind assailants chasing him through his stupor.

To my surprise we shared the cell with the two shadowy figures with whom I had earlier made my hidden acquaintance. In the harsh medicinal glare of the halogen bulb they were immediately recognizable by the shapes of their bodies and the language of their posture, but they seemed strangely shrunken, as if the obfuscating fog of darkness had previously endowed them with a terrible authority that broad daylight - or a reasonable facsimile thereof - could never hope to match.

But they were punks. Punk kids - older than me, but kids nonetheless - with frayed leather jackets, and who looked in over their heads. They looked dreadfully, deeply afraid, morbidly distraught. Possibly high.

The cell was small and dry. There was a slight draft whistling down the hallway, just enough of a breeze to chill the room. There were no shadows.

The bed where my inebriated companion had settled to sleep was little more than a metal plank jutting from a concrete wall. We weren't trusted with bedrolls or pillows, apparently – which made sense, I suppose. Certainly the drunk kid barely noticed.

There's a dream where I'm falling down a dark hole for an indefinite period of time. The air is hot and fetid and damp. I reach out to touch the walls but all I feel is something wet that gives but slightly to my touch – something like a lung or a chest cavity pulled inside-out.

I'm falling through the dark and I can smell something deep and old, something that was born before the stars were lit and something that makes my sleeping body recoil in horror.

Eventually I reach the ground. I don't hit the ground with a great impact, somehow I merely touch the ground and begin to walk, to explore whatever strange underworld in which I've found myself. I'm in a cave and I can see the walls vaguely flickering like the vestigial memory of a flickering pre-digital nickelodeon. I continue walking for what seems like forever, with surging flotsam around my feet, my body borne along by strange faint breezes from further down the tunnels.

I'm lost and I can't seem to see anything but the ground immediately in front of me. Its dark and the waters are rising and I am slowly aware of noises, loud and tremendous, filling the air and echoing through the living corridors of the maze.

Sometimes when I'm lying in the hazy netherworld between sleeping and awakening I imagine that I'm going to be wandering through hell for the rest of my life. I'm choking on shit and I try to move my arms to grasp at the walls but I'm asleep and I can't move, I'm paralyzed and my limbs only respond in sharp imprecise jerks.

We were in the cell for the better part of an hour before the violence began.

3

When I was twelve I spent a month in a mental hospital. I try not to remember much about what actually happened during that month – lots of jigsaw puzzles and television. We were forced to participate in long nature walks through the surrounding wilderness. There was also therapy and there were tests but mostly, in between torture sessions, I remember being very, very bored.

I learned very quickly not to talk about those things I feared. People think you're crazy when you start talking about red walls and purple nightmares – its best to avoid such discussions altogether.

It was an old building, I remember that, a very nice institution set on a sloping green estate in a quiet rural town many miles from the city. There was well-maintained but rarely-used playground equipment in the building's front yard. Only the windows betrayed the building's deeper motives: dark and furtive, laced throughout with metal wire to prevent them from shattering when crazy people tried to break them with chairs - which they would try to do in order to escape the intense pain of "treatment".

When my mother sent me to the hospital I think she was relieved. It's not hard to see why. Ever since I had been three she had been afraid of me, casting suspicious glances in my direction every so often as she became increasingly convinced that not only could I see more than she could, but that I saw things which would forever be invisible to her. I also saw things inside her of which she was ignorant.

The painful outbursts decreased in frequency as I grew older. Partly this was due to the growing realization that I had to normalize my behavior to survive unmolested in the mainstream, and partly this was due to the fact that I grew inured to the chaotic and daily betrayal of my five senses. The event that precipitated my first and final institutionalization was my last major episode before puberty, as well as the last major episode I had the weakness to share with the world outside my mind. Also, it should be noted that the medication I was given succeeded in preventing these outbursts as well, but not without extracting a cost.

(I can only imagine the relief my mother felt as I left for college. In the space of eighteen years she had traversed an emotional gamut the likes of which I could never hope to understand – from maternal affection to cold disdain to naked betrayal. For much of my youth she regarded me as a coiled snake held close to her bosom, and she would probably have had more consideration for the snake.

But eventually she softened. Trauma and anguish change a person. I would never say she warmed to me, but perhaps she grew accustomed to the idea that I was eventually going to leave. This allowed her the luxury of feebly attempting to recreate the sensations of her initial maternal affections. I appreciated the attempt, even if I knew it to be specious.)

The walls of the hospital were made of gray bricks, stacked one on top of the other and whitewashed over throughout the long subterranean hallways of facility. The dormitories were made to appear warm and welcoming, with friendly colors on the walls and picture books on the tables, but the hospital was still as uninviting an institution as could be imagined. I remember the gray-white walls and the blue metal doors that swung shut behind the orderlies and doctors with loud swooping thuds. It was harsh and loud because there was so little atmosphere, it seemed as if we were eight miles high and the air was thin and brittle, but we were really underground, deep beneath the surface of the earth.

To my disdain I would later discover that the hallways in my college dormitory were whitewashed gray-brick as well. Only, the atmosphere at school was as far removed from that of a hospital as could be conceived: the air was heavy and jellied, caked around the doors and windows. It was not a new building and the rot and mildew of previous tenants hung in the air like meat on a hook.

Of course it goes without saying that I despised my collegiate peers. Once you've been in the mental hospital and seen the clouds melting around your mother's face you learn the lesson that life is a painful bitter and redundant struggle. You work hard and your soul becomes callused. You fight and you fight against the prevailing winds to gain a footing on what you have no choice but to call your own "achievement".

But you're surrounded by privilege and affectation. Everywhere around you are reminders of just how callow and disproportionate the world your peers inhabit actually is. Had any of them been in the mental hospital? Did they understand what true, profound privation and suffering were? I doubted it.

There's a world that I will never inhabit. The inhabitants of this world believe that art and literature are fashion accessories, and that having fine prints from the Met on your wall and Pablo Neruda on your shelf somehow absolves you of having to struggle. Well, art is powerful for exactly the reasons that these people will never understand.

It's powerful because it can destroy as easily as it can create. It's harder and harder to appreciate beauty the deeper you explore misery. That's why its so important, so vitally intrinsically important that people have their conceptions of beauty and truth, so that we can somehow manage to keep living even when we're seeing three thousand people die on the television in our living room in real time.

If you don't understand this, if you've never suffered, how can you claim any appreciation of beauty? It's callow and selfish and delusional to pretend at depths you cannot fathom.

So I spent a great deal of time in college sitting behind the dorms near the garbage dumpster and chain smoking. I would sit against the fence and read my books in the shadows of the streetlight and pull my jacket closer to my skin because it was getting chilly outside but I didn't' want to go inside because they would all be sitting around playing video games and listening to MTV. It seems petty, doesn't it? But I don't want to have to pretend I care, that would just be needlessly unpleasant for all concerned.

I'm already a loner with a reputation for sullen disrespect. My mother calls every few days and we actually have long meaningful conversations. Perhaps she misses me – if for no other reason than that I was the closest thing in her life to a constant? The closest thing in her life to an actual living breathing confidant, based on the fact that even if we didn't like each other we still had a shared background of distrust and codependence?

She missed my father, I could tell. When she had been thinking about my father I would come home late in the day after high school classes and find her sitting in the kitchen in front of a cold cup of coffee and staring at a half-finished crossword puzzle or possibly a romance potboiler that she had placed before her and simply forgot. She had loved my father and she regarded me strangely as her only link to him, a mystifying mixture of keepsake and indictment. He was gone, she was still here, I was still here with her, why was this so?

In the habits and attitudes of those who come into money late in life, I have come to recognize a certain mortified stiffness of demeanor, a pallid rigidity that reflects an inherent uncertainty. My mother was never comfortable in her own skin after the day she became a millionaire. Her mind, the body which imprisoned that mind and the world around that body became perfect strangers, reflecting only distrust and anxiety. There is a constant fear that the sky will open and God will descend to Earth flanked by a chorus of angels in order to explain in very reassuring yet firm tones that the money was a mistake and he's going to take it all back.

So the money became a burden. If the wealth had been intended to ease the suffering my father's passing had left, it was a total failure. My mother would have been happy to be poor in his presence – now that she was rich in his absence she felt shame.

Of course, all of these things appeared in my thoughts in the duration of a mere instant as I sat uncomfortably in that dry and stuffy cell, with my inebriated friend for company and those two anonymous criminals with whom my fate had become temporarily and inexplicably tied. It had been a busy night for the campus police. There were drunken and disorderly frat brothers and sexually assaulted coeds running everywhere, it seemed, and the cops were just too busy to actually do anything about any of it.

As we had been booked there was a girl in the front of the station begging and crying and screaming for help, claiming she had been raped and that a group of boys at one of the fraternities had ganged up on her when she was drunk. She had been wearing the remains of a nice outfit, a short plaid skirt and a white blouse that she had sweat right through. She had been drinking and was still somewhat drunk but there was a fevered hint of sobriety at the edges of her voice, a hysterical glint in her words that betrayed a deep and portentous suffering. Of course, she was ignored.

So the ceiling is low and the lights are flickering. It's late at night and its pretty hot outside because I'm sweating underneath my coat even through its supposedly air-conditioned inside the jail. I'm going to be sweating for hours tonight, even when I'm back in my apartment I'm going to feel my body sticking against the sheets. Nervous shivers rack my body. I am calm.

There's a girl down the hall in my apartment building who I initially found attractive but who has since fallen in my estimation. She's rich and comes from a background of privilege and license, and I find myself unable to mask my sarcasm when I'm around her. She seems functionally intelligent but lacks the kind of essential hunger that is necessary to succeed in this world, unless you have already achieved success by virtue of your birth.

Of course, this is the same problem I see all around me. Everyone seems recklessly intent on squandering their advantages and wallowing in their own concupiscence for mediocrity. It's a depressing world to have to live in because no one seems at all worried about what they're going to do with their lives.

These thoughts are still bubbling in my head when the action occurs.

I had been nodding myself to sleep in the quiet interim when I was woken by the struggle. The two men who shared our cell, the two shadowy figures who had killed the police officer as I watched in horror, who I had later seen to be punk kids little older than myself, were speaking in loud and agitated voices. They became increasingly angry as the minutes of captivity passed into hours, and finally the agitation erupted into desperation and violence.

The smaller one stands and runs to the opposite end of the cell, trying to stand out of the larger man's reach. The larger one leans down and pulls something small out of his sneaker, I can't quite tell what because I'm trying very hard to seem like I'm totally ignoring what's going on even though I can't look away. It's a small cell so my attempts at ignorance go unrewarded.

The small man is wailing like a cornered animal as the

larger man strides confidently across the cell. There's something in his hand and his eyes are fixed, like inanimate objects, rocks or stones set against the pasty backdrop of his face.

The small man is screaming louder and louder for help, for any kind of help but there are no answers. Everyone in the jail is looking at what's going on in our cell but everyone is strangely quiet: all the petty crooks, all the drunks, all the hookers and all the brawlers. I get up and move across the cell to where my inebriated friend is laying, the only person in the cellblock oblivious to the drama, pursued by his imaginary demons.

On the opposite end of the cell, nearer where I had been sitting, the larger man has the smaller man backed into the corner and he's holding him against the wall with the collar of his dark leather jacket balled in his fist. Suddenly there's movement and then there's blood everywhere, like he had reached into the smaller man's chest and turned a faucet, because it's on the man's jacket and splattering on the floor.

The larger man turns away from the victim and tosses the knife away, into the hallway. His hands are covered in grimy, dark black-red blood and he's got a strangely distracted look on his face. The smaller man slumps to the floor, his hands limp and his face ashen. His blood is everywhere it shouldn't be and he can't put any of it back where it's supposed to be and he seems mildly amused by the irony as he starts to quietly cough and the blood drips down his chin.

Finally, after what seems like an eternity the police respond to the commotion and move into the cellblock en masse, opening the door to our cell and pushing the larger man to the floor and running to the smaller man but he's already dead. Of course, my friend and I are overlooked and that's for the best all things considered.

The smaller man dies before they can do anything and

the larger man is mute, he seems tired and he doesn't want to communicate anything, he just wants to go to sleep from the way he acts. He's still got blood all over him and even some spurted on his face, shading his mouth and his eyes so that it looks like he put on war paint. He's on the floor and he's handcuffed and the police are yelling and shouting at him but he just looks like he's about to fall asleep right there in the jail cell as he's being held to the ground.

And of course I never found out what any of that was about, not until much later.

4

My father was a killer for the CIA.

He was involved in the Deep Shit, the type of vitally important national security matters that necessitated his total and unequivocal silence. It has only been through the painstaking and laborious process of investigation that I have been able to piece together the fragments of his life.

The twentieth century was not kind to the African continent. The aftermath to hundreds of years of colonial repression was decades of war – both civil and external. My father was a mercenary in darkest Africa for the greater part of the 60's and 70's – fighting in the Congo and Angola and Zambia, killing on the side of those remaining white colonial governments who were being secretly supported by the United States through the CIA.

Throughout my childhood and early adolescence there's the recurring presence of a One-Eyed Man, a tall and swarthy individual who would sometimes make himself visible to me when I was at the playground or playing soccer or shopping with mother. He would appear and I would look at him and he would acknowledge me, just long enough for the mutual recognition to register, and he would be gone.

I knew without having to ask, without having to say anything, that he had been sent by my father to watch over me, to keep an eye (one eye, at least) on me and ensure I was safe. I am certain that my father made many enemies during his tenure with the agency, enemies who would have liked nothing better than to strike out at my absent father through his vulnerable family – but he was always there to protect us, even when he wasn't.

The One-Eyed Man stopped coming sometime after I hit junior high. Perhaps the people who had threatened my father were finally dead, or perhaps, as I secretly feared, the One-Eyed Man had finally been eliminated. All I knew was that the final link to my father's secret life and career had been severed.

I never told my mother about the one-eyed man. She lived in a state of forced ignorance in regard to my father's activities – I suspect she knew more than she admitted, and had perhaps been in some way complicit in my father's death - but her sanity depended on keeping these disparate parts of her life compartmentalized.

My newfound drunken companion and I were released from police custody around sunrise. Trevor, as I later learned his name to be, had slept through the entire altercation, waking only after the body and the murderer in question had both been carried away.

He was holding his head and squinting in the crisp winter morning. Apparently the events which had led to his arrest involved drinking contests and video games – more than that he refused to remember. For the immediate future he was concerned mainly with finding coffee and shelter.

The campus police station was situated on the far end of the school from where my apartment and Trevor's fraternity house were both located. It was a Saturday morning and the school was quiet.

It turned out that I had indeed met Trevor before, although I would not have remembered this if he had not been the one to mention that we shared the same chemistry section during our freshman year. On a campus filled with tens of thousands of unfamiliar faces it was almost a miracle to find recognition in a stranger.

Trevor was wearing a simple white T-shirt. He had been sweating throughout the night and now he was very cold. There was a pancake restaurant off the main boulevard as you rose up through the campus buildings. We decided to stop in and have breakfast together.

We were certainly a sight. I hadn't slept all night and there were spatters of blood from the murder all over my shirt and coat, droplets which had inexplicably flown across the cell to land on me. Trevor looked like he felt, horribly hung-over. His skin was coated in grease and his eyes were crimson.

The restaurant was empty. The waitress led us to a booth towards the front of the restaurant and filled our coffee cups. She was a student at the school, dully attractive in a soft and unfocused manner, although her breasts were recognizably pert through her starched uniform.

I ordered a plate of pancakes and a glass of orange juice. Trevor nibbled on an English muffin with some strawberry jam smeared clumsily across the face. After he downed two cups of coffee, he opened his eyes wider and engaged me in tentative conversation. He asked me why I had been in the jail. I told him the truth: that I had been walking around campus late at night and had had the misfortune to witness a shooting.

I explained roughly what had occurred last night from the time I spotted the two men arguing near the entrance of the Life Sciences building. I omitted mention of my air rifle.

The same officer who had collared Trevor had apprehended me. We met in the back of his cruiser, which Trevor did not remember. He didn't remember much from around the time he was doing tequila shots with Arthur

Magnusen from Delta Kai to the time he woke up cold and throbbing in the cell next to where a brutal murder had recently occurred (a murder which he also did not remember).

He mentioned in passing that the police had arrested him after pissing in a mailbox on Warring Street. He didn't remember doing it but that's why he had been booked.

All throughout our conversation he was drinking coffee at a furious rate. In hindsight it seems perfectly sane – drinking copious amounts of coffee enables his body to flush the system of toxins. I wasn't dealing with an amateur, apparently Trevor knew his way around the world of extreme inebriation.

And as we chatted quietly and as Trevor continued the slow and awkward process of working through his hangover, I looked over his shoulder towards the opposite side of the restaurant and saw a familiar face staring back at me across the sterile café. It was the One-Eyed Man, ten years older and none the worse for wear, unmistakable.

The One-Eyed Man was staring directly at me with a look of inconsolable melancholy writ passionless on his face. Whatever had brought him here, ten years in the future from the last time I had seen him, set down directly into my life and my world again, from out of the dim recesses of my ancestral past, was obviously a grim chore.

Suddenly I wished that I had discussed the man with my mother. I wished I had been able to overcome my natural reluctance to communicate with her and explored this mystery further because I found myself inexplicably unable to deal with the sudden numbing possibilities which his presence reopened in my near future.

Trevor had stopped speaking. He had lifted his head and was looking right at me. I snapped back to our conversation but I didn't have the slightest notion what we had been discussing.

When I looked again the One-Eyed Man had gone, paid

his check and left the restaurant. But I knew I was going to see him again, and soon.

5

Trevor invited me to a party later that week at his frat house. I usually made a habit of avoiding parties but my inexplicable affection for Trevor overcame my better judgment in this instance.

The fraternities are arrayed in a row on a long street jutting south from the main campus. On any given weekend there are dozens of parties ongoing, dozens of ancient houses filled to the brim with drunken children. You could walk down the street on party nights and feel as if the entire campus was on fire, as if all the houses were actually part of one greater party and everyone was invited.

Of course, that was an illusory effect - and in reality, most parties are illusions. There's an aching solitude at the heart of them, a cloying adolescent loneliness that won't be alleviated merely by mass drunkenness or group sex. Perhaps I just don't get it. I don't know. I do know that parties usually don't entertain me.

When I was fourteen there was a party at someone's house . . . someone's birthday party, I don't remember exactly. I dressed nicely and had my present wrapped, I don't remember what I got, it must have been something my mother picked out.

So as bad as college parties are it goes without saying that junior high school parties are worse. There's not really a lot to do because you're not old enough to be outside of the immediate purview of adults and you're not young enough to think that's OK. You want to be older but you're stuck being what you are for however long you're there. If I could go back in time with a fresh keg of beer and present it to my fourteen-year-old self he wouldn't have the faintest clue what to do with it.

And of course its impossible to cast my mind back without stumbling across memories of Lauren.

There were years in my life devoted to abnegation, entire periods of my youth blacked out between the time of my father's death and my departure from home. My childhood was given over to phantom deliriums, and my adolescence was almost entirely consumed by a negative burning lust aimed inwards and fueled by self-hatred.

Sometimes I crept out of the house and walked across the long and luxurious fairways of the nearby golf courses. I lay on the grass and looked skyward, slowing my metabolism down until I could feel the movement of the Earth in orbit beneath my fragile pulpy body. I dreamt inky purple seas of molten grief, and my father's face spinning high above me, unable to see me or to hear me.

Lauren was beautiful, of course, and looking back across the years I can see now that she was irresistibly innocent as well – a virtue that would have appealed to me. Of course I was unable to do anything, to act on my impulses, because in all seriousness I was just a kid, and a pretty fucked up kid at that.

But I remember snippets of the year and I remember moments from that party in particular – a magical moment towards the end of the party. We were sitting on the couch waiting for our parents to come, sitting in a darkened living room somehow, inexplicably alone. I don't remember thinking anything so much as wondering how this could possibly have been allowed to happen, it seemed so odd in a house full of people to be alone with Lauren in the living room . . .

And it was dark and we were sitting there together looking out the window and seeing the headlights pass by on the road and feeling the faint glow of reflected light on our pale youthful faces. It was dark in the house but there was white light from a lamppost outside and it played across our faces through the vertical bars of the venetian blinds.

I don't remember what we said, and I don't think we said anything important. But I remember that one single shining moment for what it was worth. Not much.

Trevor was nowhere to be found when I arrived at the party. The house was already filling with people, younger coeds and older members of the fraternity, in addition to sorority sisters and athletes and perhaps even a few townies somehow thrown in the mix. There was liquor everywhere, domestic beer in cheap plastic cups and ugly liquor in small shot glasses on coffee tables.

There were a few people I vaguely recognized. A younger girl came up to me and asked if I knew where the bathroom was. I told her that I didn't and she thanked me and walked away. She was attractive in a preening slutty way, in much the same manner that most of the younger girls were.

The house itself was beautiful, an old gothic residence with high vaulted ceilings in the living room and elaborate winding staircases throughout. It was a perfect house in which to throw lavish parties, and a perfect house to entertain guests. I began to lose awareness of my surroundings and my eyes stretched off across the ceiling and into the spaces between spaces.

I turned my head and looked over towards the corner. There was a keg of beer set on a thick wooden table with a few younger coeds milling around. Looking closer I saw an older gentleman whom I hadn't recognized when I first entered the room, but who I soon remembered. I strolled across the room and reached my hand out to him.

"Hello, my boy," he said, taking my hand in a firm shake. "I'm so glad you could make it. Trevor told me you were coming and I'm very happy to see you here."

"Thanks," I said. He was holding a small plastic cup of beer in his hand. He reached over to the keg and poured another cup for me.

"Here you go," he said. "I am happy to be of service to you."

I took the beer and drank deeply. It was warm, room temperature, but it slid down my throat easily enough. It was good to see my friend, and he looked well. He was wearing a nice dark suit, with the tie pulled slightly loose from his collar, just casual enough to look at home anywhere he went. His complexion was a healthy light red, his black hair slicked back behind the tiny little horns poking out just above his forehead and to either side of his widow's peak.

"Seriously, my boy, I've been meaning to have a talk with you for a good long while here." He reached out and put his hand on my shoulder, comfortingly. "I've heard some pretty special things about you. You're going to have a good year, you know that?"

"Really?" I asked.

"Yes, really. Once you get out of here," he gestured around the room with his free hand, "and get home, you've got some big decisions to make."

"Connie."

"Yes . . ." he paused. "She's certainly a big decision. But there are some even bigger decisions on your horizon."

"Huh."

"Yes, yes. It's a damned good thing I found you when I did, because I have some very important advice to offer you. Come with me . . ."

He grabbed my arm above the elbow and escorted me out of the living room. We found ourselves in a smaller area, perhaps a family room, with a much cozier space. There were fewer people here as well. My friend sat down in a chair to the side of a plush sofa and I sat down on the sofa nearest to him.

"There's one thing you've absolutely got to remember, I mean, above all else this is vitally important. Are you listening?"

"Yeah."

"Everything is important. From this moment on in your life, everything that happens to you has a reason. Like a puzzle. You have to be smart enough to put everything together because everything is going to mean something."

"I don't quite understand."

"Of course you don't understand. Not yet you don't. You're going to be in the middle of some crazy shit, my boy. You're going to have your hands full."

"Hmmm. So, I'm not going to marry Connie?"

"No, I never said that. But I think you're going to want to take some time off after school, go find yourself. This is a big country and you've really only seen a tiny sliver of it."

"Yeah, I was thinking of doing that. Road trip out to see New York maybe."

"Yes, New York. Maybe you could see Ground Zero?"

"Yeah, I did think of that."

"You're not the only one. Anyway. In the coming days and months there's going to be a lot happening around you and you have to be very careful to make the right decisions, to choose the right paths, or the consequences could be much more disastrous than you or even I could possibly foresee.

"You just have to remember one very important thing." At this he leaned down from his chair and pressed his index finger into my chest. "Everything counts. Everything that happens to you from this day forward is important, it all means something, it all adds up. Pay attention and see if you can discern the shape and texture of the patterns that surround you, the patterns that dictate your existence. That's the only way you're going to get ahead."

"I'm afraid," I said meekly.

"Don't be. I've seen this kind of thing before – a kid like you, fresh-faced, straight out of college. Takes some time off, finds himself. You've just got to figure our where you're going, is all. Its not that intimidating, is it?"

"Not when you put it like that it isn't."

"See, that's just my point. You've got to take it easy. You've got a lot of power now, a lot of potential. You can do anything in the entire world if you want and nothing can stop you. The only thing that can stop you is fear, and you can't be afraid of anything, OK?"

"OK."

"That's what I like to hear." He slapped me on the back in a jovial fashion. "Would you like another beer? A cigar perhaps?" He opened his coat to reveal his inside pocket, crammed with freshly-wrapped cigars. "Just got in from Cuba – fresh as a daisy."

"No, no thank you, I don't smoke."

"Fine, fine. I can respect that. Anyway," he said as he rose from his seat, "I really should be on my way. I've got a busy night ahead of me yet."

"It was good talking to you," I said dully, lifting my hand up to grasp his.

"Don't let it get you down, kid, just go home and get on the road. Things will start happening, I guarantee you'll end up on the right page in the end. I have it on a pretty high authority that you're destined for greatness. Just be on the lookout for synchronicity – it's the secret story of everything all around you. Figure out how that story ends and you'll rule the world."

"I will, I will. Thank you, thank you so much."

"No problem. I still owe your dad . . . we go way back, you know that. He was a good man."

"Yeah he was."

"Cheer up, kid," he said with a smile, "you're on the right track."

He grasped my hand and left, turned abruptly down the hall and disappearing into the party.

I sat in silence for a moment, ruminating on the

conversation. My friend hadn't said anything which I did not strongly suspect to already be true, but it was heartening nonetheless to hear it said by a voice besides my own.

The party grew louder and louder with every moment I sat thinking. There were more people streaming in from the outside and there were already more people than I thought possible packed into the house's cavernous basements. The faint but insistent throbbing of music from deep in the building's foundations was strangely, ominously comforting.

I looked up from my reverie and saw Trevor approaching from the main foyer. He had a broad grin and was carrying two more plastic cups of beer. Without a word he handed me one and took a long draught from the other.

"Dude," he pronounced solemnly. "You made it. I was beginning to think you weren't going to show."

His face was flushed, I could tell he had already been drinking heavily for a while. Did he ever stop drinking, I wondered? He sat down next to me on the sofa while I spoke.

"I've actually been here a bit," I answered. "I was talking to a friend before you came in."

"Fuckin' wild. I told you you'd see someone you knew."

"Yeah, I'm glad I came."

"Dude, you saved my ass the other night, you know that? I mean, seriously, dude. I was hardcore fucked up, seriously fucked up. I don't even remember any of that. But I sure got some blood on my T-shirt to, uh, commemorate it by."

I chuckled and took another sip from the beer.

"So, like, I'm glad you could make it, but you are just so not being where the party is going, dude . . . I am afraid I am going to have to insist you come on down with me and see what we can see. Seriously, dude."

He rose on shaky feet and I followed. We turned the

corner and found a long thin hallway leading to a dark stairwell at the end. There were kids lined up all across the hall, in various states of disrepair. Some were making out with others, some were fast asleep. I tried to be as careful as I possibly could, lifting my feet to ensure I didn't step on anyone's fingers or knock over any beers. The floor was already sticky with liquor.

The stairwell proved narrower than the hallway had been, curving down into the hill on which the ancient house stood. The music came up to me, thicker, meaner and bloodier in my ears. Slowly my eyes adjusted to the viscous darkness that enveloped us. We were surrounded by people all around us as we descended the stairwell, sweaty figures in the fumbling dark, leant against the crumbling masonry of the walls. There was smoke, tobacco and marijuana and more.

The stairs came to an abrupt end and we were suddenly in a large, dark enclosure at least thirty feet below the first floor of the house above. I had underestimated how deeply the foundations of the house had had to be cut into the hillside in order to build the house.

There were people everywhere, dancing sluggishly or lounging against the walls. The confidence and languor of these guests assured me that the basement was obviously the epicenter of the party. There was a small bar set jutting from the wall at the opposite end of the room, with half a dozen men whom I recognized as members of the fraternity taking turns pouring beers from a large metal keg and taking shots with the other revelers.

There was a DJ in the corner, two turntables and a mixer set atop a long piece of plywood perched on two piles of cinder blocks. He was in deep concentration as I entered the room, his headphones half ajar on his head and scrunched up against his shoulder. His fingers were slowly and methodically turning the record as it spun on the platter, speeding up or slowing down the incoming music to match the song that was already playing.

The crowd was lazy, however, and inattentive to the music. There were dozens, hundreds of bodies moving slowly across the dance floor, propelled by liquor past the point of exhaustion. Here was the dense hard core of the party, the people who had been here for hours and had no intention of going home, and the people for whom this permanent state of Bacchanal excess was home.

There was a thick iron chain hanging from the center of the ceiling, and there was a large iron-wrought cage hanging from this chain – like a birdcage, only bigger. Suspended about three feet off the floor, the cage contained a girl.

I don't know if you could call the caged girl beautiful, because a latex mask covered her face. She was wearing some shiny fetish gear over her body. Her body language seemed dazed, slightly disinterested, perhaps bored. I think I would have been, in the same situation.

Trevor tapped me on the shoulder and motioned for me to join him at the bar. The bar itself was surrounded by what seemed to be thousands of swarming lowerclassmen screaming for beer. The bartenders gave a cup of beer from their keg to every third supplicant, in between downing cups of beer themselves.

The music was good but no one cared. I pressed into the crowd with Trevor, gaining ground on the bar as we slowly came through to the gate. Trevor swung the gate open and we emerged on the other side in the small area behind the bar. There were two chairs off the side, next to a television that was bolted to the wall. There were neon beer signs – flickering orange "COORS" and "BUDWEISER" talismans that gave you a headache to look at them.

Above the bar, on the ceiling behind where the cabinets were situated, there was a large poster of a naked lady, perhaps a Playboy model? I didn't recognize her. It was an old poster.

Trevor leaned over and spoke in my ear, loudly through the noise: "Having a good time?"

I nodded my head dully. One of the seats was empty so I sat down, careful not to spill my beer.

As I situated myself, Trevor leaned under the bar and found a half-empty bottle of whiskey. He found a pair of shot glasses and slammed them onto the arm of my chair with an audible thunk. He filled both shot glasses, motioning me to take one.

We clanked our shots in mock toast and threw the liquor down our throats. It had been a while since I had drank whiskey and I was reminded, briefly, of just how foul it actually tasted. It ran down my throat as quickly as I could manage, and it landed in my stomach like a drop of molten lead. I was growing quite drunk despite myself.

Trevor turned away and shared a shot with his fraternity friends. My mind slowly tuned out the crowd beyond the barricades of the bar, focusing on the music and the light, soft and hard on my senses. The girl in the cage was still bored and looked drunk or stoned, and from the other side of the room I commiserated with her. I wondered, obliquely, how much she was being paid.

Then it occurred to me that I had seen the One-Eyed Man just a few days ago, after having missed him for almost a decade. It was an upsetting thought, and for a moment I fought feelings of paranoia rising out of my stomach and into my brain. It was a reptilian feeling, a pure conception of the primal ego that left my skin feeling vaguely like coiled scales. I felt the harsh fabrics of my shirt against my naked flesh and I was repulsed by my physicality.

But what was left? I was drunk and I had nothing to fear, at least for the time being. I found myself enjoying the party despite myself. As was to be expected, I had nothing to do and nothing to say to Trevor's companions – anymore than I had anything to say to Trevor himself – but I enjoyed the party from my vantage point at the far rear of the basement, observing from a position of serene detachment. Life was good, at least for the time being.

After a few indeterminate minutes, Trevor turned back to me and we downed shots again. I was smiling, I could feel the grin across my face, and I could hear the blood pumping through my brain. It's an odd sensation, drunkenness, and I am rarely prepared for the disassociation, of perceiving my surroundings in crystal clarity but being unable to speak or act in a rational manner.

For a moment, at least, I relaxed into the dull soft-focus of the party, enjoying the brief high and putting all unpleasant thoughts outside of myself. I would pick them up later, when the voices resumed and I was free to act on my friend's advice. I had the rest of my life ahead of me, and the rest of my life started tomorrow.

6

The first few days after the bombings were days of panic and fear, days of attenuated perceptions stretched past the breaking point.

The broadcast news networks began running their coverage around the clock and the television feeds changed their design. Small running text feeds stretched across the bottom of the screens, buffeted by pictures and computer graphics moving like video games around your field of vision. As hard as it was to grasp the realities of a geopolitical universe grown suddenly much harsher, the hyper-kinetic paranoid television presentation brought these changes home to our living rooms. Here was the altered world, splayed and dissected and splattered across the TV.

There's a point where you realize that the world you live

in is no longer the world you grew up in. There's a moment of hideous recognition, a sensation of horror that passes across the membrane of your consciousness like a bubble in oil. Everything feels wrong, jaded, corrupted.

When I turned my eyes from the television the running text strip at the bottom of the screen was burnt into my eyes. I was seeing the news as it happened with my eyes closed.

I dreamt of burning bodies and the smell of gunpowder for weeks after the towers fell. There was nothing I could do to cleanse my mind, nothing I could possibly wish for but silence, blessed silence, but as soon as I turned on the television the noise in my head was replaced by the noise on the news, voices and mouths speaking in clipped tones of urgency, saying nothing in particular in a very forceful manner.

And so I began, in the hazy days following the destruction, to gain a unique and comprehensive understanding of the strange world in which we now lived. Everything was compromised. Every layer of perception in our world had been dominated, purchased and pasteurized, coated with liquid latex and made to look new and agreeable and exciting. We saw mass murder unfold before our eyes and reacted as if we had just seen a television commercial. Where was this new product? How much did it cost?

Everything in our lives has been replaced by cheaply manufactured simulacra. I wondered when they had got to my mother. But then I realized it didn't matter: she had been only too happy to be appropriated. She was positioning me for my replacement, working diligently to achieve this goal.

The Saturday after September 11th saw me the guest of Connie's parents, Mr. and Mrs. Gooding. Connie's school schedule was such that she left for classes at the end of August, while my school year didn't commence until

September.

I enjoyed the company of the Goodings far more than I enjoyed the company of their daughter. They were honest and scrupulous, I felt, much more so than my own duplicitous mother. They were very comfortable with their lot in life, and both worked decent and respectable jobs. I felt at least partially safe in their home, removed from the constant struggle of the running captions that moved across the bottom of the television screens and which had sprouted across everyone's forehead during the preceding week.

The Goodings' house was impeccably and classically furnished. The furniture was strong and resilient, and when I returned home after dining with them I felt incredible shame at my mother's gauche taste in modern furnishings. There wasn't a piece in my mother's house I didn't feel that I could break apart at the slightest provocation, and I was deeply afraid of the impermanence represented by broken furniture.

I sat at the head of the Goodings' cozy kitchen table, opposite of Mr. Gooding and flanked by Mrs. Gooding. They regarded me as their son-in-law in deed if not in word, making every accommodation to my eccentricities. Truth be told, they understood better than their daughter the difficult upbringing I had received, and felt almost grateful for the chance to help me.

In any event, theirs' was the first house I had entered in a week's time that did not have the television playing. They were as impeccably presented as they had ever been, and they welcomed me with unfeigned warmth and generosity.

Mr. Gooding asked me how my week had been. I told him that I had been fortunate enough to be able to spend most of my week at home, reading and relaxing in preparation for returning to school. He inquired as to the date of my departure, I answered that I was planning on returning on the 20th.

They had been in close communication with Constance

all week. Her classes had apparently been canceled on the day of the attacks and the school had remained closed for an additional day. Classes had resumed on Thursday but there was still campus-wide paranoia. It occurred to some that in the event of another proverbial shoe dropping a small liberal arts college in Oregon was hardly the most likely target, but logic and fear are rare bedfellows.

I asked Mr. Gooding what he had been doing at the time of the attacks. He had been doing paperwork in his office at the bank when he had received a call from his wife, who told him to turn on a television – any television. It was very early in the morning and few people had yet arrived at the bank, so he was alone as he marched into the small break room hidden at the rear of the bank and flipped on the small portable television that sat on the main table.

He was transfixed for a good ten minutes before he realized it was time to open the doors. By this time the morning shift were arriving and most of them had heard nothing yet. As they arrived he informed each of them that something terrible was happening in New York.

He opened the front doors anxiously and returned to the break room. By this time the first tower had fallen. He succumbed to temptation and carried the television into the lobby, installing the small receiver on a podium at the center of the room. He turned the volume loud and sat down in a chair near the loan office.

After a few early-birds, no customers came to the bank that morning. Everyone was hunched around the television together, unwilling to miss a moment of the history.

Mr. Gooding made the decision to close the bank when the first calls arrived for the parents. Schools had closed early and the children were being sent home, and most of the tellers needed to leave. It was really no decision at all – the take-out Chinese food restaurant situated across the way from the bank in the strip-mall had already closed, along with the insurance agency next door and the dry cleaners on the other side. The coffee shop across the highway was doing good business, though - there were dozens of trailer-trucks and cars packing the lot, having stopped in town after hearing the news on the radio.

Mr. Gooding saw each of the employees out the door and locked the building as he left. It was a surreal feeling, to close the bank before even the lunch hour had struck on a sunny Autumn Tuesday. He imagined millions of people across the country in similar positions, finding themselves impacted by distant events they could not easily comprehend. Aside from the out-of-town traffic at the coffee shop, the town had grown preternaturally quiet.

Mrs. Gooding was a doctor – an orthopod at a sports clinic downtown. She canceled all her appointments soon after seeing the first images on television. She called down the list and most admitted that they had had no intention of coming. Mrs. Gooding changed out of her white coat and was the last person to leave her office, the secretaries and other physicians having left earlier.

The Goodings' voices were soft and assured, well suited to calm descriptions of tragedy. I remember feeling somehow reassured listening to them speak, assured in a way that I hadn't felt listening to the same stories passing from my friends or my family's lips. They were all the same, all the stories, anyway, it was simply in the act of telling that they were able to gain any semblance of significance.

Everyone's story was essentially the same, and this was both boring and horrific. I longed to find someone with a different recollection of the day's events, someone who hadn't seen the towers fall, and still sees them standing today. That would be a story worth telling.

In any event I woke up the morning after the frat party with a pounding headache. I was back in my room although I didn't remember in perfect detail how I had returned. I had never had a hangover like this before, and I was suddenly very glad I no longer had roommates to contend with.

I stayed in bed for most of the day, drinking water and coffee and trying to read but mostly just laying in bed with a pillow over my head. I remembered with a sudden viciousness why I disliked drinking.

I made myself get out of bed as the evening wore on and proceeded to find some food. It was only then that I saw the note, scribbled hastily and left on my computer screen the night before –

> Had a great time? Hope so, lover . . .
> Kristy

My brow furrowed and I felt a searing pain through my head. Whatever I had drank the previous night had done a complete number on me, and the more I strained the less I remembered.

There was a Chinese take-out place down the street from my building. I pulled on my coat and left the apartment carefully, trying to walk as gently as I could. The sun was beginning to set but I wore my sunglasses anyway.

I had given up on studying the year before. Thankfully – or not, depending on your outlook - I had been gifted with the kind of memory that enabled me to make it through my courses on nothing more than willpower. I read all the assigned books but never gave the classes a second thought until I had to take the tests. Sure enough, I had been rewarded with A's and B's, an admirable scorecard by any definition. My time was left free for other pursuits.

Sometimes I wished that I could work harder, that I could enable myself to fail at something, anything. But it was all so damned easy, and I felt frustrated for caring.

As I walked down the street my friend's words of the previous night came softly back into my aching head. I had felt aimless, adrift – unable to focus my life and my energies on any goal or suitable vocation. But his words had opened dark reservoirs of secret purpose at which I had only ever previously realized vague hints. Perhaps all of this was merely just a test, or a passing phase, and I would eventually perceive my current life as if it were a platform of phantoms and ghosts. Something was up there, waiting for me, watching.

If someone was watching my I had to be very careful. I cast a glance over my shoulder but the street was remarkably quiet. It was the weekend and there should have been some activity, I reasoned – but there was none. Simple preternatural silence was the only thing I heard.

The streets were composed with a mixture of ramshackle and modern architectures, a surreal jumble of old and new piled high one on top of the other. There was ivy everywhere, ivy and broad leafy trees bunched across the streets. There was something cozy and dark about the city, something that seemed to simultaneously repulse and welcome the stranger.

But now I became convinced that every corner, every cranny and nook in the crumbling civic masonry held a set of anxious eyes eager to find and dispatch me. There was nothing I could do but go about my business because I knew that to give so much as the slightest foreknowledge that I was aware of their presence would lead to my inevitable doom.

The feeling of being watched is one of the most unpleasant and helpless sensations in life. There is no earthly reason why you should be able to feel as if you're being watched, and yet you know, with a certainty that belies proof, from the evidence of the downy hair on the back of your neck. You can almost hear the whispering voices as you turn the corner, the spies in their long duster coats and their faded porkpie hats, recording data and transmitting it back to their secret headquarters. It's just like you've seen in all the movies, only worse and filled with loathing.

I sometimes wonder if the people watching me at night are even human anymore. There's a part of me that hopes not.

I carried my Chinese food back to the apartment and locked the door behind me. My head was still pounding and my eyes felt shriveled. I still couldn't remember a damn thing about what had happened last night after we started doing those shots behind the bar.

Connie was a good girl, better than I deserved. I hoped she wasn't compromised by any of this.

Her parents had related their stories to me quietly, with the plain and humble authority with which they communicated everything in their lives. Here was a couple who had succeeded, who had found everything they wanted in life. Their daughter was a tribute to their conceptions of morality and decency, a good girl who reflected well on them both.

Except that she wasn't really their daughter. Her mother was dead, her father was somewhere else. She had been abandoned by life and it was only her extreme good luck that she had found the Goodings – a childless couple who were willing to adopt an older daughter. I found out later – much later, and accidentally – that Mrs. Gooding had had a tragic miscarriage early in their marriage, and this misfortune had taken from her the ability to bear any children.

They had wanted a child, they had wanted children, the perfect keystone to the perfect suburban American life. Sometimes things don't work out the way we plan. In any event, I've known Constance for longer than her parents have. I remember seeing her biological parents, when they were still alive and together.

That was a long time ago.

7

I've got these pills I'm supposed to take but I don't. They make me sleepy and give me headaches and I just don't want to take them because I'm not sick.

I get the bottles every month in the mail from my doctor but they just stack up in the closet. My mother always asks me whether or not I'm taking them and I lie to her, say "yes, ma," and leave it at that. She wants me to take my pills so I'll be vulnerable to her, vulnerable to the machinations of her and her fellow ghouls. I don't want that to happen, I can't allow them to dull my perceptions, so I just smile and nod when the subject of my medication comes up.

But she's no dummy, she knows I'm not taking them. She knows because they haven't got me yet. When I take my pills it dulls everything, like there's cottonwool around my head and I just can't think straight. I know they're out there but I can't see them or hear them and that makes me paranoid as fuck. So before it gets too bad I stop taking them and soon I can hear their footsteps behind me as I walk through the neighborhood, and I find that oddly comforting because at least that way I can hear them coming.

I don't think my dad heard them coming, which is why he's dead. I don't know exactly how he died but I imagine it happened in a similar fashion. They wanted him dead and they waited and waited and waited but he was too smart and too canny for them, until he finally let his guard down enough for them to slit his throat in the night and that was the last we ever heard of Pop.

In any event, the people who got to my dad are still out there and I know they're still after me. If I had ever had the luxury to forget that, the One Eyed Man was back in my life to remind me of this fact.

So I began to formulate a plan.

My father was dead because of what he knew and what he had. There were hundreds of millions of dollars still out there, unclaimed, that belonged to him – belonged to me – and I had to figure out where it was before they did. Because if they did, I knew there wouldn't be a place in the world I would be able to hide from them.

I felt sorry for Connie sometimes. There were times where I wanted to run away from her and never return, but I knew that at the end of the day I was important to her, deeply important in a way I couldn't begin to understand. We had been friends from such an early age that it would simply be impossible to imagine life without her, for better or for worse. That probably goes a little way towards explaining why I'm such a goddamned chickenshit with her. I don't want to marry her. I don't really even know how we got engaged. But somehow it happened . . . and I can't really explain that.

And I certainly can't begin to explain it to her. I don't want to hurt her because, ultimately, she's going to be hurt enough by life before all is said and done. That's just the facts.

Ultimately I suppose I was afraid. I didn't want to let go of the life I was living, blissfully unaware of all these raging undercurrents beneath my feet, ignorant of the perfidy that sublimates us on a daily basis. I didn't want to step out of the shell of college, where I felt relatively safe and secure, because I knew that I was going to be hurt, that the same people and the same forces that had wanted to hurt my dad were going to try and hurt me. I knew that the series of events which began with my father's death and led eventually to those two planes falling into the World Trade Center could only end unhappily for me.

But I had a responsibility – to my father, to Connie, even to my mother as much as I hated to admit it. She was compromised, hidden away and demolished by their subterfuge and their hatred, but she was still my mother.

There were maps, maps and graphs and legends of all the places I needed to go and to see and to investigate, long charts of names and numbers relating back to the late 1800s. The same colonial forces that had thrown Africa into perfect disarray had also been working behind the scenes, slowly and confidently, in order to use this chaos to their greatest advantage.

My father was a mercenary in Angola – I've mentioned this. But I didn't get into the part where my father was also smarter than his paymasters gave him credit for. He was a killer, yes, but he also kept his eyes open. It was no problem for him to see what the Company was really doing, to see that their covert activities were just masks for deeper machinations, masks atop of masks atop of masks. He was smart enough to see all the pieces as they fell into the tumblers, all the small clicks inside the lock that no one but a trained thief would be able to discern.

So that's what ultimately killed him – the fact that he knew more than he should, and the fact that he had used this knowledge in ways he shouldn't have. He was rich – very rich – and his wealth was a threat to the Powers because the fact that he had gotten his money in the way he did meant that he knew exactly how their little Ponzi scheme was supposed to happen. It made him the most dangerous man on the planet, and it also made him the most wanted.

And so he was killed. They cut his throat in the night and took his head clean off with a garrote, leaving it sitting in a chair on the opposite side of the room from his cot. There was a picture of me and my mother in a frame next to his cot, a picture taken when I was no more than two years old. I was the last thing he saw before he died.

Graduation is a quiet affair. I spend a lot of time packing my boxes and preparing for the trip home. I'm putting my books away with extra care because they might be in storage for a long time. They're going to sit in the attic of my mother's house until everything is over.

I was glad that I had been able to find this apartment, off the beaten track and without the necessity of a roommate. Many of my former dormmates had been forced into unpleasant circumstances because of the housing shortage, and I was incredibly lucky to be where I was. I realized this, but I didn't really consider myself lucky. I considered myself bored.

So here was my crummy room – a few bookcases filled with books, a computer, a bed and a miniature refrigerator. Magazines and comic books and newspapers strewn across the shelves. There's a bag of stale pot in the toe of an old workboot, pot I bought a long time ago but never really wanted to smoke. I don't like smoking alone and I don't like being around people.

I expected to feel some nostalgia, some sympathy for my past and my lost youth. I just felt tired, tired and bored, as if it had been time to leave a long time ago. I had overstayed my welcome.

There was a pile of Chinese food cartons piled in the wastebasket near the door. I dislike Chinese food but it was close enough that I didn't care. I didn't have a kitchen and I didn't want to use the kitchenette that I shared with three other apartments on my floor. I'm just funny like that.

But I couldn't stop thinking about my dad. In the last few days I had been reminded of so many important things that I had seemingly allowed myself to forget. I was still just a callow, raw youth, a child alone in a world of men.

My landlord was in on it. I knew because my apartment was right above his. Late at night when it was quiet outside I could hear him talking on a secret radio with the men who killed my father. The voices on the other end of this radio are raspy and harsh, just like the sound of brambles brushing the concrete. These are the voices I can hear on a clear day when the wind is low, and I stop just in time to turn and see the hint of my pursuers.

There's a sweet scent in the night air, like ginger and chamomile, and I know it's them.

I'm packing my bags and going home. I have a notebook filled with maps and numbers and names and plans for my trip. I think they are very anxious to see where I'm going and what I'm going to do. They would kill for my notebooks.

8

I retrieved my car from the parking garage and filled it with stuff. The rented trailer was big enough to handle all the boxes of my crap. I reached home late that night after a nerve-racking drive.

My mother pretended to be happy to see me. She helped me unload the trailer in the morning and drove with me down to the U-Haul center.

I mentioned in casual conversation that I was going to be leaving on a trip in a few weeks. She seemed nonplused. It was obvious to me that her reaction had been precisely calibrated to make me think that her feelings were hurt when in fact she didn't care. She didn't care and she didn't want me to know that but she was out of luck as far as that was concerned.

After college the old hometown is invariably gray and pallid. I'm not going to say I was in love with college one way or another, but it does enable you to get your head out of the dirt. I am grateful to the university for giving me four years away from my life to prepare for my journeys and labors.

And I had a nice piece of paper on my wall certifying that I was an expert in the field of history, with a minor in mathematics. It was an odd mixture but it worked. I was already fielding offers from graduate programs across the country, but I sincerely doubted graduate school was in my future. I think I would like to be a teacher, if I live that long.

The worst part about being home is having to put up with my mom's "boyfriend." She says they met at the supermarket but I'm pretty sure that he's her handler. Have I mentioned that while I was gone they took the opportunity to wire every length of the house? I'm certain that nothing I say or do in my mother's house goes unnoticed by the men who killed my father. Ironically, given the fact that I'm under constant surveillance I think I'm fairly secure here. If they wanted me dead they could have killed me the moment I set foot inside my mother's door, but as it is they want to watch me. They're probably unsure how much I know and I'm damn well not going to tip them off.

The first day I was back we had a big dinner, with my mother's boyfriend and Connie. He was pretending to be amicable for the sake of the ruse, which I at least appreciated in Connie's presence.

He says he went to Stanford and I don't have any reason to disbelieve him. He's probably been instructed to tell me as much truth as he can get away with, so as to allay my fears. He tries to build some conversation from the fact that Stanford and my school are perennial rivals. I gave him a tepid response and he smirked. I told him I'd never attended the "Big Game" and he was vaguely disappointed.

Constance was overjoyed to see me. She had returned from her school a few weeks before me and had been very impatient for my return. She was as beautiful as ever. My mother was very eager to press the subject of our impending nuptials. As we ate I watched her hands, watched her engagement ring bouncing gaily in the bright light of the dining room chandelier. My mother had given me the money to buy it and I had bought a very nice ring. I just didn't feel it.

But it was on her finger nevertheless. We had postponed the wedding long enough, my mother insisted, and now it was time for us to get down to the nitty-gritty in terms of planning. When were we planning on getting married? Where were we planning on living? Connie could conceivably get a job anywhere but my decision was the vital one, because I had yet to decide whether or not I wanted to attend graduate school.

Or at least this is what my mother thought. My goal was to string her along as long as I could without actually upsetting her plans, under the notion that this would be the best way to ensure my plans went unmolested.

So I let slip in the most casual way that I was planning on taking a trip at the end of the month. Constance was disappointed that I hadn't thought to ask her along but she assented readily enough when I told her this would be the last delay before our wedding. It was time to relent. I said we would spend the next few weeks before my trip planning the wedding and then while I was gone Connie and our parents could focus on the planning.

I suspect that women are generally disappointed when men fail to share their interest and enthusiasm in wedding planning. At the least, I will say that if I had been planning on actually marrying Connie we would have eloped, far from the prying eyes and ears of my mother and her "boyfriend." If I was actually her husband I would have to spend the rest of my life keeping Connie safe and secure from the forces that wish to harm me. In the long run, it's better she have as little to do with me as possible.

It was in my interests to keep my itinerary as vague as possible. I mentioned possibly visiting my grandparents in the southwest. Most importantly I gave them to infer that this was merely the last fling of my boyhood, one last great adventure before being shackled to the "ol' ball and chain". These were phrases which I think appealed to them on this issue, gave them reassurance that everything was above-boards.

These are the reassurances I had to proffer in order to

buy my freedom. I dislike lying but what is left of my life but subterfuge?

So I spend the next few weeks in a fugue. Before I know it I'm looking at invitations and banquet halls and registering at department stores. Strangely, I think Connie herself is only halfway concerned with the wedding preparations. Perhaps she is merely going through the motions, trying to convince herself that this is what normal people, people with real parents and affectionate fiancés, actually do. Again, I am stung by the reminder that she is very fragile. Undoubtedly in the end I will have hurt her, but it's best this way.

We make love and it is unsatisfying. She caresses and protects me but she is not stupid, she knows there is a reserve which hides those things that I do not share with her. I imagine she considers it her fault, and so sex becomes wilder and more primal, more desperate and pleading on her part. She believes that orgasm can bridge the gap.

There's nothing I can do but wait these last days out. The summer is coming meekly across the mountains and I grow weary of pretense. Every night I check my notebooks where I have hidden them, in order to ensure it has not been stolen. It is safely hidden away where no one can find it.

At night I watch the blinking lights in the sky as the jets mark their passage through the night. I'm sitting in the backyard at our picnic table and drinking a beer. It's very quiet and the night is just barely chilly.

I think I'm ready to leave.

9

If women ever truly understood the nature of lust, they would lock their doors en masse and never pass their thresholds again. Lust is inescapable, it's ubiquitous. It's the cultural currency and we live in a masculine culture. Rape is the subliminal undertow that carries across every transaction in our lives.

I feel slightly bad leaving Connie in the proverbial lurch - as I know I am doing - but there's nothing for it. She fell in love with me. I feel gratitude, slight affection, some friendship towards her . . . but no love. Certainly no lust. I envy those who feel love, I envy the feeling itself. Just to feel anything besides the constant white background noise of painful trembling fear would be a relief.

Perhaps that is love. I know that I envy Connie her assurance. I envy her and I also despise her. I despise her deeply and with every fiber of my being.

I rise with the sun and drive south. I have a few odds and ends in the car but mostly I've packed light, for reasons that will soon become obvious. I have a cassette in the tape deck that I recorded off the late-night campus radio, some DJ or another spinning fairly decent acid house with some Goa trance thrown in for good measure. It's going to be a hot day, I can feel the sun just starting to tickle the skin on my neck through the window pane of the drivers' side window.

There's a recurring dream sensation from my childhood that I can't seem to get out of my head. For some reason I'm grasping a balloon, holding onto it as it grows larger and larger. It grows until It overwhelms me and I feel it all across me body, pulsating like living tissue under my arms and hands. I can feel the muscles in my body recede with this until the feeling of weight and gravity grows distant and dim. My jaw moves like a marionette on strings. It's a strange disconnect.

For some reason this recurring childhood hallucination has returned to me on this august morning. I'm grinding my teeth as the miles pass me by behind the windows of the car, I'm grinding my teeth to feel the mass of muscles and ligament come loose and unattached in my face. I feel liberated.

I set out on the freeway heading due south in the morning haze. I reach my first destination after about an hour of driving.

Although the town where I grew up is situated in a strange pocket of desert suspended between massive mountain ranges, the areas to the immediate north and south are composed of rugged hills. I get off the freeway next to a small town on the shores of a large lake. Everything is tight and winding, with roads hewn close to hillsides and strange houses built upon isolated hilltops.

I've driven through the area before, a few times, on leisure trips of one sort or another. There's one place I know very well.

It's a beautiful drive. The sun is just starting to settle in as I hit the thick green forest near the lake. Its an artificial lake, an eyesore reservoir built into a series of dammed canyons in order to provide water for farmers and municipalities further south in the state. Its easy to make out the shapes of the original canyons and gullies that marked this area originally, before the waters came.

There's a side road somewhere on the east side of the lake, overlooking a tepid and forgotten tributary of the sprawling reservoir. There aren't any houses overlooking the ravine. There aren't any fishermen out on the stark rock outcroppings that stand for beaches. Over the side of the thin dirt road there's an almost perpendicular fall down around one hundred feet of hard red clay with harsh rocks set against the waterline.

There was a guardrail along the side of the road, sometime a long time ago. There are a few wooden posts with rusted bolts still attached, but mostly the railing was demolished by time, by rust and drunken drivers. I park the car in the middle of the road and grab my duffel bag. Everything I need is here, my clothes and maps and notebooks.

I shift the car into neutral and turn the wheel towards the ravine. It's a light car, a compact, and it pushes relatively easy. Before I know it the front wheels are over the cliff and the car is tumbling down the long face of the ravine.

It makes a God-damned noise when it hits the rocks at the water line. I half-expected the car to blow up, but I guess that only happens in movies. It just sat there, easing into the soft mud exposed by low tide and hissing softly in the morning air. Probably burst the radiator, undoubtedly popped the tires.

From the road, you'd have to be looking down to see the wreck juxtaposed against the rocks. No one comes along this way anyway. I imagine someone in a fishing boat will see it in a day or so, and then they'll need a crane to pull it up and there'll be an investigation. But by the time any of this happens I'll be gone and they won't know where I am, or if I'm even alive.

There are sinister forces at work in this world, forces that killed my father and engineered the tragedy at the World Trade Center. The evidence in my notebooks, the evidence that I have carefully compiled since my father's tragic passing, makes me the most dangerous man in the world.

The only problem is that they'll eventually figure out I'm not dead on account of the fact that my notebooks are missing. My notebooks and my maps, all that I have to prove the conspiracy, are safely tucked into my duffel bag. They'll know this, and then they'll come for me. Hopefully by then I'll be ready.

10

I dreamt about a bug my dad used to tell me about when I was a kid. When my dad was in the bush he saw something called a Buju Buju which he later says was one of the most unsettling experiences of his entire military career.

He said the Buju Buju was about the size of a normal tick, except it was quite a bit nastier. Instead of merely biting you it would use its teeth to burrow into the flesh on your arm, and work its way into your body like a mole. There it would lay eggs that would hatch and grow into larvae that would eat their way out of your body and destroy you as they did so.

He saw a man with a Buju Buju infection once. They woke up in the bush and the man had the telltale divot on his arm that told him he had been infected. The man could feel the bug burrowing up his arm, slowly, and they could see a deep purple bruise up the side of his arm where the bug had made his path. They had to cut him open right there in the camp, wrapping a length of rope around his arm for a tourniquet and digging into his shoulder with a Bowie knife.

I've always had nightmares about the Buju Buju and I woke from one of those dreams that afternoon, shivering and shaking in the back of a flatbed pickup truck, nestled between a bale of hay and a cooler filled with beer and sandwiches. I had been picked up on the freeway by a farmer and his son heading towards Sacramento, and after hopping aboard the back of their truck I fell asleep for the remainder of the trip.

They stopped for lunch at a Denny's in Woodland and I thanked them for the ride. The sun was high in the west, it was late in the afternoon. Perhaps the car had been discovered by now, perhaps not. I was far enough away that I felt relatively safe for the time being.

I set out from Denny's with my thumb stretched towards the west. A late model minivan stopped and the back door slid open to let me in.

The driver was ten years older than me, maybe fifteen. He was remarkably well-preserved, however old he was. There was a young girl in the passenger seat of the car and a dog in the back.

"Come on in, buddy," the man said. "Where you heading?"

"Berkeley," I answered.

"Well, that's perfect, we're heading to San Jose. Through your bag in the back and climb in with Rufus."

Rufus lay sprawled across the back seat of the van, his outstretched reaching from window to window. He was a rottweiler, and a large one at that.

"Come on, Rufus," the man exclaimed. "Make room."

I wasn't afraid of the dog but I was slightly intimidated. He cocked his eyebrows at me, as if to tell me that he didn't have any desire to move on my account. But move he did, as the man continued to cajole him up from his sedentary position.

Finally I was able to settle myself on the edge of the bench. After a moment he ascertained that I was no danger and placed his head on my lap and returned to sleep.

The van pulled out of the breakdown lane and rejoined the freeway traffic.

"So," the man began, "what's a young fellow like yourself doing hitchhiking in this day and age?"

"Heh," I replied, slightly nervous, "Don't have much of a choice, really. My car broke down in Redding and I didn't have the money for a bus ticket."

"I can certainly understand that. I just wanted to ask because, well, most hitchhikers these days are kind of surly fellows, older . . . I haven't picked up a hitchhiker in years, and certainly not with Princess in the car. But you looked like a regular stand-up kinda guy, and we got Rufus back there in case you try any kind of funny stuff." He chuckled at this.

"Thank you Sir," I said.

"So, you in college?"

"Actually, I just graduated last month."

"Berkeley?"

"Yeah," I said.

"Well, I'll be damned," he said. "You didn't look like a Berkeley man to me! If I'd have known that I wouldn't have picked you up. I bleed Cardinal Red, myself."

I smirked. "Well, you don't have to worry about me. I was never very much of a partisan."

"You weren't, eh? I can see that."

"I mostly just got frustrated by the traffic on the Big Game weekend."

"Yeah, I'll bet it was something else."

We drove in silence for a few minutes. I was curious as to why the girl in the front seat was so quiet. She didn't seem old enough to be very quiet for very long. Maybe she was shy. I put my hand on Rufus' muzzle and scratched his chin. He seemed appreciative.

"Rufus likes you," the man said. "Sometimes he doesn't like people."

"I'm glad he likes me," I said. "I would hate to be on his bad list."

He laughed again at that one. "Oh, his bark is definitely worse than his bite. That's the thing with rottweilers that no one really knows . . . they have this reputation as big toughies but really they're all just babies. I mean, you've never seen a gentler dog than Rufus, have you, Princess?"

"No, daddy, I haven't," the girl said with a very quiet voice.

"That's right. And even among rottweilers Rufus there is the king of slugs, you know?"

"I can tell."

"So, buddy," the man said after another moment, "I've heard great things about you."

"Um, what?"

"Don't play dumb. There are a lot of people watching your career with great interest. I'm one of them . . . or, should I say, I represent their interests."

Immediately I felt the cold sweat on my backbone and a

ball of molten ingot in my belly. The car wasn't slowing down. I was trapped. I remembered suddenly that my mother's boyfriend was a Stanford graduate as well.

"Don't look so scared," he said. "You look like you've seen a ghost." He adjusted his rear view mirror in order to get a better look at me.

"But," I said slowly, gulping for air, "but – but who are you?"

"A friend. Maybe a friend of a friend would be better to say. You know how these things work, I know someone who knows someone."

"I see," I said, trying to regain my cool.

"I knew your father."

"You did?" I didn't believe him.

"I fought with him in the Congo. We were both Thompson gunners working for the colonials. I remember he used to talk about this stash of diamonds he had supposedly stolen, a huge cache."

This didn't make any sense. My dad didn't have a huge cache of diamonds. He certainly wouldn't have talked about it if he did.

"I wonder where those rocks got to, all those years ago," he said absent-mindedly, trying to act coy.

"I don't know," I answered.

"Oh, I think maybe you do," he replied. I caught a glimpse of him in the rear view mirror he had trained on me. His teeth were glinting in the sunlight. He was grimacing.

"I don't. I don't know anything about my dad. I don't think you do either."

"Don't be petulant. No one likes a brat."

"No, I'm serious. I don't think you knew my dad. You've told me as much about my dad as you'd pick up from a pop song."

"Ah, perhaps, perhaps. You are very astute."

He reached to the dash and turned the radio dial. The

cabin was filled with static for a moment until he found the right channel.

"Frequency 109.9," he said clearly into the air, "this is Operator 8 calling from Interstate 80 roughly between Vacaville and Vallejo. Over."

There was a voice on the other end of the radio, speaking back at him. "Yes, we read you, Operator 8. Please report. Over."

"I have the Prodigal and am en-route to Berkeley as per his request. Subject is docile. Over."

"Very good, 8. Proceed according to plan. Over and out."

The radio went dead. The man – whose name I began to realize I had never been given – turned the radio off and began to smile.

"I'm so very glad I was able to be here, to see you and help you on your way. You're going to do some very important things, my friend. Very important."

I didn't know what to say, how to reply. I looked to my side and there was a large white eighteen-wheeler passing us on the left. The driver was large and hairy, and was staring at us very intently.

"That's Jerry," the driver said, "he's Operator 11. He's here to insure nothing goes wrong. Whenever you see a white truck like that, unmarked, with no bumper stickers and a government license plate, you can assume it's us, doing our best to keep our eyes on you, keep you out of trouble."

He waved the truck past us, passing the thumbs-up sign to the driver. The truck sped up and was soon passed us.

"That went well. I'm glad you're taking this in good spirits. Really, we just want to help you. We know where you're going and we know why you're going there, we just don't know how. That's what you're going to show us."

"I'm not going to show you anything."

"Yes, yes, we kind of figured you'd say that. Hey, you

want a magazine?”

“A magazine?”

“Yeah. Reach into the back and there should be a big cardboard box. Grab a handful, however many you want.”

I reached behind me and there was indeed a cardboard box filled with magazines. I grabbed one and pulled it out apprehensively.

It was a thick magazine, with slick brightly-printed covers. A large neon ink logo announced the name of this magazine to be "YOUNG MEAT". There was a girl on the cover, a young girl no older than nine or ten. She was licking a lollipop, feigning a seductive pose but failing badly, in the disgusting way of small children who pretend to be sexual creatures.

I flipped through the pages and there were children everywhere – preteen boys and girls playing with themselves, playing with older men and women. Some of them were tied up, some of them were being brutalized and raped, covered in purple bruises. Some of them were dressed like sailors and shepherds.

“Do you like it?” the man asked eagerly. “That’s my little Princess on the cover. She’s going to be a star, you know? She’s got that quality to her. It’s magical when she gets in front of the camera.”

I took a closer look at the picture on the front of the magazine.

“Flip to the middle spread, that’s where her pictures are . . .”

I did. There pictures of her being tied up on a wooden table and sodomized, just the worst filth you could imagine. There was blood.

“This is sick,” I said.

“No, it’s business. We all got to pay the rent. You want it? You can have it, I’ve got boxes and boxes full.”

I placed the magazine back in the box. I felt ill, physically sick and dizzy. I didn’t have a clue where I was and I felt vaguely ashamed. I wouldn't be able to sleep tonight, wherever I was.

"Don't worry, we'll set you down safe and sound in Berkeley, just like you said. Just relax and rest, and leave the driving to us."

I didn't say anything for the rest of the trip. Rufus slept with his head in my lap, blissfully unaware of anything that went on around him. I felt bad for the dog, in that life, but he seemed well fed and taken care of.

He took the off-ramp in Berkeley and stopped at a gas station to let me out. I grabbed my duffel bag and jumped out the door as fast as I could.

"Hey," he said, calling out to me, "you be careful now. There's some bad people out there, and they don't all have your best interests at heart like we do."

"Thanks," I said weakly, still quite confused. I looked once again at the girl in the front passenger seat. Her face was blank, unresponsive, uninterested in me or in her father or anything. I wondered, for as long as I could stand, just what horrors she had seen in her short life to inspire such awestruck silence.

11

I never knew what to do in college. I used to walk around by myself and stare at the baleful moon, shooting rats and staring through the windows of the houses down the street.

You learn a lot about cities while they sleep, and Berkeley is no exception. For one thing, a college town doesn't really sleep. The closest you get is the gray haze of the last hour before sunrise, when the only folks awake are night owls burning the candle at both ends. That's the hour I love the most, when you can smell the potential in the air, like the crisp taste of cloves on your tongue.

I loved Berkeley, but I never felt at home there. Somehow, even though I felt a great affection for the city and its inhabitants, I never felt as if I were a part of the organism. There was always something keeping me away, setting me apart from the normal course of events. I often wondered why it seemed as if I was cursed to stand apart, to walk alone . . . but now I have come to understand that it was merely my destiny, if such a word is appropriate. I don't know if I believe in destiny but I know now that I was set apart for special things. There is no such thing as coincidence: I see that now.

The town is built around the University like a cocoon protecting a soft pulpy mass of flesh. The campus is set into the base of the hillside, with the cyclotron and the defense laboratories resting on the roof of the town, overlooking the entire bay. Because of the research they do up on the hill there are spies everywhere, but most of the students and faculty are unaware of their presence.

I met a spy once. It was during those happy and carefree days when I had managed, against all odds, to forget the constant and unremitting danger I lived with. It was the pills I took, the pills my mother made me take that dulled my senses and were fattening me for the eventual kill.

When I stopped taking them I began to perceive the world as I once had, with all the colors and sounds and shapes that I had forgotten. I had allowed myself to be lulled into a false sense of security, and as unforgivable as that was I knew I had no one to blame for this turn of events but myself.

There's something strange in the Berkeley air. I don't know if I could find it at another school, in another school-town in another state or country. But as you rise up on the gradually sloping eastern hill on which the town as built you also pass up and through and into a different state of mind, as if you are passing through and up and apart from the constraints and conceits of mundane life. College has its own mundane, its own sense of normalcy, but it is far removed from gas stations and pharmacies.

You ride a bus up from the freeway. If you took the freeway through to its terminus you'd either end up in San Francisco or San Jose. If you needed to go to either place you could simply take BART, but BART only stopped at Shattuck, a block west of the campus.

The closer you edge to the campus, the more conventional civilization begins to fall by the wayside. Amazingly, there are no fast food restaurants inside the campus or, in fact, anywhere east of Shattuck. Of course, you can find a Taco Bell, a McDonalds and Burger King all within about a quarter mile radius of each other. I had McDonalds every Wednesday afternoon and it was a treat after the bland and starchy stink of dorm food.

On the last block of University Avenue before you enter the University you pass Comic Relief (although I hear they have since moved) and a decent record store whose name escapes me. But then you reach the streetcorner right before the big gate and there's an administrative building right there, rather large and clunky and God have mercy on you if you have to go in there.

The entrance to the University is laid out in a large U-shaped courtyard before you reach the actual roads that line the campus. Of course, the roads themselves are closed to most traffic, with the exception of emergency vehicles and groundskeepers and the like. As you head up University drive there's a beautiful grove of trees to your immediate right, a hidden track of darkened greenery left to quiet and contemplation on warm spring days when the campus fills with the noise of city activity.

After the copse you pass two life sciences buildings. If you keep going due east you'll pass the huge library complex set at the top of a beautiful northward sloping glade. It's a straight shot to the stadium and the amphitheater, both set into the hill at the rear of the campus proper, directly under the grade that leads to the cyclotron.

But I usually turn right after the life sciences building, climbing a small hillock between the massive Dwinelle complex and the tiny Durant Hall. That's one of the most beautiful places on campus, a small glade with green grass and trees with huge spreading leaves perfect for passing an hour or two with a book, watching the people pass. In the fall and the spring, that's when the girls pass by with their sundresses on. Girls don't wear slips anymore.

Of course when you pass by Dwinelle you're almost to Sather Gate and once you pass through those great grand wrought iron archways you're in Sproul Plaza and you're in the full press of history and fully in the midst of the assembled student body. There are always people, always people at all times of the day and in all situations.

This is where the riots were held, the famous protests and the chants and the marches. Of course, all that's in the past now. There are always some token politicos on the scene – it goes without saying – but the overriding emotion on this campus, and I assume on campuses across the country, is apathy. People work hard to get into these universities. They work hard once they're in the universities. If they don't work hard, they party. They don't want to throw away their personal achievements or their equally important personal luxuries on some vague sense of broad responsibilities. There are just too many things to do, and no one cares. I didn't, and knowing what I know now I can't say that my priorities were entirely misguided.

I've been to the campus at Santa Cruz and it's really amazing how they designed it to be the polar opposite of Berkeley. It was built in the years immediately after the unrest of the nineteen-sixties, so it was planned without any central location, no unifying plaza like Berkeley had with Sproul. All you have is a string of disparate campuses set miles apart in the midst of a primeval forest. It lacks something very vital to the college experience, I think.

Opposite the Sproul building in the plaza is the King Student Union building. The University bookstore sits in the Union's basement along with a few related retailers, the college memorabilia store and a small convenience outlet that sold cheap candy. There are also a few assembly rooms in the union as well as the ballroom. A large staircase curves down from the ballroom mezzanine.

I've been to the top floor of the Union exactly once, on a campus tour during my junior year of high school. It was a good trip. I was still taking my pills during that part of my life and I suppose I was distracted by any number of things. That is maybe why I made the decision to come to Berkeley.

Anyway, after a brief meeting with an enrollment executive, we dispersed and were given a few minutes to ourselves in the union building. I found an exterior porch to the side of the main meeting room, a small rooftop alcove facing west over the city of Berkeley and towards the bay. On a perfectly clear afternoon you can see the fifteen odd miles from the top of Berkeley on through to the Golden Gate Bridge, and if you catch the afternoon just right you can see the sun setting through distant gaps in high tension cables drawn and pulled half a century ago. That's when I knew I wanted to go to Berkeley. I tried to take a picture but – of course – I ran out of film at just the wrong moment, and when I turned around the sun had moved and the image was gone, save for a lingering shiver in memory.

But memory is like that. It creeps and crawls like a chimera, tricking and taunting you from behind a curtain. You think you remember something but you don't, not really, not really in any meaningful way. Memory can be an illusion, a cruel deception. Of course, this seems overwrought, like something in an adolescent diary. But its hard to feel anything but grim resentment towards the workings of your own mind when you know you've been set upon, betrayed and trapped by circumstance. They've been lying to me since the day I was born, and sometimes I want so badly to just accept the lies and the illusions, to convince myself that I'm happy because the world says I should be, that I should take my pills because I need to be healthy.

But I don't want to be "healthy". If I'm healthy then the men who killed my father, who killed 3,000 people in New York and countless thousands more across the world, will be able to get away with it.

Once I took apart one of those pills they send me in the mail. I cut the membrane open with an exacto knife and there was a small creature living inside it, a small pink worm with minuscule antennae sticking out of its forehead. When I opened the capsule there was a brief whiff of something pungent, like valerian root mixed with sulfur. I surmised that this was the creature's atmosphere, this was the air it needed to survive in the pill until it could prosper in my innards.

After I saw this I was repulsed. I emptied my stomach in my wastebasket and lay on the hard industrial carpeted floor of my dorm and sweat in the cold for a quarter of an hour. I didn't eat for two days, rather I flushed my body with the harshest laxatives I could find. I drank castor oil by the bottle. I gave myself repeated enemas, one after another.

Finally, when I was satisfied that I had done everything I could to flush the creatures out of my system I began a regimen of white rice and distilled water, which I kept to for a full month. I dropped twenty superfluous pounds and felt better than I had in ages. The spiritual visions that had almost left me forever returned with a vengeance, and I began once more to understand things which I had imagined forgotten.

Sometimes I tried to see if there were any bugs left in my system. Once I saw small shapes burrowing in the flesh of my forearm, so I took a knife and tried to dig them out. I never found them, however. If they are still there I can't find them. Maybe they die and rot.

Berkeley is a beautiful city, a wonderful place to live and to learn. But there's also something unbearably disingenuous here as well, something rotten and sticky and covered in vomit right at the very core. Sometimes when I would walk around in the night I would see things, I would see people doing things I didn't understand, that couldn't make sense. But I saw them nonetheless, and I had no choice but to try and reconcile what I had seen with that I desperately wished to believe was true in this world.

There are garbage trucks that run in the night, making their way unobserved through the tight city streets of America's great cities. The trucks stop at a corner in a major metropolis and men in black leather jumpsuits pour out of the back. These men wear helmets that obscure their faces. They carry high-caliber machine rifles slung over their shoulders.

They pour into the ghettos and barrios and liquidate the homeless and the abandoned on America's streets. They take the bodies and put them into the back of the truck where the remains are never seen again. People just disappear off the streets. I've never seen it but I've heard tell.

After Sproul you come up against the southern border of the campus and Bancroft Avenue. Bancroft runs all the way down back to Shattuck, where the movie theaters and the Barnes & Noble are. But right down the way out of the union and by the tree-lined sidewalk you find yourself on Telegraph Avenue, the heart and soul of the campus. When I dream of Berkeley, this is where my sleeping heart brings me.

12

I once met an old man with a mermaid in his pocket. It was small, maybe half an inch long, and he had it locked in a small glass ball, about two inches in diameter. There was a tiny valve on the top of the ball that he opened every now and again in order to aerate the ball, so the mermaid's water wouldn't grow stale.

He told me that he had found the mermaid in a fishing net off the coast of the Isle of Man. Apparently it was yet a baby, fresh out of the egg, and would need another thirty years to grow to full size. Mermaids grow at a much slower rate than humans, apparently.

I met this man in the People's Park, which can be found one block east of Telegraph at the intersection of Dwight and Bowditch. The People's Park is where the homeless men live, and it's also got a basketball court and some rather scary looking public restrooms that I have never used (but which I have entered). During the daytime the basketball court is always in use, but during the nighttime I try not to go near the park for fear of any number of things.

Sadly, the night is full of stories, hidden narratives that can jump out and tear you into another world. I took a cosmology class where the professor discussed string theory, and how string theory had evolved into something strange called M theory that posited that the universe as we knew it was nothing more than a stretched membrane floating in eleven-dimensional space. There are perhaps an infinite number of separate dimensions floating in M-space all around us, perhaps no more than a quantum millimeter removed from our own universe.

Sometimes all it takes is a slight slip to move from one membrane to another, and in this way can a seemingly infinite gulf can be traversed in an instant. So it is with these strange shadowy underworlds that live and prosper underneath our feet and behind out backs. All it takes is one instant for everything in your life to change, for you to slip through one membrane and into another. There's only ever a phantom wisp of a breath standing between you and a living nightmare.

Telegraph Avenue is the confluence of all the energy in and around the campus. You have the hyperattenuated nervous energy from the student body and the paranoid menace emanating downward from the military facilities on the hill and the desperate calm of the homeless folk and gutterpunks who dot the boulevard. The energy is delirious and manic and contagious and addictive. The children who come to the University from all across the world, alone for the first time and drunk on the possibilities of life on their own, unaware and oblivious to the dangers that lurk at every corner all around them, they are everywhere. I was one of these children, when I came here, and it's a miracle I eventually managed to extricate myself from the poisonous intoxicating lethargy.

Walking south on Telegraph I can smell the same possibility that once seemed so welcoming. It has curdled, it has been soured by time and experience. There's a Gap on the right side of the street, across from a bath store. Blondie's pizza is still on the first block, with the best pizza in the city, maybe the best pizza in the world.

There are parking garages and banks and memorabilia stores where you can buy clothing items emblazoned with the school logo. Right off of Telegraph on Durant they've tucked the Tower records, which may not have the selection of Rasputin's or Amoeba's, but is still worth browsing for discounts. I spent so many hours browsing through the record bins, learning quite a bit without even trying. It allows you to be alone in the heart of a crowd. As much as I ever felt alone I knew there was a reason for isolation, that there was a purpose for my desolation. If I didn't maybe remember the reason that was OK because there was that tendentious urge in my belly, the overwhelming desire to run and fight and scream that kept me from ever truly forgetting my destiny.

Of course, looking back over those words on the page they seem amazingly callow, spectacularly overwrought. It might seem that way to you if you've never been afraid for your life, afraid of the folds in the fabric behind your head, afraid of the fragile membranes popping and leaving you adrift. I know very well how important I was and am to their plans, to their burgeoning schemes and machinations. I had to be afraid, because I was alive. I was born afraid.

I've spent hours in Cody's books. They've got a good newsstand and an even better florist positioned right outside the front door. Across from Cody's is Amoeba's, which I've already mentioned, the best of the three record stores on Telegraph. Next to Cody's there are two additional bookstores, both of which trade primarily in used and remaindered stock.

There's so much to do and see in these scant four blocks, without actually doing anything. I left this school in the same position that I arrived in – abject isolation. I went out of my way to avoid people, because I didn't want to hurt anyone. Was that wise? Healthy? I've been accused of psychotic behavior in my time.

I don't want to hurt anyone. I don't want to hurt myself. But I know I'm a target, that's why I had to leave, that's why I had to go and isolate myself while these things work themselves out. What else is there to do? I feel adrift, cast off, alone and undernourished. I'm hungry.

I don't know if I'm still being followed. My conversation with the man who had given me the ride into Berkeley still rang in my head, the man who sodomized his daughter for money on camera. If he was correct, then they knew where I was at all times. It didn't matter what I thought, whether or not I felt I was being watched or not, I was being watched. Perhaps they had probes in my body, tracking me at all times, or maybe they could even read my mind.

It wasn't that crazy to imagine that someone, somewhere had built a machine to enable them to read minds. All it would take would be the impetus to read the unconscious signals ticking off from the spinning synapses in my brain, to be able to home in on my peculiar brainwaves in just such a way as to see exactly what was in my thoughts at all times. It didn't seem far-fetched at all.

They have atom-smashers out in the desert, huge lengths of steel pipe wherein they explode tiny atoms in order to count the subatomic particles emitted by massive collisions. They can track the movement of neutrinos in heavy water, can't they read the particles in my head?

Walking down the city streets everything seems so ready, like dollhouses and doll streets and matchbox cars with Weebles inside them. The motion and the energy is contagious. You want to walk forever with the massed bulk of people, disappearing into the crowds and losing yourself and your concerns, melting down into the pipes that run along under the streets.

I'm standing on the corner of Telegraph and Dwight outside of Amoeba's when I feel a hand on my shoulder. I turn around and there's the man from that night at the jail, the large man who stabbed his compatriot while we all watched.

"Good to see you," he said. "I was hoping I'd run into you again."

"You remember me?"

"Of course. I never forget a face. Especially considering the auspicious circumstances under which we met."

"You killed that guy." My voice emerged as a dry croak. We were standing in the middle of a busy intersection in a large city. There were people everywhere, but no one was paying any attention to us.

"Yes, I killed him," he replied. "I had to kill him. He's not the first or the last or even the most interesting person I've killed. It's my job to kill people."

"Are you here to kill me?"

His eyes widened as he grinned. "You? No. I have no intention of killing you. It is very much more to the point that I wish to show you some things, to elaborate certain facts which you may, up to now, have been ignorant of."

He began walking up the block towards People's Park. The basketball court was full up again, with young men running up and down the pavement and sweating their asses off together. It was hot enough, in the middle of the summer, for the game to have devolved into shirts and skins. The athlete's broad frames glistened in the summer sun. Most of these boys looked very good – were they members of the college team on break?

My host continued up the sidewalk. He didn't pay any attention to the game, or the dozens of homeless people who were scattered among the foliage, or the handful of hippies playing frisbee in the meadow. He seemed oblivious, but I'm certain he saw everything. He wasn't as young as I remembered him, or perhaps he was and he merely looked older without his companion.

"You can call me Adam," he said, lifting his head and wiping the sweat from his brow.

"That's not your real name."

"No shit, Sherlock," he replied. "You're not as dumb as you look." He pulled a white handkerchief from his pants pocket and wiped a bead of sweat from his forehead.

"What do you want?" I asked. I was starting to get nervous.

"What do I want? What I want is irrelevant. What I am here to do, on the other hand, is of the first importance. I trust your ride into town was eventful?"

"Yeah," I answered wanly. We were standing in front of the small restroom to the rear of the park. It was tiny, just room enough for two johns and two sinks. I don't think I had ever had reason to enter it before.

"Whatever you do, if you ever see that man or his

daughter again, you have to run the other way as fast as possible. You are in grave danger every second you are in their proximity."

"I have no intention of ever seeing him again."

"I should hope so, but all the same, if you do so much as catch a glimpse of them in a crowd, you have to run, or you will most likely die."

He opened the door to the men's latrine and motioned for me to go in first. I hesitated. He repeated the invitation.

"Please," he said, "do not make me beg for the pleasure of your company." He very nonchalantly moved his hand towards his back pocket.

I didn't want to find out just what was in that back pocket. I shuffled into the small, stifling restroom and he followed behind me. The door swung shut with a metallic thud and we were alone in a very small and sweaty bathroom.

Adam walked the few feet to the far wall and kicked the toilet. A hidden panel slid away along the top of the wall. He reached up and pulled down a solid red lever, and the floor slid away slowly, revealing a flight of stairs illuminated by a train of fluorescent lights.

"You first." He motioned me to descend.

I didn't really have a lot of choices. He had me trapped, and he had a gun. I could have opened the door and ran, but I think he could have found me anywhere I wanted to hide. It behooved me to trust Adam, as for the time being I did not seem to have a choice in the matter.

I bit my tongue and began the slow descent. Our footsteps echoed against the claustrophobically tight walls of the stairwell. There were lights all around us, set into the sides of the steps and illuminating our passage with an illicit glow.

"How deep does this go?" I asked after a minute or so.

"A mile or so," he replied. "But not this stairway. This stairway actually terminates in the main mezzanine."

"Ah," I said. I didn't understand anything.

"We should be just about there."

Sure enough, the stairwell soon came to an end. The mezzanine was a large metal expanse, with industrial-grade carpet spread from wall to wall and large florescent lights embedded in the cavernous ceiling. There were three large leather couches spread throughout the room, and along with a handful of small end tables festooned with magazines and ashtrays, they were the only furnishings in the entire lobby. There were numerous doors on either side of the room, leading to unknown and mysterious passageways far beneath Berkeley.

The room terminated in a far wall with three large doors. The doors were the kind you see in hospitals, swinging gates with large glass windows set at eye level and with tin plating along the bottom third. There was one man in the room, a large muscular man sitting on the couch closest to the stairwell. He had a magazine on his lap but he wasn't reading it, he was aiming a large assault rifle directly at us.

"What's the good word," the man said gruffly.

"Adam Alpha Nixon," my friend replied.

The guard on the couch did not lower his weapon. "How's the weather," he replied.

"Partly cloudy, with a 50% chance of rain in the evening."

The guard finally lowered his gun. "Good to see you, Sergeant."

"Any trouble since I've been topside?"

"Not a one," the man replied. "Everything's been quiet. Is this," he motioned towards me with his cigarette, "the golden boy?"

"Yeah, this is him."

I didn't know how to react to this, to any of this. The architecture of the mezzanine seemed to imply a nightmare behind padded doors. I was afraid, but I was stuck. I had to play through.

"Doesn't look like much," the guard sniffed. "Hardly worth the trouble."

"Looks can be deceiving," my friend said curtly. "We'll be going into the project now."

"Have fun," he sniffed. He picked up his magazine and began to read, successfully ignoring us before we had exited the room.

Adam grabbed my arm and led me through the room. The doors at the distant end of the great hall were smeared with flecks of paint and dirt. I wondered if perhaps this strange place didn't have a janitor.

The doors opened just like the swinging doors in a hospital. We were in a long low hallway with dim light. There were cages all along the sides, large cages with old-fashioned iron bars. There were no lights on inside the cages and I couldn't make anything out as we passed through the passageway.

"It's nighttime down here," Adam whispered as we walked briskly. "These folks need their beauty sleep."

I didn't ask anything. I had the odd feeling of being in a dream – and when you're in a dream you don't think to ask questions because there is a part of you, deep down, that knows the answers. If I knew what was being held in these cages, I didn't remember it then.

"You're curious, but you're smart enough not to let it show. I can certainly respect that, I can definitely respect that impulse. You're smart. There's a reason why your line was chosen."

I kept quiet. We were approaching the end of the long hallway, and there was another set of battered institutional swing doors at the end. We passed through these doors and we were in a small room . . . a laboratory of some sort. There were metal counters all around the wall, with empty examination tables set throughout. The pungent aroma of scrubbed antiseptic hygiene permeated everything in here. Even the air was harsh and sharp in my lungs, crisp and devoid of any life.

There was no one else in the room. If it was nighttime for the prisoners held in their cages, perhaps it was nighttime for whomever operated this laboratory. I wondered, in an odd, absent fashion, whether or not this lab was connected to the labs on the hill, or maybe to the greater Livermore complex.

Adam walked over to the far end of the room. There was something under a long blanket on one of the metal exam tables. I didn't want to take the blanket off because I was afraid of what I would see if I did.

"Now, I don't want you to get upset," he told me. "You're about to see something that might upset you. But you're one of maybe a dozen people who actually know what is going on in this room. This is very, very important."

He pulled the sheet off the table, revealing a naked corpse. Or, at least, parts of a naked corpse. The body was shaven and half of the face was removed. The left leg was missing, and the skin had been flayed off the torso. The corpse was open from stomach to sternum, revealing the body's innards.

"You're not vomiting, good. You never went to medical school, you're not used to being around cadavers. I'm proud."

I wanted badly to vomit. But I swallowed the bile in my throat and tried to breathe through my nose, not my mouth. Thankfully, there was no smell.

"This fellow here didn't have a lot of use for us, unfortunately. You can barely tell with his skin removed like this, but he was a pretty bad alcoholic. Most of his organs were horribly pickled. He had some interesting brain chemistry, though, that was very useful to us."

I had been silent since we had entered the room, but I finally spoke up at this. "Brain chemistry?"

"Yes. Before he died, he was under extensive

observation. He had something wrong up there – he was bi-polar, or schizophrenic or something to that effect. In any event, he didn't respond well to mind-control. His cerebral cortex would light up like a Christmas tree when we tried to read his thoughts. Unfortunately, that's what killed him. One day his brain just melted through his nose."

"So you can read my mind."

"Well, of course," Adam said, reassuringly. "We can read everyone's mind. It's what we do."

He put sheet back over the body and walked to the far side of the room. There was a door in the wall and he motioned me to enter the room on the other side.

"This is where it happens," he said with pride. The room was smaller than the last, cramped with machinery. There were computers everywhere, and television monitors, and EKGs with bouncing electric streams of consciousness floating all around us. Most of the television screens were playing blurry pornography.

There were a few people scattered throughout the small room, glued to computer monitors and quietly tapping on keyboards.

Adam leaned over whispered into my ear: "They're very busy. They can home in on any mind out of hundreds of millions. It's their responsibility to keep us all safe. They take that responsibility very seriously."

Adam grabbed my arm and pushed out of the room. "They don't like to be disturbed. They do twelve and sixteen hour shifts and it's vital that they keep their concentration strong throughout. It's amazing though, that they can do all that from such a tiny room. You couldn't have done it at all, fifty or seventy-five years ago - the computers necessary to sift through all the data just didn't exist. But now you can fit the appropriate processors in the palm of your hand."

We were alone again in the laboratory. I felt very pale but I knew I was sweating. I hadn't regained my composure from seeing the flayed corpse laid out on the table like that.

"What's the matter, chum? Not feeling too good?"

"I'm a little bit nauseated."

"Ah, I should have expected as much. I'm very sorry, but I didn't have time to prepare you properly."

"I don't know how you could have prepared me properly for that," I gestured over towards the table where the corpse lay.

"Oh, that's nothing. We have to be strong, my friend, in order to protect the people who have been entrusted into our care. All of them."

"How is this protecting them?" I nodded over to the table where the corpse lay.

"Oh, very simple. This isn't a good example of what we can do. Things have been kind of quiet lately, to be honest. But a few years ago we were very busy. We constructed the hijackers out of spare parts we picked up around the park – an eyeball here, a deltoid there."

I didn't know what to say to this.

"Of course, we have our fingers in everything, these days. You have to control all the different players, make sure every piece on the chessboard moves exactly how you want him to move, or you will never succeed. Everyone from the President to the lowliest bum in the street, we can read all their thoughts, and we can tell anyone what to do. Of course, none of this would have been possible without your father."

"My father did this?"

"Oh yes, he was instrumental in creating all of this."

"I don't believe you."

"Well, that's certainly your prerogative. It doesn't really make any difference whether you believe me or not, but it is true."

"I believe you about as much as I believed that pervert."

Adam blanched. He looked genuinely wounded, as if I had slapped him. "You wound me, sir. I am nothing like that monster, or the men he serves."

"I don't know anything about any of this. For all I know you and him could be working together with all of this."

"Let me show you something." Adam grabbed my arm and began walking towards the door that led back out to the mezzanine. We passed through the door and were in the hallway again. Adam reached across to the wall and flipped the light switch.

The hallway was filled with flickering light. I didn't realize how dark these rooms had been until he flipped the switch – I moved my arm to cover my eyes.

After my eyes adjusted to the light I saw Adam walking over to one of the cages that lined the hall. While my eyes had been adjusting he had grabbed some sort of long metal pole and put on a pair of leather gloves. He turned a key in the wall and one of the cells opened, a wall of iron bars swinging out into the hall.

"Look in here," Adam said. He gestured with the metal pole into the cage. There was something moving slowly inside the cell. It looked like a pile of rags and blankets. I couldn't see what it was. There was no furniture in the cell and the floor was covered in hay.

"Get up," he began to yell. "Get up! Get up!" He moved the pole in his hand to gain better traction on the long instrument, and then shoved it into the mound of rags on the ground. It wasn't a pile of rags, though – I heard a man scream. There was electricity coming out of the end of that pole, and there was a man writhing in the floor, covered in hay.

"This is what we do for you, my friend," Adam said to me, turning his head to look at me as he continued to poke the man on the ground. "This is what we do for every living soul in America, to keep you safe and secure."

I could smell something burning. The man on the ground didn't say anything, he just lay in a heap and shivered and moaned as Adam kept jamming the cattle prod into his flesh.

"This is sick," I yelled. "What are you doing? What does this prove?"

"I'm conditioning him. He has to be prepared. Tenderized. Traumatized."

"You're insane."

"No," Adam said serenely. "I'm not insane. You are."

"Fuck you." I grabbed the cell door and swung it shut as hard as I could. The key was still in the lock – I pulled it out and threw it as far as I could down the hallway. And then I ran.

I ran through the hallway with Adam's laughter ringing in my ears. He didn't care that he was trapped in the cell, I'm sure his friends would get him out in a moment's time. He was still getting his jollies from zapping the prisoner, as I could hear the muffled cries of protest, almost inhuman in their savage pleading, echoing down the prison walls.

I flew threw the doors and into the mezzanine. The guard was gone. His magazine was where he had left it, and his cigarette was still burning in an ashtray. Had I gotten lucky? Bathroom break? I didn't stop to reflect.

The stairwell leading to the surface was longer than I remembered, and the metal steps were slippery with condensation. Was it raining in the park? I didn't even remember. I didn't think I'd been underground for longer than twenty minutes.

I ran and I ran, taking the steps two at a time until my lungs were burning. I realized that I was holding onto the strap of my duffel bag so hard my knuckles were white. Finally I came to the top of the stairs. The passageway had closed behind Adam and I, but there was a big red bottom on the side of the wall. I pressed it and the trapdoor slid open: apparently they are less concerned about people finding their way out than finding their way inside.

It was dark outside, dark as pitch and I stumbled the moment I left the bathroom. Hadn't it been daytime when I had gone down the stairwell and into the complex? I hadn't been in that underground laboratory for longer than twenty minutes. I couldn't have been.

It had been raining - the ground was slick and wet. There was yelling and screaming in the distance. I turned and ran into the park.

All around the perimeter of the park, the homeless people establish little tents where they keep their belongings and sleep. There were flashing lights all around the park, and I could see movement in the darkened streets.

Someone started screaming over to my right. I turned and saw one of the park's homeless residents sprawled out on the grass next to the copse of bushes where his sleeping bag and knapsack were stashed. He was yelling and pointing and I couldn't make any sense of what he was saying but everyone else in the park was beginning to panic.

There were black shapes moving in the darkness, dark boots crunching the leaves and the grass between their feet. I moved to give the man who had fallen my arm, to help him to his feet, but he pushed me away and pointed towards where he had been sleeping. There was a large man covered in black – black leather pants, black armor, gleaming black riot gear. He wore a featureless black helmet and was swinging a truncheon as he walked towards me.

I put up my hands to block the blow but before I knew what was happening I was on the ground, splayed on my back. I wasn't moving. My eyes were open and I could see very clearly what was happening but when I tried to make my arms and legs move, in order to pull myself to my feet and run to safety, it didn't work. I just couldn't do it.

There were more of the black-clad stormtroopers, streaming out of the darkness and into the park. They were swinging their clubs indiscriminately, pushing over the tents and trampling the bushes.

I lay there for a few moments, quietly watching the carnage unfold, before I realized that I could move again. My head was hurting badly. I reached up and felt my forehead – sure enough, there was something very soft and wet above my right eye, a pulsating wound where the stormtrooper's club had found my forehead.

I pulled myself up and began to crawl towards the street. No one was paying any attention to me, it seemed, as the homeless people were being routed and rounded up into a large black wagon, about the size of a dump-truck. They were screaming and protesting, and many were badly injured.

There was a flash of light and fire, and one of the stormtroopers ran into the street, panicking, covered in fire and waving his arms like a madman. He fell to the ground and rolled, trying to dampen the flames. Two of his fellows ran after him, trying to pat down the fire as he rolled on the bare concrete. I could see the fire reflecting against their sleek and smooth black helmets - like motorcycle helmets, with no facial features whatsoever, just a blank.

Whatever it was that had set the trooper on fire wasn't isolated, because I looked back towards the park to see that the treeline was beginning to burn. The homeless people who weren't badly hurt began to move and scatter, pouring out of the park and away from the van and into the side streets of urban Berkeley. The guards tried in vain to enforce order, but they succeeded only in clobbering a few random stragglers. There had been dozens of homeless people sleeping in People's Park that night, and it looked as if most of them managed to get away.

But the fire was still burning, and the flames began to gather intensity. I pulled myself to my feet as quickly as I could, hoping that I had been totally forgotten in the scuffle. But I saw two of the troopers turn and lumber towards me before I could begin to run.

"Hey," I heard a voice behind me, "come here."

Someone grabbed my arm and pulled me away faster than I could respond. My legs were shaky under me and everything was spinning. I turned and I saw a man pulling me towards a light brown van parked at the corner of the street.

He pulled me the remaining way towards the van and threw me into the backseat, where I landed with the grace of a slaughtered cow. The man who had pulled me to safety jumped into the van and pulled the door shut behind him.

"Gun it!" he yelled. The vehicle lurched and we moved into the night.

"Yeah!" my savior yelled as he looked out the rear window. "They can't catch us – they've set the whole neighborhood on fire."

I was laying on the floor of the van in a pile of crumpled sleeping bags and blankets. I couldn't lift my body up to look behind us, but I saw the lights from the burning trees flickering against the walls and ceiling of the van.

"You've been hurt," I heard a voice say. "Don't move."

I blinked for a moment and when I opened my eyes there was a girl hovering above me, young, with long brown hair pulled back into a ponytail.

"Stay where you are," she said. "I'll clean your wound."

I was in no shape to argue. I tried to at least stay conscious but it was a losing battle. She pressed a wet towel against my forehead and it felt good. I could feel the bus vibrating as we skidded over the wet pavement on our way out of town.

In the last moments before I totally passed out I was able to make out a the outline of a poster tacked to the ceiling of the bus. It was black, with a field of stars and an image of planet Earth floating in space in the foreground. A bolt of energy burst through the heavens and down onto the surface of the Earth. I could barely make out the script printed across the bottom of the poster as I drifted out of consciousness for the final time:

"The New Universe sold here."

13

I woke up in a campground in Truckee. It was late in the afternoon and I had been asleep for well over twelve hours.

I couldn't remember a damn thing from the moment I fell into the van at the park. My head was throbbing, and I was aware of the fact that there was a thick bandage covering my forehead.

The sun was just starting to set beneath the distant mountains, but of course I couldn't see that because the campground was set in a grove of trees. We had climbed a good few thousand feet in elevation since leaving Berkeley, and the air here was crisp.

Truckee sits at the heart of the Sierra Nevada mountain range, about twenty minutes from Lake Tahoe to the south and twenty minutes to the Nevada border in the east. I found out later that they had had an Olympics here – or rather, in Squaw Valley, which is about ten minutes outside of town, between Truckee and Tahoe City. The Soviets beat the pants off everyone else, with seven gold medals, five silver and nine bronze. Of course, back in 1960 there were only thirty nations participating in the winter games, and there were only twenty-seven events.

I could easily imagine how living in such a beautiful town could be a headache. There are ski resorts everywhere, along with tourists and traffic congestion. Nice place to visit but I wouldn't want to live there, as the saying goes.

My sleeping bag was hot, so I slowly undid the zipper to let some cool air in. The metallic buzz of the zipper's teeth rang softly through the thin air. I felt woozy, light headed and hungry. There was only one person still at the campsite with me.

"Hello?" I called out meekly.

"Oh, you're awake!" she answered. It was the same girl who I had seen in the van for a moment before I passed out. In the daylight, she was still beautiful, but she was also very young. Maybe twenty. I would have been surprised to learn she was old enough to drink. She looked like she could use a meal.

She was sitting at the picnic table reading a book. Placing the book on the table behind her she walked over to where I was laying. There was a large tarp stretched across the ground, and there were four empty sleeping bags next to mine.

"How's your head?" she asked as she knelt down next to me. "Does it hurt badly?"

"It's OK. It feels better, I suppose. I feel weak."

"Well, of course you do, that was a nasty hit you took. It took twenty stitches to patch you up, and I could see the bone."

"You took me to the hospital?"

"No, we did it ourselves, by the firelight. John is an EMT, he knew how to do it just fine. We figured you might not feel kindly towards waking up in a hospital bed."

"Yeah," I sighed. "Do you have something to eat? I'm starving."

"Let me get you a sandwich," she said as she rose. "You're probably not up to much more than that right now."

I lay back down on the pillow. She was right, of course – my stomach was empty but it was also feeling rather hostile. I closed my eyes and tried not to think of the pain as she prepared my sandwich.

After a few minutes she returned with a peanut butter and jelly sandwich and a bottle of cold water. I didn't even realize how thirsty I had been until the water hit the back of my throat.

The sandwich tasted as good as anything I had ever

eaten. Before I knew it I had eaten two more, along with having drank a few additional bottles of water.

"You have a healthy appetite," she said playfully. "I'm glad to see you're feeling better. We were all worried after that bad scene in the park."

"Yeah," I nodded vaguely. Images and events from the previous days came rushing back over me. I was a log in the tidewater, bobbing lonely in deep waters. Suddenly my stomach wasn't so secure.

"What was going on, anyway?"

I looked up at her and tried to speak. I didn't know what exactly to say. My mouth opened, and closed. Nothing came out.

"It's OK," she finally said, "if you don't want to talk about it now that's all right. You look like you been through hell, 's all."

I felt very much as if I had been through hell, but I wasn't about to tell her that. I didn't really know her, and I had no desire to entangle her in my problems.

"Where are the other guys? I remember other guys." I asked.

"They went into town to get some supplies." She motioned towards the distance. We were near a freeway, I could tell from the loud diesel trucks groaning in the distance, hitting their Jake brakes as they rode down the steep incline on the way down into the Truckee basin. The town proper lay a mile or so in the east, huddled around Interstate Highway 5 for protection. I was going to have to get back on that road and keep going before someone found me. I wondered how long I could keep going down the road with these strange people, who had already been so kind to me.

I was still sitting up in the sleeping bag when I heard the others return to the campsite. There were three of them, and they were all carrying groceries. One of them held a flat pizza box in front of him, arms outstretched in a peaceful offering.

"Hey there," the one with the pizza called out. "Debbie!"

Debbie . . . Debbie was her name. Debbie ran out to meet them and helped them carry the groceries to the table.

"He's up," I heard her say. The three men turned over to where I was sitting, noticing me awake for the first time.

One of the men walked over towards me. He was taller than the other two men, broad-shouldered, and looked to be at least a few years older as well.

"John?" I inquired as he crouched on the ground next to me.

"Yep, John Long. How's your head?"

"Feels pretty rough," I answered. "But I guess it could be worse. I have you to thank for that?"

"I put some stitches in you."

"Well, thanks, I guess."

"Want some pizza?"

Even after three peanut butter and jelly sandwiches I was still hungry. "Yes," I replied. "Help me up."

He held out his arm and I grabbed his hand. His fingers were unreasonably strong. I was weak and my head started to swim as I rose but he steadied me.

The pizza in a big box labeled Pizza Junction tasted as good as anything I'd ever eaten before – and certainly a far sight better than those sandwiches. I tried not to eat more than my share but Debbie volunteered to give me a slice of hers because I was so hungry.

After we had finished off the pizza the five of us sat in silence for a moment. Even taking into account the presence of a stranger such as myself, there was an unease in their company, the silence of unspoken words.

After a few moments, John finally spoke. "Tell us, where were you going?"

"I'm heading across the country. I wanted to see it from one ocean to the other."

"Admirable goal," he mumbled. John's voice was low

and graveled, like a rural road. It seemed as if speaking was an effort, or at least an inconvenience. The longer I sat in his presence the more I became impressed with his physicality. He was wearing a thin white T-shirt that showed his muscles - perhaps you could say it showed them off.

"Where are you four headed?" I asked.

"We're off to see America," John answered blandly. "You ever read Kerouac?"

"Yeah, in high school I guess."

"Like that, sort of. I'm Dean."

I didn't know how to take that one, but after a few more seconds his stolid face creased into a sly smile. He was an odd one.

I wondered why the other three were so quiet in his presence. I hadn't even caught the other two mens' names.

John and Debbie were seated on the opposite bench from where I sat next to the two others. I turned to my right.

"I didn't catch your names."

The one immediately to my right turned his head towards me before he spoke. "Lyle," he answered. He extended his hand over the table and I met his grip.

"Brent," the other one answered. He waved, probably because he didn't feel like reaching over Lyle. Neither of them seemed very enthusiastic about keeping the conversation going.

"So," John began quietly, almost as an aside, "what happened last night, anyway?"

"I wish I could tell you," I replied, as honestly as I could manage. "There was some kind of riot going on and I just happened to be caught in the middle of it."

"Hmmmm." It was a long, low rumble that emanated from deep inside his barrel chest. His sun-creased brow furrowed.

"I'm lucky your four were there, or I'd probably be in jail or the hospital by now."

"Yeah," John answered. "It was lucky. Do you live in Berkeley?"

"No, no . . . I went to school there. I live further north. I just wanted to start my trip there, looking over the harbor out onto the bay and out through to the Pacific. It seemed as good a place as any to start."

"It's beautiful there," he agreed.

"So, where have you seen?"

"What?"

"Well, you said you were out to see America, what parts have you seen?"

Debbie exchanged looks with John. He was nonplused, but she seemed nervous.

"We've been all over. We were down in Mexico for a while. Baja is beautiful in the spring."

"So I've heard."

There was another moment of silence. John seemed to physically discourage further conversation through sheer force of will. He rose slowly from the picnic table.

"I'd like to take a closer look at your head, if I could," he said.

"Sure." He motioned me over to the van. It was already getting dark, long shadows growing underneath the pine trees.

It was a mess inside the van, as you would expect from any vehicle that was carrying four people across the country. He nodded over towards the bench at the rear of the vehicle and motioned for me to sit.

He rummaged in a bag and pulled out a small flashlight. Leaning over me, he shone the flashlight on my scalp and poked the stitches with his finger.

"Um, should I maybe get a tetanus shot or something?"

"No need for that." He lay his hand on my shoulder and squeezed firmly. "You're going to be just fine, my friend. Does this hurt?"

He poked at the stitches again.

"No, not really," I answered.

"Then I did my job well," he said.

"OK."

He finished examining the wound and leaned back on his heels, crouched on the floor of the van before me. His eyes were still focused squarely on my wound.

"Where are you going?" he asked.

"I told you. I'm going across the country."

"Yes," he replied. "that's what you said. But I know you're not telling us everything. What kind of game are you playing?"

I rose up in the seat, pulling myself erect and returning his stare.

"I don't know what you're talking about."

"Of course you don't." He smiled. "I'll be frank with you: I don't know what you're doing, or who you are. But I know enough to know that there is something about you, something particularly nasty. There's a reason we found you in that park last night."

"I was caught in that riot. What were you doing there?"

"We were trying to score some hash at the dorms, is what we were doing."

"I still don't understand why you think I'm anything other than what I keep saying."

"Because I know. I don't perhaps have the exact details, but I have connections in government and espionage. I have spoken with men who have spoken with men. I have seen many things I cannot explain, and I believe your presence in my life represents an anomaly as well."

I grew very quiet. We could hear the muted sounds of quiet conversation outside, as the other three spoke softly at the picnic table. No one had moved since John and I left the group.

"I don't understand," I maintained. I was trying to remain calm but I honestly had no idea where this was going. I didn't think there were any squirrels with video cameras out there focusing on me, not yet, but there would be, perhaps.

“You’re after Debbie,” he said. “Don’t fuck around with me.” He lowered his voice and leaned closer to me. “I know what you’re after. You don’t think I know? You don’t think I know what my enemies are capable of? If you’re in league with them, I have to know."

“You’re being paranoid,” I replied. “I don’t have a fucking clue what you’re talking about.”

He was silent for another moment. Finally he reached over and patted my leg. He was smiling again.

“No,” he laughed,” Of course you don’t. Come on, let’s get back to the others.”

Again, I didn’t know what the hell was going on. The lights that used to flash around me when trouble was afoot were nowhere to be seen. I was in unknown lands, with strange allies. The sun was going down and the shifting winds were beginning to carry a slight hint of a crisp evening chill.

We sat for a while longer in awkward silence, drinking soda pop and swatting at mosquitoes. Finally, after what seemed to be an unbearably long moment of tense silence, John rose and stretched his arms. His physique was truly impressive, and I could see the gnarled muscles stretched taut over his ribcage.

"Time for dinner", he said with a laugh.

The other three rose from the bench and walked towards the firepit. They arrayed themselves neatly on the benches which surrounded the small pit in a semicircle. John walked back to the van and retrieved a small metal box, olive green like a military locker, with a large combination lock placed on the latch.

"Start the fire, Lyle," John commanded. I grew uncomfortable as I began to perceive that John's three companions were definitely in a subservient position to their strange muscular friend.

Lyle gathered a small pile of kindling and placed it gingerly at the bottom of the pit. He walked back to the picnic table and returned with a bag of our garbage from the previous meal, dirty napkins and the empty pizza box. He threw the paper waste in the pit and reached into his pocket for the matches.

Debbie was eyeing my warily, as I noticed after a few minutes of watching Lyle attempting to start the fire. There was definitely something odd going on here, and I didn't know what it was. The fact that my head was still hurting didn't help matters either - pulling my thoughts together was like pulling at taffy, sticky and unresponsive.

What did she want? What was she looking to me for? I didn't know. She was watching me but I saw her eyes darting back and forth from me to the box John held in his lap.

After a few frustrating minutes Lyle succeeded in starting the fire. After the kindling was lit, he picked a few larger logs from besides the pit and placed them in the flames.

John accepted this as an unspoken signal. He moved the box in his lap and began to open the combination lock. Although I was still confused, I must admit that my curiosity had long since been whetted.

As John fumbled with the lock, drawing out the process to elaborate lengths, I could see that the other three people around the fire were all poised expectantly, almost reverently, waiting for the box to be opened.

Finally the tumblers of the lock clicked open and John open the latch. He reached inside the cavity and drew out a gun.

It was a large gun, well-oiled. It gleamed in the flickering light of the firepit. It was a revolver, and John made another elaborate show of checking the six chambers and ensuring that there was a bullet in each one. Finally, once he was satisfied that his weapon was in adequate condition, he reached into the box again.

He pulled out four lengths of rubber tubing, and passed them around the fire until everyone - except for John - had taken one. He pulled out four more spoons, and passed them around as well. Finally, he gave us all an empty medical syringe.

Debbie, Lyle and Brent were watching his hands with a maniacal intensity. I sat dumbly, holding my length of rubber tubing, my spoon and my needle, still bewildered. John stopped a moment and addressed me. As he spoke, the others grew stiff and tense, anxiously awaiting the final component from the box.

"My friend," he said with a smile, "have you ever shot heroin?"

The tumblers kicked in my head and I suddenly became very aware of the strange objects I was holding in my hand.

"No," I answered.

"It kicks pretty hard the first time. I'd enjoy it while it lasts."

I stared at him. He was still holding the gun, but as he spoke he lifted it until it was aimed squarely at my chest.

"It's a funny thing though, about opiates . . . heroin is an opiate, you know. When you're just started using, its the greatest feeling in the world. But of course, soon it goes downhill, and you find yourself needing more and more junk just to feel the same high. Eventually you find the highs have dwindled away to nothing, barely even a glimmer of the rapturous joy you once felt. But even though you can't get high you still have to keep using, or you go into withdrawal. It's an instance of diminishing returns, and its a sad thing to see . . . very painful. Heroin withdrawal is one of the most violently painful things a man can experience."

"Why are you telling me this?"

"Oh, come on. Don't be coy. We all have our crosses to bear." He reached into his box again and pulled out a small plastic pouch of heroin. He reached across the fire and offered it to me.

"Take it," he said. There was something hard and unyielding in his voice. "Take it. You'll have a good time."

His gun was in his left hand, on the far side of his body from where I sat. He was growing impatient.

I reached out and took the pouch from him. I felt it between my fingers: beneath the plastic I could feel something fine and granulated, like talcum powder or flour. He smiled at me as I accepted the pouch.

"We'll show you how," he said. He reached into his box and pulled out another pouch, this one for Debbie. She accepted it eagerly and began her preparations, pulling the cord around her forearm.

Lyle and Brent were focused on Debbie, their own hunger masking their awareness. John leaned away from me for a moment as Debbie prepared her batch. I stood up suddenly and threw the pouch on the ground in front of John.

Brent and Lyle saw the pouch leave my hand and land on the ground. John turned and saw in a moment what I had done but before he could speak he was knocked flat on his back by Brent and Lyle, who had both jumped across the fire in order to seize the fallen packet of heroin. The gun jumped out of John's hand as he fell backwards on his back.

The gun was in my hand before John had regained his feet. I motioned for him to put the box down on the bench in front of him, and he did. Lyle grabbed the box and began rifling through the contents.

Debbie was almost totally oblivious. In the long moments since I had grabbed the gun she had finished boiling her batch and placed the needle in her arm. First she pulled the depressor out, filling the syringe with her blood, and then, after it had mixed sufficiently with the drug, she slowly pushed the depressor with her thumb and sent the blood, mixed with the heroin, coursing back into her veins and through to her heart. She turned her head slowly and saw that I had the gun - a groggy, half-sleeping smile crept over her beautiful face.

I slowly backed away from the campfire. John was standing alone, focused on the gun in my hand while his former compatriots sat around the fire and greedily divvied up their shares of the heroin that had been in his box. Still walking backwards so as not to lost sight of John, I walked to the van.

"Hey," I called out to John. "Where are the keys for this thing?"

He didn't say anything.

"If you don't think I'll shoot you, you're sadly mistaken." I aimed the pistol and shot in the general direction of his feet.

The pistol jumped in my hand, spewing fire into the dark twilight and resounding through the nearby wilderness in an echoing boom.

"Motherfucker!" John yelled. He fell to the ground and clutched his right foot in agony.

"OK, I'll ask again. Where are the fucking keys?"

He didn't say a thing, but he reached into the pocket of his jeans and pulled out a small bundle of keys. He tossed them in my direction and they bounced on the dry ground.

"I'll leave the van down the road." I struggled another moment, trying to summon something appropriately pithy. Finally I just let the silence fall and climbed aboard the van.

The engine started and I pulled out of the campsite as hurriedly as possible. I wanted to put that extremely bizarre scene behind me. The gun lay where I had set it on the passenger seat.

Forty minutes later I pulled the van into the parking lot of a large hotel and casino a few miles east of the California border. Numerous flashing billboards all across the interstate pronounced that this was Boomtown.

I followed the snaking roads that lead to the parking lot

and disembarked. I grabbed my duffel bag and the gun as well. Briefly searching the van, I concluded that there was nothing of value left inside, do I left the keys sitting on the drivers' seat and locked the doors.

There were half a dozen restaurants inside the massive building, but I chose the most modestly outfitted coffee shop on the premises. I ordered a cup of black coffee and sat, trying to ignore the pain as I scanned around the casino. Finally, I found who I was looking for.

Morris was tall and sunburnt, a muscular man in a leather jacket and dirty jeans. He was having an early breakfast and watching the news on a muted TV screen above the bar. He was heading to Denver with an eighteen-wheeler full of Chinese DVD players. We made small talk for a moment before he agreed to let me hitch a ride across Nevada.

14

Morris was a big man, surly and jovial. He was fat, but he didn't seem corpulent: his largesse had been baked into a solid and imposing mass of flesh. Standing near him you felt subdued by his potential power. Fingers like sausages gripped the steering wheel with potency.

He was a private trucker, owned his rig and traveled the country at his leisure. He had been a trucker for twenty years, had owned his rig for ten, and was beginning to eye a retirement condo in Idaho, near where his mother had passed away the previous year. It was either Idaho or Texas -- he found the Texas weather congenial.

I learned all of this within the first five minutes or so of riding shotgun down I-5. Driving with a professional trucker is a bewildering experience at first. They make their living driving and do so as casually and as confidently as you or I might walk across the street. Of course, driving an eighteen-wheel diesel trailer compares to driving a normal car in the same way that shooting a water pistol compares with firing a Howitzer.

Morris liked the company, which was one of the many reasons he was happy and proud to be an independent operator. Most corporate rigs were fixed with devices to deter the practice of taking hitchhikers - usually in the form of gadgets that recorded when your passenger and drivers' side doors were opened, where and how long. But Morris was convinced that this was a dangerous practice, regardless of the company's policies on freeloaders, because having a friendly hitchhiker to talk to was better than a bucket of methamphetamines.

"You see, it's a lonely life on the road - not that I would have it any other way. I like driving, I like seeing the scenery and getting a feel for the mass and density of this here country, getting a feel for the undulating plains and valleys and mountains that carry the road from one end of the continent to the other. I suppose I could have been happy doing something else - if I'd have never driven a rig, or never had the pleasure of being my own boss.

"You going to school?"

"No, I graduated just a month ago."

"Oh, good on you. College was some of the best years of my life, I can promise you . . . made me the man I am today sure as I'm sitting here next to you. Of course, Ma always said I never did anything worthy of my talents, but I just turned right back and told her that I was happy driving a truck and seeing the country. There's a book to be written about this country, one of these days, a picture of this country as it is, not as it was or as someone thinks it will be. Someday someone with a feel for the geography of this place, the massive monolithic loneliness of the great empty spaces that lie in between here and there, someone is going to put something down about those places. That's the best part of America, that's where the heart is - where it's still empty. You ever been to Utah?"

"No, not yet."

"Utah has a bad rap because of all the damn Mormons but it's really a beautiful space. You keep following this road and you'll come out on the Great Salt Desert, and let me tell you that is a sight you will remember for the rest of your life. Nevada is full of real desert - sand and cactus and lizards and red mountains on the horizon. But Utah is unique and special because the desert there is hard and brittle, covered in chalky natural salts that crunch under your boot. Its about a hundred miles across and flat as a pancake . . . it's unlike anything else you're likely to see anytime soon. Driving across it is like driving across the ocean, just flat and clear and reflective, so that you see mirages made by the glare of the sun on the distant salt. It's a lonely place, but it's also majestic, powerful in a way that no other part of the country is - empty and barren and deep as a well. It's a magical place, maybe even the heart of the continent. How do you communicate the language of emptiness, of dry expanses and lifeless tracts of time stretching into either horizon like receding sunlight? Someday, someone's going to figure that out, because that's something bigger than us, bigger than you or me or anyone, and it's been waiting for a long, long time. It can stand to wait a little longer, I figure, but soon enough someone's going to figure out how to speak to the heart of this country. It's not in Washington, I'll say that.

"People is small and tragic and full of themselves, building this and that and tearing down Lord knows what to put something else or whatnot. It's all well and good but if you drive around the country you get a feeling for the shape of things, how they really are, and you see that there are a whole load of things that seem really important to some people but just don't really matter much at all."

I nodded in general agreement. I could tell that Morris was a man who liked the sound of his own voice, especially considering the fact that he was often alone.

"So, boy, you horny?"

"What? I don't know . . ."

"Simple question: are you horny?"

"Um. I don't really know how to answer that."

"There's only one rational way to answer that question: you say yes, yes I fucking am. Heh. We're gonna stop up here and damned if I don't know a little hole-in-the-wall that can do something about that for both of us."

I didn't say anything. I thought I had an idea of what he was talking about but it seemed a remote, almost comical idea on the face of it.

"Oh, don't worry about it," he laughed. "First time with a hooker's no different than you're first time with anyone else . . . you're not a virgin, are you?"

"No, no."

"Well, good, good. You got that much OK. The first time you pay for sex is a little like the first time you have regular sex . . . you get a little bashful, you blush and you're not quite sure what you're doing. But you know what, it always turns out OK in the end, because unlike little Mary Sue in Junior High, these gals are professionals and they know how to make the experience as pleasurable as possible. They have a vested interest in making sure you are satisfied with what you're paying for, because bad word-of-mouth for a whore can take money right out of their pockets. Truckers and businessmen both go to hookers, and they both gossip like housewives. You better believe that if Maggie down here or Eustace over there don't know how to give a blow-job to save her life she'll be hungry in a week."

"I imagine that would be a pretty basic skill in that line."

"You'd hope so, I guess. Anyway, you don't need to worry, I'll steer you right. Its a big, bad world out there and there's a lot of people who mean to do you harm, but if you watch your P's and Q's things usually turn out sunny-side up when all is said and done."

"Hmmm. I guess you're right. I mean, about it being a hostile world and all."

"Truckers can be paranoid motherfuckers, because we all sit up late at night listening to the nuts on the AM radio - you got the Jesus freaks who are all saying the end is coming next week, you got the UFO nuts saying that 9/11 was really the first salvo in an interplanetary war and the government is covering it up, you got a whole other mess of tinfoil hats saying no, it was the CIA who did it all and then you got everyone in between, like the crazies who believe shit like the Pope is a pawn of Israel and they're trying to bring about the end of the world by contaminating our water supplies. The world is full of nuts."

I once again nodded my general agreement. I was staring out the window, looking at the cars coming toward us in the opposite lane, their bright yellow lights streaking through the sentient nighttime with an implacable purpose. They never blink.

"Anyhoo, we'll see about getting you a hole to dip your wick into, you see if we don't. That's one of the fringe benefits of riding the roads: you get to go out and get some pussy whenever you feel like it. Sure, sometimes it ain't so easy to find . . . not every state is as amenable to mankind's natural urges as Nevada. But if you know what you're looking for you can pretty much find it anywhere you want, that's a basic truth in this world. I know there's a few men on the road who know where to find other men, and even a few lonely women who know where to go for what they want. There's sex everywhere, but not very many people are willing to pay for it on the free market, and that just smacks of hypocrisy to me."

Morris was still talking as we pulled off the freeway and onto a thin frontage road. We were on the outskirts of the desert, where thin trees nestled into the hard dust and shivered in the shadows of hard clay mountain ranges. The asphalt stored and radiated a great deal of this ambient solar energy, and the further we drove down the frontage road and away from the freeway the colder it felt.

I didn't know what to expect when we pulled into the parking lot of the whorehouse. It was a large house, the type of cozy two-story building that could have been a happy home to any family in any state in the union . But instead of a well-manicured lawn the front of the house was a dry dusty parking lot, filled with a half-dozen eighteen wheelers and a few more smaller vehicles nestled close to the building. There was a bright light shining over the wooden porch, and a neon orange OPEN sign hanging over the front door. It could have been a coffee shop or a rural doctor's office.

Morris parked the truck and stopped the engine. The great rattling diesel motor shuddered to a crashing halt, and the sudden dearth of movement produced a strangely dizzy sensation in my extremities. Morris grabbed his keys and his wallet and jumped out the truck. I left my duffel in the back of the cab, but while Morris was locking his door I quickly grabbed the gun I had taken from John, and slid it under my belt on my lower back.

The building was quiet. I don't know if I had been, on some subconscious level, expecting an Old West saloon, complete with a creaking player-piano and a bartender in spats, but the reality was perversely anticlimactic.

It was dressed as you would expect the lobby of any mid-level motor inn to be decorated: there were fake potted plants and nice sofas, and a muted TV hanging from a platform on the wall. There was a conscientious majordomo at the desk, handling clients and punching numbers on a computer. They even had a large sign under the counter, loudly proclaiming that they happily accepted Visa, Mastercard, Discover, American Express and Diner's Club, but No Personal Checks (Please). There was even a slot machine in the corner, another reminder to me of Nevada's pervasive and inherent strangeness.

The majordomo was busy so Morris motioned to one of the nearby sofas. We sat down to wait. Morris stared at the television idly - it was some sort of late night comedy program - while I grabbed a magazine off the table to the side of the sofa. I was reminded that this was not a motel by the fact that in addition to the standard issues of Newsweek, Golf Digest and Sports Illustrated, the lobby was also outfitted with the latest numbers of Penthouse and Club.

It's difficult to say what was going through my head at the time. Just six hours ago I had survived John's attempt to turn me into his drug slave. Twenty-four hours ago I survived a strange riot in Berkeley. Forty-eight hours ago I was sleeping in my own bed at home, under the same roof as my mother for perhaps the last time. I had the cold metal of a gun barrel resting against my ass and a large bandage still taped to my forehead. I wasn't really thinking about having sex at the moment: I felt drained, like an empty vessel that hadn't yet been refilled.

After a few minutes of aimlessly flipping through the pages of Penthouse, the previous customers finished their business at the counter and the majordomo signaled to us that he was ready.

"Gentlemen, if you are ready?"

We rose and approached the counter. The majordomo was a large man, tall but not especially well built. His lank figure seemed to be having trouble filling the black turtleneck and sportscoat he wore, a particularly unobtrusive uniform for a professionally discrete gentleman.

"You pay when you're finished but we require a deposit beforehand."

Morris had already produced his wallet, and was pulling out an imposing Platinum card of some variety. He laid it on the counter and the majordomo retrieved it reverently. He reached under the counter and produced a clipboard and a sheet of paper.

"May I see your license?" he asked. Morris slid his license across the counter and the majordomo examined it, ensuring that the name on both cards was the same. He handed Morris his license back and wrote Morris' name on the sheet of paper, before he placed his credit card under the clipboard's wire tongue. He placed the clipboard with the empty invoice and Morris' card in a small cubby hole to the side of the desk, alongside perhaps a dozen other similarly prepared clipboards.

"And how will you be paying?" he addressed me.

"Cash."

"We require a deposit of one-hundred dollars for cash transactions, please."

I pulled my bankroll out of my front pocket and peeled off two fifty-dollar bills. The majordomo accepted them and placed them in a small envelope. He reached for another clipboard and placed the envelope of cash under the wire tongue.

"And what name shall I report on the invoice?"

"Er. John. John Smith."

"Yes," the majordomo smirked. "John Smith. You spend a lot of money here."

Morris turned to me and grinned - I could tell he was trying hard not to laugh.

"You crack me up, kid," he said as he slapped my back.

After the majordomo had placed my clipboard next to the others he stepped out from behind the counter and motioned for us to follow him down the hallway. He led us to a large room that had been outfitted with far more elaboration than the lobby, a red barroom with elegant fixtures and plush carpeting. There were burgundy sofas in the corner, and framed reproductions of certain particularly arousing studies . . . I recognized a Titian and a John Singer Sergeant, among others.

There were a few other men lounging around the room,

one at the bar and two sitting together on a sofa and speaking softly. I didn't know if they were waiting or if they had already been, and were merely enjoying a post-coital cocktail.

Morris led me to the bar and ordered a beer. I demurred, and asked the bartender they had any soda. He poured me a glass of Coke and left us to talk.

"Oh, come on, you can't have Coke in a whorehouse." Morris found the situation increasingly amusing.

"I still have a little bit of a headache from this," I pointed to my forehead. "I don't want to push my luck."

He was silent for a moment as he took a sip of his beer. "OK, I can see that. You get a 'by' this time, kid." He resumed chuckling.

After another moment a woman entered the bar. Morris turned and his face lit up. The woman ran over to the bar and wrapped her arms around him.

"I thought I saw your truck in the lot! When did you get in?"

"No more'n ten minutes ago," he said. "I was hoping I'd see you here."

"Well, I'm so glad you came. Seems like it's been forever and a day."

"I've been over in the South and the East . . . haven't had the chance to swing by the desert."

She turned and noticed me. "Who's your shy friend? Does he have a name?"

"Heh. Call him 'John'. That's what he told Peter up front."

The woman laughed. "Oh my, I guess this is your first time, then. They're all 'John' the first time . . . nobody has the intelligence to think up something less predictable."

She was a beautiful woman, with golden blonde hair hanging loosely around her shoulders and a small black barrette pulling it back from her face. She looked older than I would have expected, with a mature beauty that seemed to radiate comfortable experience. Maybe she was forty but I wouldn't have said a day over thirty by the looks of her.

And I could definitely see enough to judge. She was wearing a translucent slip, almost sheer, underneath which all she had was a black lace bra and a thong. Her stomach was firm and flat, her breasts full and round, and her body had an alluringly lived-in look to it. I imagined that making love with her would be like slipping into a pair of comfortable slippers after a hard days work, albeit slightly more eventful.

"You wait here a minute," she said to John. "I think I know just the gal for our friend John here. I'll go get her and then you and me can have some fun." She smiled at John and then at me before rushing out of the room.

"She's a great gal," Morris said after she had left. "I been through here dozens of times but she's my favorite. She's got a way about here these younger gals just couldn't beg borrow or steal."

We lapsed into silence as we awaited her return. Finally, after a few more minutes, Gwen returned with another girl in tow.

The new girl was younger, maybe my age or even a little younger, with dark hair cut fairly short on her head. Her lips were narrow and her face slightly angular. But her features were not severe, rather they seemed almost perfectly proportioned, with high cheekbones obscured by the kind of soft skin that diffuses direct light into an ambient glow.

She was dressed slightly more modestly than Gwen, in a skimpy black skirt and low heels. Her body was less full than Glen's, her breast and thighs less pronounced but no less appealingly, more subtle for their intimations.

"Hey," she reached out her hand to me. "Gwen said you're new. My name is Erica." She blushed slightly as she said this. I wondered in that moment whether or not her slight embarrassment was feigned or genuine, but I understood that I would never know the answer to that. A magician never reveals his tricks.

Gwen wrapped her arm around Morris' and they left the bar, him still drinking his beer. Erica correctly sensed that I would appreciate a more measured approach. She asked the bartender for a scotch and soda.

"So, John. You're not a virgin are you?"

"Uh, no. I'm not."

She looked at me for a moment in silence, her eyes narrowing into shrewd slits. "Yes, I can see that. No one ever admits it, and many are lying. But you're not. I can tell. You would also be a suspiciously handsome virgin."

I blushed, and she laughed.

"What did you do to your head?"

"I got hit," I said. "Someone hit me, rather."

"I see. That sounds very painful."

"It wasn't fun, I'll say that. I'll probably have a little scar for the rest of my life."

"Everyone has some scars," she said wistfully. "Um. I realized right after I said it how pretentious that sounded." She giggled slightly as she sipped her drink.

"Oh, that's all right. We're all guilty of pretense sometimes. It's unavoidable."

"Yeah. Like this. What are we doing? You're embarrassed: you shouldn't be. There's no shame here." She reached over and grabbed my hand, guiding it over to her thigh. She pressed my fingers into the flesh above her knee, and pulled my hand slowly up her leg until my fingers were reaching under her skirt.

"This is just how I make my living. I think you're a philosopher, from the looks of you - you look like you spend a lot of time thinking. Don't think, it's unnecessary."

I didn't know how to reply. I took another sip of my soda, only to realize that the glass was empty and had been empty for a while.

"Let's go," she said softly. She rose from the stool and

began to lead me away from the bar.

The hallway leading from the bar to the stairway was, like the bar, dimly lit. We rounded a corner and climbed the stairs leading to the second floor. The entire building seemed to be lushly carpeted, and every step was a soft thud, dull and distant. It reminded me of walking across a field of snow the morning after a snowstorm, with fresh powder crunching almost imperceptibly under my feet.

Her room was at the end of the upstairs hallway. She opened the door and motioned for me to enter.

It was a small room, or perhaps it merely seemed small on account of the king-size bed which dominated the center of the room. There were two medium-sized bureaus against the walls and a small stereo on a bedside table. There was a small bathroom just off the side of the room.

She closed the door behind us and stepped in front of me. She was tall for a woman, only an inch or so shorter than me. She reached out and put her hands on my shoulders, squeezing them slightly. She didn't say a word but she lowered her hands, sliding her palms down over my chest and my stomach, all the while keeping her eyes focused intently on mine. I didn't know if I was allowed to kiss her.

Finally her hands were pressing against her abdomen. She began to slowly undo my belt buckle. I remembered something and motioned her to stop.

"Let me take my own pants off," I said. "Please. I need to unlace my shoes."

She was confused but she pulled her hands away. She turned her back and walked to the side of the bed to fiddle with the stereo.

While she wasn't watching I switched the gun from its place in the small of my back to my back pocket. I undid my sneakers and pulled my pants off quickly, so she didn't have any time to see the bulge in my back pocket.

Something soft wafted through the room, acid jazz or trip hop or some hybrid thereof. She turned back and I was standing with my pants off, folded on top of my sneakers placed neatly on the floor. She wasn't paying any attention to my clothes because she immediately noticed the large erection in my underwear.

"My, my my," she said. "You must be happy to see me."

"Yes," I replied. "Yes." I couldn't think of anything else to say.

She reached down and grabbed my penis through the tight cotton briefs. She was looking at me again, more intently than before. Either she was genuinely aroused or she was a pro . . . either way, I wasn't in any condition to complain.

After she pulled my underwear down over my butt and to the floor, she knelt down and began to suck me. It was soft and eager, not harsh and violent. I wondered -- or at least, the part of me that could wonder at that moment did -- why I had never been attracted to Connie. She was beautiful too, her tits were bigger than Erica's, her fellatio was perfectly competent. I had never wanted her at all, and I had never wanted anyone in my life as much as I had Erica at that moment.

After a few minutes of leisurely head, she rose again and smiled at me. She reached behind her and unzipped her dress. It fell to the floor around her ankles with a ghostly sigh. She was only wearing a small black thong, barely anything at all. Her breasts were almost perfect, rounded and firm with pert nipples. She was staring at me.

"Do you want me?" she asked.

"Yes," I replied, still unable to speak more than a one syllable at a time.

"Then take me. I have everything you could possibly want, but I don't think you want to whip me or beat me or tie me up. I think you just want me. Am I right?"

"Yes."

She got on the bed -- or perhaps it would be more appropriate to say she glided onto the bed, because it seemed at that moment as if friction could not effect her movement. She was liquid, seeping into the cracks of my body.

15

I slept across most of Nevada, waking intermittently throughout the late night and early morning. Every now and again I woke up to the noise of talk radio, to which Morris gave his extensive commentary. He was used to being alone, and spoke with company in much the same manner that I imagine he spoke to himself.

The state of Nevada is almost pornographically empty, its vast featureless expanses stretching from horizon to horizon. Of course, there are mountains and valleys and peaks and gullies, but the mountains are neither so tall nor the valleys so low as to impress the viewer with anything but their massiveness.

Of the few towns I saw in the state, I can report little save that they seem singularly oriented around the care and patronage of travelers. Every thirty or forty miles as you cross the interstate, there's invariably a small town of some kind, filled with fast food restaurants, gas stations and convenience stores. They stand out from the blackness of the nighttime desert, oases of neon splendor set at intervals throughout the featureless void.

Traveling across America is a hypnotically effacing process. There is so much emptiness spread across the fifty states, so many vast tracts of undeveloped and unheralded nothing that the spirit rebels in opposition. I can barely imagine the existential terror of astronauts, who face larger tracts of vastness on a scale to make the greatest terrestrial void pale. There's so much distance in the stars, so much room to get lost.

As a youth I was a fighter. Before I learned better than to

trust my perceptions around strangers, I lived a violent life of psychiatric repression. I have already mentioned the mental hospital where I was a patient sporadically during my upbringing. I have not mentioned the abuse, both physical and mental, which was heaped on me every day.

The orderlies and attendants at these mental hospitals are taught that the best - the only - way to properly treat their young wards is through harsh physical punishment. There are many who may perhaps profit from such a treatment: I do not know. I merely know, based on what I have since learned, that this treatment was specially designed for me, in order to better combat the growing realization of who and what I was and would come to represent. The masters and overseers of my father's enemies were undoubtedly well pleased by my institutionalizations.

I am unaware as to whether or not the technology to read minds existed when I was hospitalized, but I suspect now that those techniques were utilized in a far more primitive and inspecific manner. In particular there were certain orderlies who seemed to have access to the deepest recesses of my private thought processes. They carried small invisible radio receivers in their ears and these receivers broadcast the content of my mind.

When they believed my thoughts to be dangerous, I would be set upon by the staff. They would encircle me and press in close, grabbing my limbs and forcing me into compliance. They wrestled me to the floor so that I was on my chest with my limbs spread out and isolated, with a large attendant pushing down on each part of my body. I was effectively immobilized, being pressed down close to the floor and suffocated for hours at a time.

It's easy to grow inured to pain and confinement when it is all you know from a very young age. At the very bottom of an enormous pile of flesh, I limited my breathing to very shallow channels and constrained my thoughts to minimize the trauma. I recall that sometimes I would enter a state near to spiritual ecstasy, confined and restrained by a half-dozen muscular orderlies on the dirty tile floor of the hospital, pressed in by a half-ton of flesh on a hard cold surface, but perceiving myself as floating free, numb and weightless through the ether of unattached ego.

I would wake after an undefined period with bruises across my body and purplish-yellow welts from their grips. I would have been moved, in my catatonic state, into a "safe-room", a padded cell with constant observation. Slowly I crept back into consciousness, feeling the perimeter of my being for any signs of persistent threat, finally returning face down in a puddle of drool with my body leaden.

The repressive forces who insured my continued imprisonment would later learn, to their eternal dismay, that I was absolutely insensate during these disassociate episodes. I was therefore immune to all of their torture protocols: the same painful treatments which they inflicted on my unfortunate peers in the mental hospital would have no effect on me.

I do not doubt that many of the children with whom I shared my interment were legitimately ill. But the programs and prerogatives of the system in which we were placed were designed not with the goal of helping and healing, but of breaking and nullifying. Many times I saw otherwise happy and well-adjusted children taken away to the torture chambers, only to return with hideous scarring and sometimes permanent disabilities.

Once I recall a particularly willful patient who was treated to a gradually escalating regimen of painful torture. He remained stubborn and brave throughout, as they increased the level of torment according to his increased resistance. He was burned and whipped and beaten and hobbled, but he remained stoic.

Finally one day he returned from his session, groggy from anesthesia. They had rendered him unconscious and he awoke with a scar across his belly and a hard lump in his abdomen. There was a short wooden straw pointing out from his belly button.

Over the course of the afternoon as he awoke from the anesthesia, he became more and more aware of a blinding pain in his belly. The lump grew larger and began to move, tearing and gnashing at his innards. He began to cough blood and other viscous liquids, the bile bubbling from his mouth uncontrollably. Finally the stitches came undone and his stomach burst open like a smashed melon.

They had surgically implanted a hypnotized possum into his belly. The creature breathed through the straw which we had found poking through the boy's belly button. As it awoke from its hypnotic stupor, it tore through the layers of flesh and blood until he was free.

A possum is a particularly unpleasant animal. Their teeth are small, sharp and placed at odd angles from their mouth. Coarse gray fur covers their bodies like wire bristles, and their long tails resemble those of rats. This creature emerged from my friend's stomach covered in blood and ichor, sticky with the ersatz amniotic fluid of its brief imprisonment.

At that moment, as the possum spewed forth onto the tile floor of the dining commons and peered around, dazed, confused and wary, I finally knew the depths of distrust and hatred which I had come to regard my immortal enemies. It would take me years of my life to become absolutely acclimated to the constant terror and loathing that had surrounded me, but in that moment the full impact of heavy fear hit me with a sudden and terrible wrath. I was essentially adrift, cast off and abandoned on the shores of a great and mysterious continent of paranoia.

And so I took the steps I needed in order to become adept at hiding my emotions, of suppressing the fears and suspicions that I constantly felt. There were constant warning signs of danger all around me, ever present symbols of incredible danger in everything I saw. But I knew then, as I know now, that to acknowledge the fear is to invite disaster: you can't let them know that you know what you know.

Morris stopped in Wendover, a small town poised on the border of Nevada and Utah. It was oddly split, with one half of the town filled with the vice of Nevada and the other emptied of anything remotely evocative of sin. You have casinos and pornography stores just a few hundred yards away from the border, where pious and noble Mormons sniff the air for signs of indecency like gourmands inspecting a plate of rotten ham.

We ate breakfast at a Burger King directly off the highway. It was an interesting town, built on a series of high rock outcroppings where the Great Salt Desert of Utah met the sandy wastes of Nevada in mortal combat. Like many places in America, it seemed to have been built primarily for the edification of travelers: it was hard to imagine actually enjoying life in such a desolate limbo.

Our meal was relatively quiet, with Morris uncharacteristically taciturn. I suspected he was growing tired and would want to rest soon - I wondered what I would do when he decided to pull over.

"I think I'll stop in Salt Lake," he announced. "I know a place to stop for a few hours so I can catch some shut-eye in the cab. You wanna get off now or then?"

"I guess I'll ride with you into the city," I replied. I didn't know exactly where I was going, but I knew I needed to continue east at a fair pace. "But I'll probably hitch another ride when you stop."

"OK, good. I don't think you'll have any trouble finding a ride where I'm going - there's hundreds of truckers stopped for gas or a shower and there'll be someone heading east who can spare a seat. I'll vouch for you."

We finished our meal and threw away our refuse. Morris returned to the cab but I told him I needed to go to the restroom. I did my business and exited the restaurant.

I pulled myself up to the cab of the truck and opened the door. Morris, however, was gone. In his place sat a stranger holding a gun.

"Get up in here," he said. I was still standing on the side of the truck with my hand still on the door. I didn't move.

"I said, get up in here, boy." He moved his arms as he spoke and the gun hung limply from his hand as he gestured in my direction. He was entirely comfortable with the weapon, like a man with a pen in his hand who completely forgets the presence of the implement.

"Where's Morris?"

"He's not here, that's all I'm gonna say to you. Get on up here." He leveled the gun in my direction, aiming it directly at my head.

I hesitated.

"I don't have to be patient," he said, clearly exasperated. "I get paid whether you come in warm or cold, and I'm hardly picky on the subject myself."

Finally I climbed into the cab and slowly pulled the door closed behind me. Morris was probably dead.

"Strap your seat belt on," the stranger said. He turned the key and started the engine. It seemed that he know his way around an eighteen-wheeler.

We left the Burger King and soon the truck was back on the freeway, thundering down the road with irresistible momentum. My new captor was tall and thin, almost wiry, dressed in jeans and a tight white T-shirt. His arms were muscular in a dangerous, sinewy fashion, as if he had grown up hungry and scared, and never managed to eat enough to catch up. A toothpick dangled at a rakish angle from his lip.

"You can call me Leon," he said after we had been thundering down the road for a few silent minutes. His gun was still in his right hand, resting casually in his lap as he steered with his left. When he switched gears he switched the gun to his left hand.

I reached around to the back of the cab, gingerly, to try and find my duffel bag. Leon turned his head casually and smirked at me.

"If you're looking for your gun, you can forget about it," he said. "I already got that. And I got a couple more I'll bet you didn't know your friend had, too."

"Who are you with?" I asked.

"Wouldn't you like to know? There's a few different groups out here, criss-crossing the highways and byways looking for you. I can't tell you who's signing my checks. All I can tell you is that I'm here to make sure you get to where you need to go without any more distractions."

"Distractions." I echoed the word dully.

"Like whorehouses and heroin gangs and shit like that," he grinned. "You are going to New York, and you are going to get there as quickly as possible. That's why I'm taking you to the airport."

"The airport?"

"There's a private plane with captain and crew engaged simply for the benefit of getting you across the country with the minimum of fuss. I've got a few friends waiting for me who can assure you'll be a quiet and peaceful passenger."

"I don't want to go on a plane."

"I didn't say you had a choice." Leon spat this last word like an epithet. "I merely said you were going. And you are, so there's no use crying in your beer about it."

"But . . . I was heading in that direction anyway."

"Yeah, but that was starting to get messy. The longer you're allowed out on your own recognizance, the more these complications just start to build up. One minute you're seeing the labs in Berkeley, the next you get some heroin cult after you, then you fall in with the Russians . . ."

"Russians? I haven't even met any Russians."

He laughed at that one. "Well, golly, do you think that

Morris was just being nice to you because he was your friend? Hell no, he's been on the Kremlin's payroll since Jimmy Carter was president."

"I don't believe you any more than I believed any of the others."

"Well, if I were you I'd be skeptical too. But the fact of the matter in this particular case is that you are far more important than you could ever realize, and there are easily dozens of individuals and organizations who would love to have a piece of you."

"I don't care. They can't have me. I know what they want. They can't have it."

"Eh, it's immaterial whether or not you want to give anything to them. They'll get it, or someone will, eventually . . . there's just too many folks after your hide right now, the odds of you making it through are just not very good. Best just to sit back and let me deliver you to the airport."

He lapsed back into silence as we drove. We were well into the salt desert now, with the Nevada hills receding in the west and the sun rising proud in the east.

The radio lit up and started making noise. "Operator 12, Operator 12 ... do you copy, repeat, do you copy?"

It was a familiar voice, even if I didn't recognize it. Leon stared at the dashboard where the radio sat and said nothing. He looked nervous.

"Operator 12 ... Operator 12? Can you hear me? Please respond, Operator 12, Please respond or we will initiate Maneuver Delta, repeat, we will initiate Maneuver Delta."

"Fuck. Fuck fuck fuck." Leon became agitated as the voice on the radio droned on and on.

"What the hell is Maneuver Delta?" I asked.

"I don't know. I don't want to know."

The radio suddenly stopped making noise, the signal cutting out as quickly as it had began. We drove another few miles in silence together, the tension steadily rising.

We heard a car horn blaring to our right side. I turned to

look out the window and saw a large black SUV pulling close to the right of truck. I couldn't see through the tinted windows but they were still honking even as they grew steadily closer to the cab.

"Fuck," Leon repeated the word like a mantra. I don't think he had the slightest clue what was happening, and that made for two of us.

The car horn was still blaring to the side. Leon hit his own horn and pressed down on the gas pedal. The engine groaned and rumbled but we began to slowly accelerate, racing across the great salt desert heading straight for Salt Lake City.

I heard a loud bang, like the explosive sound of a tire popping on the road. I looked back through the window and sure enough there were people standing out of the SUV following to our side, shooting pistols at us as we accelerated. I pulled my head away from the window and told Leon that we were being shot at.

"Well, whoop de doo," he replied. "That just makes my day, don't know about you."

We were going faster and faster, faster than the speed limit and far faster than I had expected an enormous machine like this to be capable of achieving. They were still shooting at us, and the sound of bullets hitting the side of the cab filled the congested atmosphere of the truck cabin with loud metallic thunks.

"Hey, kid. I just noticed something," Leon said.

"What? That people are shooting at us?"

"No, smartass. Look around. There's no one on the highway."

I looked down the horizon and sure enough there wasn't another car or truck for as long as we could see, coming either way.

"They've cleared the whole road for this," he said, as much to himself as anything. Whatever Maneuver Delta was, it was pretty thorough.

The shooting stopped. We were going about 90 miles an hour and the motor was groaning from the strain. The black SUV was still trailing us, however. I could see shadows on the roadway - were there helicopters chasing us down?

"Are they still on our tail?" Leon asked.

"Yeah." They were hugging our side, less than two feet from the cab.

"Well, then, time to have some fun." He gunned the engine, pushing the truck about as far as it could go. Then he jerked the wheel to the right, hitting the truck and sending it wobbling across the lane. And then, with one motion he righted our course and pressed a large red button on the dashboard.

I looked out the rear window and the trailer began to separate from the cab, pulling away slowly as we continued to accelerate. The SUV, still struggling from behind and wobbling from having been hit at such a high speed, veered into the careening trailer and crashed. The large truck was a toy next to the enormous trailer, and it crumpled as soon as it collided, the hood catching directly under the bottom lip and forcing the trailer to flip over and onto the SUV, instantly crushing the truck flat against the road. We had been going around 90 miles an hour when we let the trailer go and the truck following us had been going the same, so the collision was spectacularly destructive.

The twisted mass of metal that had been the truck and the large trailer rolled and skidded another few hundred yards, twisting and tearing sheet metal and rubber like construction paper. After a few more seconds there was an explosion as the SUV's gas tank caught a spark.

"I didn't know we could do that - with the trailer like that."

"It's not factory standard," Leon grunted. "Your friend Morris had a few special features added, probably by the people cutting his checks, for situations just like this."

As he spoke he pulled the cab over to the side of the

freeway and stopped. I opened the door and jumped out, anxious to get my bearings. There was a swath of damage all across the side of the truck cab, huge black and silver trails of torn metal.

"Wow," I said. The scars were still hot to the touch.

"Come here," Leon said. He was standing in front of the cab, looking directly to the east.

"You see that?" he pointed down the road a ways. I couldn't see much but I did see a few small square objects against the horizon.

"What's that?"

"It's a roadblock. Whoever else wants you is doing a good job making sure they get you."

As he spoke I became aware of a loud beating in the air above my head - another shadow passed over our heads and I knew we were being watched.

"I'm sick of this shit," Leon said slowly. he was still chewing the same toothpick he had had twenty minutes ago when we had met in the Burger King parking lot. He reached into his back pocket and pulled out his pistol.

"What the hell are you doing?"

"I told you I didn't care if you were alive or dead - I get paid either way. My bosses will be pissed but I could honestly not care less at this point - maybe if you're dead I can get out of this one alive." He raised the gun and aimed it at my head.

"Nothing personal, kid. I've known you twenty minutes and I'm already Mac-fucking-Guyver. I didn't sign up for this shit."

I breathed deeply and tried my best not to seem panicked. The barrel of the gun was less than a foot from my face. It was hot in the desert and I was sweating.

I began to slowly back away from Leon, putting my hands up and placing one foot behind the other. He finger was tensing on the trigger and I could see him begin to squeeze.

But before he could shoot there was another thunderclap in the distance. He turned to look towards the sound but there was a flash of light and an enormous sound as the truck exploded.

I was thrown aloft by a blast of intensely hot air, carried at least twenty feet before landing on my ass on the hard white salt. I came to consciousness maybe half a minute later, still seeing double and smelling burning rubber and diesel fuel. My eyebrows were singed from the heat of the explosion.

Leon lay a few yards to my side, face down and unconscious. There was blood around where his head had landed.

My legs were unsteady under my body as I rose but I forced myself to rise and evaluate myself. I didn't seem to have anything broken, and although my clothes were singed I did not seem to be badly burnt. I had a headache and my ears were ringing but other than that I seemed to be alive.

Leon's gun lay a few feet away from me. I picked it up and put it in my back pocket.

As I regained my bearings a feeling of panic rose in me. What had been the cab of the truck lay in a twisted pile of scarred wreckage about twenty yards away. The heat from the fire had scorched a block smear across the pavement all around where the truck had sat. There were strips of burnt and torn rubber lying all across the white desert for as far as I could see.

But where was my duffel bag? If I had lost my notebooks after all this time, then all this would have been for nothing.

There was nothing left of the cabin's interior. Everything had been blown apart by the blast. I peered through the twisted metal from as far away as I could come, given the heat of the flames. There was a charred body lying under what had been the grill of the truck - patches of bone and torn clothing were visible on the blackened skin. Morris had been killed and placed in the back of the cab where I wouldn't see him. His body hadn't even begun to rot before he was violently cremated.

As a stood there and watched the wreckage from a distance, the sound of a helicopter grew louder and I could see a shadow growing on the ground. I turned and there was a chopper in the air about fifty yards above me and slowly descending.

When it was about twenty yards over my head and the wind from its rotors was whipping my hair, they heaved something out of the door of the chopper. It fell to the ground and landed with a blank thud about twenty-five feet in front of me. The helicopter rose swiftly in the air and was gone again.

I walked towards the object and quickly saw that it was my duffel bag. There was a note, written on white paper with a black pen and duct-taped to the outside. It said, very simply: "YOU'RE WELCOME, YOU CAN THANK ME LATER, YOUR FRIEND FROM STANFORD".

The bag seemed to be unharmed. I unzipped it and ascertained that my notebooks were where I had left them, and so was the gun I had taken from John. I put the gun I had taken from Leon's body in there as well.

Standing next to the wreck of a diesel truck on the side of the road in the middle of the Great Salt Desert, I realized that I was in a slightly awkward position. I wondered if the roadblock was still there, and whether or not I would be apprehended. Then again, I reasoned, if they had wanted me dead they wouldn't have returned my duffel bag after having reclaimed it from whomever Leon had given it to after killing Morris.

West down the road about half a mile was the still-burning wreckage of the black SUV and the trailer from Morris' rig. The back-end of the jackknifed and crumpled box was open, brown cardboard boxes spewn all across the road. The road was so flat that I could see the boxes themselves ripped open and burning across the asphalt. There were hundreds of tiny shapes whirling through the morning air, large ashes from the wreckage.

After a moment I realized that they weren't ashes. The wind picked up and carried a few pages down the road to where I was standing, and I discovered that Morris hadn't been carrying Chinese DVD players. The pages that came flapping down the freeway, carried by the force of the wind out across the great salt flats, were burnt but recognizable. Morris had been carrying hundreds of boxes of "YOUNG MEAT", the neon lettering of the title page unmistakable as I held the thick glossy cover - singed at the edges but otherwise undamaged - in my hand.

I was shaking and sweating, feeling sore all over and more than a little bit thirsty. My duffel bag was heavy but I swung the strap over my shoulder and began to walk down the road, heading east into the hazy afternoon.

16

After I had walked a few miles down the road a few cars began to pass me on the road. I stuck my thumb out and the fourth car, a compact sedan, stopped and motioned me to get in the passenger side.

It was an older woman, with light brown hair cut so that it fell loosely around her shoulders. Her frame was large but she carried herself with a discrete and purposeful authority. Despite the fact that she was probably a bit heavy she was still strangely attractive, attractive in the way that only an older woman can be - confident and assuredly, with the full experience of a lifetime partially lived under their belt. She didn't have any makeup on, but her complexion was such that it would probably have seemed garish.

I threw my duffel bag into the backseat and sat down

gingerly. Her car was fairly cluttered, and it was not hard to guess that she had been driving for some time.

"Hey there," she said as I sat down. "You look like you've been through a war."

"Really?" I didn't know.

"Yeah, your face is covered with soot and your clothes are singed. I'm assuming you had something to do with whatever was going on back there?"

"Um, I guess."

She chuckled at my cagey reply.

"Well, if you've got secrets I don't care. I've got a few myself."

"You sure you don't mind giving me a ride? I mean . . ."

"What, because I'm a weak and puny female? Do I look like I was born yesterday to you? I'm just wondering because if I do I've been going to the wrong gym." She laughed at her joke and I laughed to. She seemed like a very friendly person.

"Well . . . OK, you got me there. Most people don't want to pick up hitchhikers at all these days, let alone single male hitchhikers."

"Life is too boring if you never take any risks. Besides, if a weak and puny little thing like yourself can overpower me, I guess I deserve to be raped." She laughed again.

Unconsciously, I looked down at myself. I hadn't realized it but I had become rather scrawny. I chuckled too.

"My name's Joanne. Where you headed?"

"East," I answered. "As far as you want to take me."

"Ah, well, I'm heading to Salt Lake. Not permanently . . . I'm actually on something of a tour. I'm a salesperson. I sell computers."

"Computers?"

"Well, not really computers . . . I sell software and a few specialized bits of hardware required for small-scale heavy manufacturing."

"Um, OK . . ."

"It's not very interesting, honestly. But it's useful: all around the country there are small manufacturing firms that don't have the resource management that companies like GM does. But they still need ways to manage their inventory and keep track of materials and access orders and basically do all the stuff that the big companies have spent billions of dollars to be able to do automatically. Well, actually, most small manufacturing outfits have already outfitted their computer systems, but what they don't have is the kind of network capability that will allow them to manipulate their resources in a fully competitive infrastructure . . ."

Her voice trailed off. "I'm boring you. I'm sorry, I've got this palaver down so well I could say it in my sleep."

"It's OK," I smiled. "It's good to hear a normal person talk."

We had been driving for about five minutes and had yet to see a roadblock. I asked her if there had been one in the direction she had come.

"Yeah, a big one, with the Highway Patrol and a few rescue vehicles. I guess it was that crash. We were stopped in dead traffic for about an hour before they let us through, and by then whatever it was had been cleaned up. I guess it was a hazardous materials truck or something . . ." Again, her voice trailed off, but this time there was a hint of expectation in her words. She was understandably curious.

"It wasn't a hazardous materials truck," I answered. "Not really. But there was a big chase and a couple explosions."

"Yeah, I could have guessed that part, from the looks of you. Shouldn't you be going to the hospital? Weren't there paramedics?"

"No . . . I just got up and walked away."

She frowned, momentarily, her brow furrowing.

"Whatever," she chuckled.

"I was a hitchhiker in the truck before it blew up. I wasn't hurt."

"And let me guess: you don't want to talk to the police?"

"Not really."

"I can't say as I blame you in that regard," she said after a moment. "So," she continued, "what are you really doing? I mean, why are you heading east?"

"I want to see the country before I get married."

"Oh, well that's certainly romantic . . . er, not romantic like love, romantic like the 19th century. Very Byronic."

"Heh. I like that. I hadn't thought of that."

"I mean, there is something enduringly appealing about a young man off on his own like that, seeing the world and getting some living under his belt before returning home triumphant . . . kind of like the prodigal son, only not really. More like 'Easy Rider', but not really I guess . . ."

She was quiet for another moment as we drove.

"So, tell me about your fiancé," she asked after a bit.

"There's not a whole lot to tell. I'm getting married when I get back . . . we've sent out invitations, I think . . . sometime in August. I'm supposed to be back by then."

"You don't sound very enthusiastic about it."

"Can you tell?"

"It's written all across your face when you talk about it. You look like you'd rather cut off your arm than do it."

"Well I guess that's an appropriate analogy, then. I'm not terribly excited about it. I don't love her, I never really did. I've just known her for a long time, longer than I've known anyone except my mother. It's sort of been expected for a while now."

"That's shame. Marriage is not something to be entered into lightly. I should know: I entered quite lightly into two of them myself. I don't think I'd get married again if you put a gun to my head - well, maybe if it was Antonio Banderas."

"I just don't have the courage to call her and tell her I don't love her. But I know if I don't I'll regret it."

"For the rest of your life. I at least thought I was in love when I got married - I was wrong, of course, but I didn't find that out until later. Or maybe I was in love, I don't know. I don't know how long love is supposed to last, but these didn't last for long."

I didn't say anything. I hadn't thought about Connie in what seemed like forever - but I had seen her just three days ago.

There was a newspaper on the ground, in a disorganized pile. I fished around for the front page and pulled it open on my lap.

There was a headline in bold black letters across the top of the page: AL-QUAEDA KIDNAPS VICE-PRESIDENT. In smaller letters below this ran: PRESIDENT SUSPENDS POSSE COMITATUS, MILITARY OPERATIONS BEGIN IN DELAWARE AND PENNSYLVANIA.

"When did this happen?" I asked her.

"What? What are you talking about?"

"Um, this," I held up the large headline for her to see as she drove. She glanced at it and shrugged her shoulders.

"I dunno, I wasn't paying much attention."

It seemed slightly odd to me that I wouldn't have heard anything about this. But then, perhaps there were reasons behind why I had seen what I had seen and heard what I had heard. If Morris had been one of them, who knows what he could have been hiding from me? Could Joanne be one of them? I couldn't know.

After a while we could see the Great Salt Lake emerge on our left, and the spires of the city in the distance, nestled at the base of a great mountain range. Salt Lake City is an odd place. Effectively built up from nothing in the space of a hundred years, there were no outlying communities or real suburbs, not in the same sense that older metropolises with more diverse geographies possessed. When approaching from the west, you enter the city suddenly. The whole thing is set in the valley between two mountain ranges, running north-south from the top of the Salt Lake in the east.

Joanne was pleasant company and I was glad she had picked me up. I was sorry that we would have to part soon.

"Where can I drop you?" she asked as we entered the city limits.

"Well, where are you heading?"

"I've got reservations at a motel, I need to check in and make some calls before I do anything else."

I didn't reply. I began to realize that I was very tired. I had dozed in the truck as Morris drove across Nevada, but before that I hadn't slept well since Truckee. Additionally, I had been in a high speed car chase, caught in an explosion, threatened with guns twice, and been to a whorehouse. The accumulated weight of these experiences suddenly seemed very heavy.

"I'm very tired," I said, unexpectedly.

"I could guess that. You look like you haven't slept in days."

"Well, I slept . . . yesterday. But I've been through a few things since then. I think the adrenaline from the accident is starting to wear off."

"You look like you've been in a war. Your clothes are singed."

"Yeah, I maybe need to buy a new shirt." It seemed as if I was a puppet, and whatever strange hand had been manipulating me and animating me had been removed, leaving me overwhelmingly tired.

My eyes drooped and I tried to stay awake. The passage of time grew a bit fuzzy and before I knew it we were pulling into the parking lot of a Motel Six off the freeway.

"Are you OK?" Joanne asked me.

"Yeah . . . I think I need to sleep."

I opened the car door and walked into the office. Joanne had reservations and she went first, signing her credit slip and accepting her key. I went next. I paid in cash and the clerk gave me funny looks.

I retrieved the duffel bag from Joanne's car and walked up the stairs to my room. The number on my key said that my room number was 207. The door to room 208 was open and Joanne stepped out onto the walkway when she saw me pass.

"What's your room number?" she asked.

"Right next to you."

"What a coincidence! Well, I'll see you later, hon." She waved at me and closed her door.

I opened my room and turned on the light. It was small: one queen sized mattress, a bedside table with a telephone, a round table with two chairs, a television on a dresser and a tiny bathroom. There's a locked door on the wall leading to the next-door room. I dropped my duffel on the floor next to the bed and closed the door behind me. After I locked the door I put the TV on the ground and pushed the small dresser in front of the door, wedging it between the door and the wall so that the door couldn't be opened.

I pulled my shirts off and undid my shoes. I was already half asleep as I took my pants off. I had just enough strength to crawl under the smooth cotton sheets and turn the light off before I was unconscious.

I dreamt of Connie's mother. I hadn't thought about her in many years, and suddenly she was back in my mind.

Connie's birth mother had been a small woman, but not meek and rarely timid. Her and her husband had lived across the lane from us in the trailer park where my family had lived in my youth. Later, when my mother and father had moved out of the trailer and into a small house, Connie's family had followed suite and moved out of the their trailer and into another house a few blocks removed from our own.

They didn't remain long, however. Soon after they had moved into their house on Chickasaw lane, Connie's mother was killed.

It was a summer day, warm and languid. Connie and I had just finished Kindergarten the previous June, and we were just beginning to understand and appreciate the concept of summer. Before school, every day is summer, and the sleepy haze that shaped the vague recollections of our brief lives had as yet been untainted by decisive tragedy. We were playing in her front yard, a small postage stamp of grass in front of her house.

Connie's mother - Helen - was sitting on the front porch and reading a book while we played. We had a pail full of those small green army men and she had a few dolls. We would place the army men in imaginary formations across the dirt and grass of the yard, placing them and replacing them to wage invisible wars.

Connie's family lived across the street from the Ackermans' house. The Ackermans had three children, Trudy, David and Gary, and the youngest - Gary - was in our class. We became acquaintances later - in middle school - but when we were young we didn't see much of each other.

But Connie's mother was friends with Mrs. Ackerman. The afternoon in question, as we were playing in the dirt and grass, Mrs. Ackerman emerged from her front porch and waved over to Connie's mother.

"Helen," she yelled. "Can you spare a minute? I've got to ask you a question."

Connie's mother rose and placed her book on her seat. She looked down at the two of us, playing innocently in the grass, and spoke to Connie: "If mommy runs across the street real quick, can you two stay right here and not do anything else until I get back?"

We both nodded our heads and returned to our play, oblivious. She ran across the street and had a brief conversation with Mrs. Ackerman as they sat together on the latter's porch. Connie's mother could still see us both from where she was sitting.

After no more than ten or fifteen minutes she rose and said good-bye to Mrs. Ackerman. I have no idea what they were talking about, in that brief, fifteen minute confab - gossip, maybe, or perhaps dinner plans. It's not important.

Connie's mother looked both ways and began to cross the street. It was a long boulevard, wide and bright. Her mother was halfway across the street when Mrs. Ackerman turned back from inside her house and yelled back at her:

"Helen! One more thing . . ."

Connie's mother turned her head and saw Mrs. Ackerman on the porch. She swiveled her body and began to walk back to the Ackerman's house but before she could go two steps from the middle of the road a large red Cadillac hit her and threw her body ten feet forward. The car lurched to a stop, and the tires left long black marks on the pavement which didn't begin to fade for a week.

She was dead the moment she hit the pavement - the impact of the car had snapped her neck. Her body lay silent on the ground at an obscene angle, her head and legs splayed around like the tentacles of an octopus, invertebrate. I was - what - five years old? Six? I was young but I still knew that the human body wasn't supposed to be in that position, its limbs couldn't bend like that unless something was terribly wrong.

The car belonged to a teenager named Henry Tork. He had just received his drivers' license the previous month. The police eventually decided he had been going forty-five miles an hour when he hit Connie's mother - forty-five in a twenty zone.

He was a minor so he was only held in juvenile detention until his eighteenth birthday. But he didn't turn out well - the stint in Juvenile Hall made him into a criminal, and he emerged from juvie confused, ashamed, and angry. He became an alcoholic at a very young age and was later arrested for burglary.

A pool of blood slowly expanded from under Connie's

mother's head, sticky red blood that stained the concrete for longer than the Cadillac's tire marks. Connie didn't understand what was happening. Mrs. Ackerman was almost besides herself but she had the presence of mind to run across the street and take Connie and myself into her house. The police came quickly, and eventually the ambulance came as well - without its lights or sirens, quietly and solemnly for the sole purpose of retrieving the dead.

Connie's father came home from work and found his wife dead. He placed Connie with my parents and left that evening to break the news to Connie's parents himself and in person. But he never made it to Connie's parents, and no one ever saw him again. Connie stayed with us for three days before we contacted her grandparents, who informed us that they had not seen or heard from Connie's father in a week. My mother was left the task of informing them that their daughter was dead over the phone.

Connie moved in with her grandparents for a few weeks, but they were old and could not become a permanent home for her. Her other grandparents - her runaway father's parents - had been dead for many years. It was at this time that the Goodings entered the picture and began, with the help of Social Services, the slow process of legally adopting Connie. The Goodings were relatively affluent and well-respected, pillars of the community, so the adoption was seen by all, save perhaps Connie herself, as the best of all possible worlds.

She grew up with three sets of grandparents: her mother's parents, who both died when she was in her teens, and the Gooding's parents. Her mother's parents eventually hired a private detective to find her father, but so far as I know he was never found.

I think the conviction that we would eventually be married was born in my mother the first night after the death of Connie's mother. Constance had rolled her sleeping bag out across our sofa but she didn't sleep: she cried in my mother's arms all night long. I crept out of my room long after they had thought me asleep, hiding in the shadows of the hallway as I watched my mother pour her fingers through Connie's long girlish hair. I resented them then, and I don't think I have ever stopped resenting them.

I'm still half asleep and I see Connie's mother hovering over me as I lay in bed. After another moment I realize that it's not Connie's mother but Joanne, half-naked and sleepy eyed, floating a foot above me as I sleep. Their faces are different. I don't know where Joanne is. If Connie's mother were still alive she would be about ten years alder than I think Joanne is, unless Joanne is remarkably well-preserved. Always a possibility.

I realize I'm still asleep when I close my eyes in my dream and open them again in reality. I am still half-unconscious, with drowsy lethargy running through my limbs and a fifty-pound weight on my chest. I can't lift my arms to turn myself over. Eventually I fall back asleep, but not before I hear someone in the room next door, quietly knocking about.

The light streaming through the curtains when I awaken is faint. I feel weak and thin, hollowed out and baked. My skin is cracked and parched.

I pull my legs out of bed and place my feet shakily on the carpeted floor. My clothes are scattered across the furniture at random, placed where I had thrown them in my half-conscious rush to bed. The small dresser is placed at a jagged edge to the door. I move the dresser back to where it had been and set the television back on top.

My clothes look like they've seen better days. The gray hooded sweatshirt I had been wearing is filthy, covered in streaks of salt from the desert, flecks of dried blood and singed all over. My jeans are in worse shape, with grass stains from Berkeley mingling from salt stains, sweat and soot from the explosions. There's probably a washing machine somewhere on the premises.

I strip my boxers off and grab my toiletries from the duffel bag. I've got shampoo, conditioner and a bar of soap. The shower is strong and hot, and the steam enters my sinuses, clearing my synapses and allowing me to think clearly for seemingly the first time in days.

Blotches of brown grime splatter across the plastic tub floor as the dirt and sweat of three day's hard travel pours from my body. I'm sore in a dozen places. I realize there's still a bandage on my forehead from John's ministrations - I rip the tape off and toss the bandage over the curtain and onto the floor of the bathroom.

After a long shower I feel slightly human again. I realize once again as I pull the towels over my torso that I have lost a considerable amount of weight in the last year: I can feel my ribs sticking through my sides. I'm hungry, in a dim and remote fashion. Clarity of perception makes the passing moments seem like pieces of film, slid through the projector and broadcast over my skin stretched thin across a metal frame.

I scrape deodorant across my body and comb down my hair. My teeth are filthy so I brush twice. I am naked but I am clean and tired. so I sit down on the edge of the bed and turn the television on.

The news report has pictures of rioters in Bangladesh and Baghdad and Belgrade. The President has yet to make a public statement on the matter of his lieutenant's kidnapping - he is being held in an undisclosed location. US Special Forces are leading the hunt as we speak. It is believed that he will be found alive.

They're talking to the families of Secret Service agents killed in the assault on Air Force 2. The TV breaks for a commercial and they're trying to sell me detergent and fast food chicken finger-foods and college tuition assistance for my newborn grandchildren through the Mutual of Omaha.

I can't understand what it is that they're saying because everyone is talking so fast. The scrolling captions across the bottom of the screen seem to have dissolved into gibberish - someone is talking about their pants and their plants and their plantains and I don't see the connection.

I put the television on mute and fall back onto the bed. I could easily stay here like this all night but before I can lapse back into a restful reverie a bolt of nervous energy strikes me at the base of my spine and I surge upwards like a marionette.

I throw my filthy clothes into a heap at the foot of the bed - I'll find a washing-machine later tonight. I pull a clean pair of boxers and some socks out of my duffel bag, along with a clean black T-shirt and a starched pair of khaki slacks (which have been unfortunately wrinkled by the process of traveling in my bag). However, the motel room has been outfitted with an iron, perched on the top shelf of the small closet. I stretch out the ironing board and iron my pants in silence, the echoes of a muted television flickering across the walls.

I hear a muffled noise from the next room and I realize that it must be Joanne, returned to her room after her appointments. After I've creased my slacks and pulled them on, I fasten my belt (it seems as if the belt is getting bigger every month), walk over to the locked door separating our two rooms and knock softly.

"Yes?" the answer comes from inside.

"It's me," I say.

"I guessed," she says, drolly. "Hold on while I get decent."

After a few moments I hear the door unlocking from her side. I unlock my side and it swings open.

"Come on in," she calls from inside. "Sorry about the mess."

Her room looks to have been hit by a tornado in the few

short hours since we arrived. Her bed is still made, but covered in papers, files, folders, compact discs, small boxes, a laptop computer and a few items of clothing. Her suitcase is sitting open across the dresser, its contents strewn across the floor.

She's in semi-formal business attire, quite different from the unflattering casual traveling clothes she wore in the morning. She's wearing a black knee-length skirt with dark stockings underneath. Despite her frame her body is forcefully curvaceous, with soft hips flexing under tight cotton cloth. Her blouse is stark white, open at the collar with the top button undone. Although I am trying not to look, I can see the beginnings of ample cleavage as it dives down her shirt.

Joanne looks nervous, frayed. She has been smoking and there are empty cups of coffee spread across the room. She was sitting on the edge of the bed and she motioned for me to sit in the chair at her table.

"Hey," I say.

"Hey yourself. You sleep all day?"

"Yeah. I was tired."

"Well, I guess. You clean up nice."

"Thanks. I didn't realize how dirty I was until I took a shower earlier."

"You were filthy. You also looked as if you had been caught in an explosion . . . which I guess you were."

"Yeah. Knocked me for a loop."

"Your bandage came off," she gestured towards my forehead.

"Yeah, it fell off in the shower. These stitches look OK, though. I was worried I'd get an infection."

"How'd you hurt your head?"

"If I told me you wouldn't believe me."

"This from the man who got blown up just this morning. Try me."

"Well, I got clobbered by a . . . riot cop. In Berkeley."

"Berkeley? How long have you been on the road?"

"About three days now."

"I was just out there. I was in San Jose four days ago, then Sacramento, Stockton, Reno, and now here. I'm exhausted."

"You had a meeting today."

She took a deep breath and lit a cigarette, running her fingers through her hair. It looked like an old habit.

"Yeah, you could say that. I didn't do too well. Seems like all the meetings I have are with people who either just upgraded their equipment or are too poor to do more than use pencil and paper. I am beginning to doubt the wisdom of this career move for a number of reasons."

"I'm sorry. Are you hungry?"

She looked up at me for a moment and seemed to brighten. "Yeah, I'm starving. I've been running around since we got here this morning and I haven't had more than a donut all day. Let's go."

I pulled a jacket from my duffel bag and she grabbed a coat. We piled into her car and headed off down the street. There were chain restaurants everywhere, garish neon-lit temples of suburbia placed at respectful distances apart from each other. We settled on Tony Roma's.

It struck me, in the restaurant's dim lighting, that she seemed more than a little tired. She asked me if I wouldn't mind driving back to the motel and ordered a cocktail.

"So," I said, after the waiter had brought our drinks (she had ordered a Bloody Mary, I had a coke), "you think you made a bad career choice."

"Yeah," she exhaled deeply. "I didn't really have much of a choice, though. I lost my job. I'm extremely overqualified for the job I have, but it's the best I could do on short notice."

"You worked in computers before?"

"Oh yeah. But that was a couple years ago by now . . . I've been a glorified salesman for a while. If I actually got a new offer for my old job I'd be screwed because I'm so out of touch. You have to stay on top of that shit or you will be eaten alive. There are guys who eat, breathe sleep and shit computers, and I was good but I could never compete with that kind of competition."

"Yeah. I can relate."

"Enough about me," she said after she took another sip of her drink, "I want to hear about you. You seem like a fascinating man."

"There's not a lot to tell. I just graduated college. I'm traveling." I didn't want to say anymore.

"And you're stuck to a fiancé you don't like."

"Yeah, you could say that."

"You need some confidence. You're a great guy, young, handsome - maybe a bit skinny - but you shouldn't have to be so afraid of everything all the time. You've got your whole life ahead of you."

I would have had to have been deaf to have missed the trilling note of self-pity in her tone.

"Don't be so hard on yourself," I said. "You're only as young as you feel. I feel like I was born old. You look like you've got twice as much energy as I do." I tried to ignore my own cliches.

"Oh, I don't feel very energized. Let me tell you, I spend half my time driving around the country trying to sell this shitty software to people who don't want it and don't need it, and the other half trying desperately to stay afloat despite the fact that I'm making half of what I used to and I'm working twice as hard. Everyone I know is in the same damn boat and it just doesn't seem to be getting any easier, because there's not a single company anywhere, in any field, that is hiring on anything other than a contract basis. I'm lucky to have medical insurance, I guess."

"You sound so sad."

"Oh, don't pay me any heed. I'm just grousing. I chose this life fair and square. You only get one and I guess I'm glad to have it, shitty or not."

"You need to think like that more often. Well, er not the shitty part, maybe."

We laughed and she ordered another drink. They brought us our food and we ate, slowly, still talking in between bites. I liked her.

I had to work hard to keep my eyes from settling on hers for too long. The room was dark and busy, with a large dinner crowd and a harried wait staff rushing to and fro. I had to work hard to keep track of everyone who seemed to be watching me - there were many unobtrusive, solitary diners who could have been monitoring my actions and conversation and reporting back to unseen masters. I had to be very careful to watch what I said.

Our dinner passed without any interruption. The ribs piled on our plates and Joanne finished two more drinks. We split a piece of cheesecake and paid the check.

She was considerably tipsy as we walked out to the car. She gave me the keys and we returned to the motel in comfortable silence. Her eyes drooped to half-shut and she wore a particularly beatific smile as I navigated the car along the wide antiseptic Utah streets.

We returned to our rooms and I saw that the door between was still open. Joanne closed it silently, leaving just a small crack between the door and the frame through which I could see passing shadows.

I flopped down on my bed and turned the television on. There were talking heads on the news stations, discussing the possibilities of nuclear reprisals and humanitarian evacuations across the Holy Land. I wondered how much of what I was seeing reported on the news was factually accurate, and how much of it was deliberately manufactured to obfuscate the truth.

In any event I changed the channel and tried to watch something else, a sitcom or police procedural or something else with less portent attached. I still had a great deal of work ahead of me on my trip, many signs left to unravel before I would be ready to interpret the code given me to protect. Somehow my father had been involved in whatever it was that was hunting me, chasing me down - probably the same beast that had turned on our own government and started the inexorable process of chewing our own legs off. America was at war with something and someone, but they were hidden, invisible, and undetectable. It was these silent forces, arrayed across the vast night of our ignorance, who I would have to elude if I was to survive the coming weeks.

A strange thought occurred to me and I found it difficult to avoid acting on rash impulse. Emboldened by Joanne's confident words and perhaps a tiny bit tipsy on the thought that she might have been flirting with me earlier at dinner, I picked up the telephone receiver and dialed Constance's number.

There was a long silence as the number connected, Finally, it rang. Once. Twice. A third time - and then there was an answer.

"Hello?"

I moved to speak but the words froze in my throat.

"Hello? Who is this?"

Nothing. Finally, tentatively, she said my name.

"Is it you?"

I wanted to speak, to tell her what I was feeling, how afraid I was.

"We found your car - what the hell -"

The receiver fell back into the cradle and the room was silent, the walls echoing with the sound of the slammed phone. What had I been thinking? I had been so foolish. The call could have been traced, I could have been caught and found out.

Which was presuming that they hadn't already found me. Weren't tracking me right now, weren't listening to every word I said and hearing every though in my head. I crept from the bed to the dresser and moved the television.

Leaning into the dresser from a crouch, I pushed it slightly on its side so I could feel the bottom - and yes, my notebooks were still where I had left them this evening, taped to the underside of the bottom of the dresser.

I breathed a sigh of relief. I was getting sloppy, and this type of stupidity could very well get me killed.

"What's the matter?"

I looked up and saw Joanne, standing in the passageway between the rooms and looking down at where I sat on the floor.

"I dropped something."

"Did you find it?"

"Yeah, yeah I did."

She had changed her clothes. She was wearing a sheer transparent nightshirt with only a bra and panties underneath. She leaned provocatively against the doorframe and motioned me towards the bed.

"I'm tired, what about you?"

I stood up and retraced my steps to the edge of the bed where I had been sitting just a moment before.

"Yeah, I guess I could turn in."

"Well, goodnight."

Joanne walked across the room and straddled me on the bed, pulling my mouth to hers and kissing me as hard as she could.

17

Regardless of their city planners' best intentions, Salt Lake City is a deceptively easy city to get lost in. The entire town is built atop a numerical street grid circumnavigated by a series of freeways, and it is remarkably easy to get lost when your only landmarks are similarly numbered street signs. The city is built on a flat plateau that allows you to keep the downtown in sight at all times.

Unique among American cities, Salt Lake is built around temples - great massive monuments erected to the tenacity of Mormon settlers. The area immediately around these monuments is disturbingly pristine, much like Disneyland, with no poverty or litter or urban blight to be seen. Of course, the further away from the downtown area you get, the more fractures emerge in the facade.

Joanne and I headed east, rising from our bed probably later than we should have but cheerful regardless. Her next destination was Denver, and our itineraries matched for the duration. We followed 80 for a few minutes more as we rose up and away from the Salt Lake City basin, and then joined with I-40 as it coasts its way across the eastern slope of the state.

It was amusing for her, I believe, to have found a young man such as myself to exploit. Older women - and women seem to become older at a much younger age as the years go by - need reassurances, and the recent fad among older women for younger trophy boyfriends served as reassurance on a massive scale that older women could still be attractive and vital.

Older women were more than merely vital, however, they seemed to have a great deal more of the perspicacity and integrity to which I found myself attracted. Of course, I was considered slightly handsome and have found myself the subject of multiple amorous encounters throughout recent years. But few, if any, have held the satisfaction for me as my brief period with Joanne, compared to whose vitality Constance was a mere flickering candle.

But of course I was conscious of the constant threat posed by my attraction to her. In having found a companion - even a passing companion - for my travels I had also managed to accrue risk upon risk upon risk. I remembered Morris' bones, flash-burnt in the desert by the intense heat of the exploding truck. I knew they were after me, and I knew that they would stop at nothing to get me. Joanne was in danger for as long as we remained together.

Unless, of course, she was one of them. In the same moment that I remembered Morris' blackened bones I also recalled that he had been carrying many tons of vicious child pornography in his truck, the very same pornography that I believed many of my pursuers trafficked in order to fund certain of their illicit activities. Was he a patsy or had he been a conspirator? Had he died believing he was carrying Chinese DVD players, or had he been reporting back to his masters the entire time I had been with him?

I put the thought out of my mind for the time being. It didn't matter if Morris had been one of them or not - he was dead. I also had no reason to believe that they were not intimately aware of my whereabouts at all times. If their resources were as broad and vast as I believed - as my father had believed - I could only imagine but that they could kill me at any time they wished. Therefore, they must have believed it to be in their interests to keep me alive, for whatever reason. With this as an assumption, I had merely to perceive and elude whatever traps they placed in my path. If i was alive, they needed something of me, and my survival might soon depend on learning just what that something was.

The eastern half of Utah is beautiful, more than making up for the vast barren deserts of the western part. As the elevation rises and you begin the gradual ascent that will lead you into the Rockies, the land becomes more fertile and green, covered in wilderness and grassland. The high plateaus of eastern Utah are covered in sage and cactus, with jagged buttes and gorgeous sun-soaked sandstone formations rising from the plain.

Whereas the drive from the Pacific ocean to Salt Lake City is a relatively straight route, eastward from Salt Lake the roads become smaller and more winding as they work their way through the mountains and valleys which compose the distinctively rugged western terrain.

Joanne and I drove from Salt Lake City to the Colorado border in the space of a day. rising at noon and reaching a motel well before dark. It's a short day's drive, but we were in no hurry. Her next appointment wasn't for another two days.

As the road wound upward through Colorado on the second day we passed and paralleled numerous mountain streams as they wound their way down the continental shelf towards the ocean to our backs. The water shimmers in the crisp rural sunlight. We stopped for an afternoon picnic with the sun high against the clouds, shaded by the tall trees at the bottom of a gully overlooked by thunderous crags.

Joanne was wearing a black T-shirt and shorts, comfortable driving clothes and definitely flattering for her figure. The neck of the T-shirt scooped down just low enough to reveal the barest curve of heavenly cleavage. Her medium-length hair was up, held by one of those brown tiger-striped clips that were persistently popular. Her green eyes hid behind dark black sunglasses.

We had been together for two and a half days but the urgency of our romance had not yet crested. I think I was in love, then, for perhaps the first time ever. I heard a man say once that whether or not love was properly reciprocated was immaterial to the essence of said love, but I now believe that to be mere sophistry. Unrequited love kills the soul because it causes one to live in the eternal shade of ineffable possibility. I could forgive Constance anything, but not her love. It killed us both, little by little.

But Joanne was, far from enervating, the most energizing relationship of my life. Pure lust, as with Erica, was ultimately frustrating, because the sensation could never be fully sated this side of death. Lust was only tolerable when leavened by love, and only then when the love was fully reciprocated.

I felt loved, and it was a beautiful feeling. In hindsight,

perhaps I should have been more careful. My responsibilities were grave and my burden heavy, and the only guarantee of my survival was constant vigilance. But somehow, without ever broaching the subject, Joanne made me believe that my vigilance was moot.

We had purchased sandwiches and potato chips at a supermarket deli in a small town near the Colorado border. There were many small rivers which presented the opportunity for picnicking, and the particular picnic spot we had chosen was well-protected from the sounds of the nearby highway. We could barely hear the road above, insulated from the noise by the trees and the persistent low rush of water in the background.

Where we sat the sunlight shone down through the gully and through the canopy of the trees directly above us. The light refracted down through the leaves, creating a carpet of green and yellow geometric shapes on the earth, swaying slightly in the breeze like a gently rocking kaleidoscope torn open and spread across the earth.

We ate our meal in silence, the wind whistling through the trees in a languid fashion. It was warm, just warm enough that we felt absolutely comforted by the wind. The hair on the back of my neck stood on end, teased by the thoroughly erotic possibilities of wind caressing my body.

I finished my sandwich and drank a soda, leaning against the side of the wooden picnic table as I watched the river pass us by. Joanne finished her meal and deposited her trash in a plastic bag, before she stood and walked around the side of thc table to where I was sitting.

Joanne's life had, on retrospect, been neither harder or easier than average. She was a strong, intelligent and attractive woman who had grown up believing everything she was told in regards to her potential and the possibilities open to her in the course of her life. Therefore she had only experienced mild disappointment when she had reached the end of her initial ascent through her chosen field: after all, it had not been sexism or the glass ceiling which had felled her, but the simple fact that there were no jobs available for someone of her qualifications.

And so she had been forced to apply to numerous positions for which her experience and acumen rendered her distinctly overqualified. Her field was computers, and after the initial boom of the 1990s, the unqualified enthusiasm of speculative investors had given way to the dignified reluctance of traditional economic indicators.

So after 9/11, before which business had already been soft, she had been faced with the prospect of her firm no longer existing. She was smarter and worked harder than most of her colleagues, but her job security was doubtful because she had been excluded from most of the commonplace rituals of office acquaintanceship. In this instance, it was not so much that she had been a woman, but that she had been an intelligent woman who refused to accept the hierarchy of office dominance. She didn't play golf, she didn't have children, and because she remained staunchly independent she was perceived as aloof despite her warm nature.

That she had been fired was a small surprise, but it had been no surprise at all when her firm was entirely liquidated not a full year later. She, at least, had escaped with a generous severance package, while the people who had been saved from the first arbitrary cullings had been lucky at the end to escape with a week's pay.

Being a confident and intelligent person, it had not crossed her mind that she would be unable to find another position. But even though her last job search had ended after only two weeks, she was unemployed for two months before she succeeded in finding a new job. The new job paid less, offered less benefits and afforded fewer opportunities for advancement - but it was a job in her chosen field, which was more than many of her former colleagues had.

So she was a saleswoman, driving across the country and selling network solutions to small companies that either already had or would never need even a small-scale computer network. Her intelligence assured her the wherewithal necessary to do her job well, but she did not possess an affinity for sales. Too often in her old position she had loathed the sales department for having oversold an underdeveloped application which she would then have to deliver to an eager clientele. Now she was the salesperson herself, and in the unenviable position of knowing full well just how little her prospective customers understood about the product they were buying - ignorance could have at least offered her the soothing balm of a clear conscience.

But she had managed to keep her house and her credit rating relatively intact since the catastrophe. She worked long hours for less pay but somehow managed to make it. It was galling to be so far behind where she would have predicted being just five years previous, but as long as she was independent, she would be happy. She did not speak of her two ex-husbands, except in passing.

She was a beautiful woman. Every trace of youth had melted from her face, and she was left with the strong and confident solidity of maturation, an allure that made a mockery of the callow self-assurance of youth. She was not yet old - far from it - but she was no longer young, and youth had been a burden which she had gladly relinquished.

We sat in silence for a long time, watching the river pass softly under the watchful eye of the hill. After a while I leaned over and put my arm around Joanne, squeezing her shoulder and pulling her slightly closer to me.

She set her hand on my leg and squeezed my thigh. Slowly she brought her hand up until she was feeling my crotch, tracing the outline of my slowly rising penis with her fingers. She undid my button and zipper, reaching inside my pants and grasping the organ firmly.

The sun was falling leisurely through the trees, and rays

of light were beginning to seep through the western face of the canopy, landing gingerly on our faces as we sat watching the river slowly pass.

I became intimately aware of the passing of time, as the sound of rushing water filled my ears and the raw loamy earth under my feet rose to my nostrils. I pulled off my shoes and socks, peeled off my trousers and my shirt ,and walked slowly towards the river. The water was clear and shone like silver in the afternoon sun.

The riverbed was covered with small rounded pebbles, smoothed by centuries of mountain water, runoff from the melting glaciers, still hundreds of miles in the east. The water was bracingly cold at first.

I had to step lightly in order not to pinch my toes between the pebbles, placing my rear foot firmly on a larger stone before each new step. I made slow progress but in about a minute I had walked ten yards out from the shore and was up to my waist in water. The river was probably about fifty yards wide.

I walked two more steps and dove beneath the surface, immersing myself in the water. I swam towards the center of the river and rose to the surface. My feet could no longer touch the bottom but the stream was not as powerful as I had feared - I could comfortably remain in place merely by treading water.

Joanne stood on the shore where I had entered, holding her shoes and tentatively dipping her toes into the stream.

"How is it?" she yelled out to me.

"Wonderful!" I replied. "It's cold when you start, but it feels wonderful when you're underwater."

She didn't reply. I dove again, heading down to the bottom of the river as quickly as I could. it seemed to be the depth of a large swimming pool at its deepest - ten or twelve feet at the most. The water was colder the deeper I descended. The comparatively warm water at the surface was displaced by increasingly cold layers near the bottom. I had become climatized to the temperature of the water at the surface but as I sank lower the progressively colder layers of water ran over my skin like ice, jagged and sharp. Finally I reached the bottom of the stream, covered in murky moss and algae, and littered with tumbled stones and sunken driftwood.

The current was stronger at this depth so I reached out and grabbed onto a large branch of driftwood wedged between two large rocks. I held on with one hand and twisted my body so that my face pointed towards the surface.

I could see the sunlight streaming down through the water, fractured and diffused by the layers of water above my head. In that moment I saw green and blue and turquoise and yellow, filtered and pixelated and magnified by the running water before finally ending its ninety-three million mile voyage in my submerged eyes.

I stared into the sun for a long moment before I realized that my lungs were burning. I had been under the water for a long minute, and I needed air. I let go of the branch I had grabbed and kicked away from the riverbed, bobbing up to the surface like a balloon.

My head breached the water and I inhaled a deep lungful of sweet, slightly earthy air.

I looked out towards the shore and saw that Joanne had left her clothes folded on a large rock near the shore and was slowly walking out towards the center of the stream. The river and the picnic grounds were hidden from the highway by the wide canopy of the outspread trees and the curve of the hill, so we were assured of our privacy.

She was naked. She wasn't thin but she was not fat - her body held no more and no less volume than was necessary to adequately fill her wide frame. Oftentimes clothes are used to hide imperfections - blemishes and dimples where there had once been clear and unmottled flesh - but in her case Joanne's skin was totally immune to the ravages of age, unbesmirched by the temerity of having lived a while on this earth.

She smiled at me as she slowly made her way out into the river. I could tell she was shivering, slightly, by the time the water rose to meet her breasts. They were ample and round, and they rose with the water level as she walked on, floating and bobbing in the water like buoys. Her nipples were sharp and solid, pointed away from her body like small bullets, thick and hard.

She was swimming out to the middle of the river, doing the doggy paddle as I treaded water. The sun was beginning to set at the mouth of the gully, sending focused rays of orange and red light down across the surface of the stream. She finally reached me and I grasped for her hand, held her close to me and we embraced. I opened my mouth and the water ran in but we kissed anyway, half submerged and hungry again.

18

The urge for perfection is an adolescent impulse, but it hardly disappears with the pimples. Moral certainty holds an irrefutable appeal which can rarely be effectively countered by experience.

I don't know very many things with any degree of certainty, but I do know this: the world is a confusing and confused place. Scratch a cynic and you'll find a broken idealist, or so they say - and I believe the same holds true for a moral subjectivist. Awareness of ambiguity breeds an overwhelming desire for control and certitude.

Which explains why teenagers are such conceited moral fascists. The world is new to them, and they are naturally disappointed in the hypocrisy and corruption that they find themselves surrounded by as they emerge from the self-obsessed womb of the American nuclear family. I have attempted at every step in my journey to combat this type of moral absolutism in my perceptions and the perceptions of those around me.

Because it's never that easy - there are always unforeseen complications. Joanne served as one such complication for me in my travels. For a time I considered abandoning my mission, turning my back on the constant, ingratiating conspiracies in which I found myself perpetually enmeshed. I wondered - if I wished merely to walk away, would they let me? If I took my notebooks - those all-important records of the ongoing international conspiracy - and drowned them in that Colorado river like some latter day Prospero, abjuring all of the special and privileged knowledge and awareness which my life has given me, would I be allowed to walk away?

If I took my pills, would they consider me sufficiently pacified? If I returned home, made peace with my mother and broke off definitively with Connie, would I be allowed to continue forward unmolested from this point?

But my thoughts perpetually caught on the responsibilities inherent in my uniquely privileged position. If I was the only man in the world who understood exactly why three thousand people had died in New York, who knew the location of the secret blueprints of the international underworld, who saw how the death of my father in the jungles of the Congo over ten years ago had set off the chain of events leading to this catastrophe, to the catastrophe unfolding on the news as we spoke . . .

An unfortunate accident at a local light industrial plant had served as cover for my father's death. There had been an explosion and a fire on the assembly line, and a handful of workers had been severely injured. The plant, one of the few industrial producers in the area, had gone out of business after it was conclusively proven that the accident had been precipitated by a preventable maintenance malfunction. The injured workers sued, and their suits were successful to the effect of hundreds of thousands of dollars.

So, at the behest of the shadowy operators who act in the interests of the secret authorities to manipulate public perception, the company manipulated events so that the general public believed that my father had been the only fatal casualty of this accident, and that my mother had grown suddenly rich not off the bounty from her husband's death paid by sinister multinational cabals, but by a simple liability settlement paid out by the defunct manufacturing plant's insurance company.

It was a perfect cover-up, as no one was given any reason to doubt the veracity of my father's given cause of death. But I knew the truth.

It was soon after my father's death when I received a crucial visit from the One-Eyed Man. My suspicions regarding my father's death had not yet been substantiated, and although he lay in the ground for less than a month at the time of the visit I had not allowed myself to mourn, for fear of losing the powerful sense of rage and indignation which, while still inchoate, guided my feelings through this initial period of loss.

"Why won't you cry?" my mother would ask me. "Your Daddy's dead - why won't you cry for your Daddy?"

And whenever she asked me this I would fix her with a stare of scathing incredulity. Of course she wanted me to cry in order to assuage her own guilt, to try and convince herself that her charade was successful and that I suspected none of her perfidy.

But she was wrong, and in the wrong, and she knew that I understood her own complicity in this tragedy. Did she want my forgiveness? She detested me. She had detested me from the very beginning, when I had emerged from her womb as an alien and unknowable creature.

I was waiting for my mother to pick me up after school, sitting on the playground equipment in such a way that I had an eye on the school courtyard. My mother was usually late, and that day was no different.

But before my mother arrived another visitor came. The schoolyard was a large rectangular lot to the rear of the actual school building, and two streets ran parallel on either side of this strip. The front of the school, where the courtyard and entranceway were, was empty. The rear of the school faced out onto a small tract of houses and fallow fields which gave way to forest.

The One-Eyed Man appeared at the rear gate of the schoolyard, at the place where maintenance trucks could swing open a stretch of the chain-link fence and enter if needed. He didn't say anything, simply appearing at the fence and waiting until I turned my head to see him.

I wasn't surprised to find him there. He was a regular enough presence in my life at that point that I was never really shocked to see him, regardless of whatever negative connotations I could infer from his visits.

This time was slightly different, however. This was the first time I had seen him since my father had died, and his visitation brought with it all the terrible associations of that grim event.

I jumped down from my perch on the jungle gym and walked towards the back fence. I had never spoke with him before, but he didn't move to go when I approached him. He lit a cigarette and waited patiently for me to approach.

When seen from a close vantage, his face resembled more than anything else the craggy texture of the naked moon. His skin was pockmarked with many tiny fissures, acne scars or enlarged pores. His nose was slightly crooked, as if it had been broken and never properly set. Eyebrows were dark and bushy, while his hair sat uneasily on his head, slicked back with cheap pomade. But most unnervingly, now that I saw him from a more intimate viewpoint, was the thin white scar that emerged the patch which covered his dead eye, running from under the patch on down over his cheek until it ended right at his chin. It was a hideous and fragile mark, unnoticeable from a distance but unavoidable up close.

When he spoke his voice was harsh but still quiet, with the rough consistency of tanned leather burnt by the sun.

"You knew my father?" I asked him.

"Yes," he said, and this was the first word I had ever heard him speak.

"You know why he's dead?"

"Yes, but it's not why you think."

"I know that. I know my mom's been lying to me about it. I don't like that."

"Your mother has her reasons for lying," he said, measuring the words like cloth, deliberately and with great caution, before cutting them upon his tongue. "She is your mother, and I suppose you will always love her, but you must never trust her."

"I don't love her. She hates me."

He was silent for a moment. "I don't believe any son should hate his mother, but your mother has done much to earn your hatred." He pulled a long drag on his cigarette before continuing, allowing these ominous and pregnant words to hang in the air between us for a moment before continuing.

"Come with me," he said, pulling the gate open.

I followed him and we walked across the empty road in silence. As we spoke we walked through the fields and deep into the forest.

"Your father," he began, "was a very important man. He was also a dangerous man, but an honorable one. Do you understand that?"

"Yes, I think so."

"He did many things which I do not believe he was proud to have done, but in the end he did them for the right reasons. Whatever else you learn in the days and years to come, you must believe that."

"I do believe it. I know it."

"Good. Because there are many who did not . . . many who opposed your father and the forces he represented. Whether or not they consider themselves to be heroes or villains in their own universes is immaterial to the current discussion. But you must never doubt that they are as motivated and as committed to their cause as you or I."

I didn't say anything because I didn't fully understand what he was saying, and indeed I would not understand until many years had passed and I had experienced these things myself.

"In any event, there have always been those who would seek to oppress humanity by fighting the forces of progress and enlightenment. There have always been secret wars waged against the backdrop of history, wars that have been fought in the private shadow of the wars you know and will learn about, and wars against which these public conflicts have been mere shadows.

"Your father was a soldier, and he fought in Asia and Africa . . . he died in Africa. In a country called Rwanda. When you're older you will learn all about the colonial period, and all the countries scattered across the world that were subjugated in the name of distant lands and foreign ideals.

"The secret wars of the twentieth century have been fought in these countries - small, isolated battlefields where hidden agendas could be consolidated away from the prying eyes of the West. The major conflicts of the twentieth century were merely feints toward greater and more potent agendas which have been in slow but inexorable conflict since the dawn of man.

"I lost my eye in Angola, fighting alongside your father. I left Africa many years ago, but I swore to your father that for as long as he remained overseas that I would look after you, protect you and guide you through until you were ready to know the truth of your father's life."

By then we were deep into the woods, with sticks and

twigs softly breaking under our feet and the coniferous trees swaying gently in the breeze.

"How did he die?" I asked hesitantly.

"They cut off his head," he said without any hesitation. "He was asleep while they crept into his hut and slit his throat. They cut his head off and left it as a warning for us. For his friends and comrades, and his family, too."

The forest was quiet. The ground was covered in a thick layer of pine needles and small brush, with manzanita growing in random clumps between the large pine trees. We walked in the shadow of a nearby hillock, and we could hear a brook in the distance, perhaps 50 yards away behind a curve in our path.

He never told me his name. As we walked together in the shade of the tall trees, he told me many things, many dark and terrible secrets which fell on my brow like a heavy burden. For the most part, I knew I could never share any of these terrible secrets with anyone, and that I would be cursed with this knowledge until the end of my days.

We talked for hours, until the sun had flown across the dome of the sky and come to rest on the distant bed of brown and red mountains in the west. Finally, when the time came he left me alone, to return to his mission, whatever it was.

The secrets he revealed to me that day became the foundations of my secret journals, the bedrock of knowledge on which I would slowly erect the framework of my investigation throughout the years. There are a few secrets which remain so terrible that, to this day, I have never recorded them. If my journals were discovered it would be a disaster, but there are at least a few important kernels of classified knowledge which they could never, under any circumstances, gain from me. Even to speak them out loud would blacken the my tongue with filth.

And of course, when the planes fell on September 11th, there were many previously unguessed items which instantly fell into place. Although it would take me a long time to pull together all the strings of the knowledge I had at the time - and indeed, I was unable to properly digest the new information until I had successfully and fully thrown off the effects of the mind-control medication I had been given - the truth, or at least the portion of it into which I had gained an insight through my investigations, was a terrible revelation of shattering proportions.

Lauren had been beautiful, but I had also been vulnerable and weak. My father's death had left me rootless. The constant perfidy of my mother remained a nagging reminder of my weakness - until I grew older I would be dependent on her for my life. I was still young enough, I knew, that I could still have been snuffed out at a moment's notice without any real difficulties.

The One-Eyed Man left me and I was alone in the forest. It was a pleasant spring evening, not sharp enough to be cold but not yet hot. In the summer, the heat grew oppressive, contorting every possible expression of life into abject squalor.

The stars were out and the sky was bright and I felt wonderfully, vividly alone - truly independent of my mother for the first time and with all illusions stripped from my perception.

I was found in the morning by a search party sent by my mother. Of course, by that time they had discovered where I had been and who I had been with. My mother's fury would undoubtedly have been great, had she been allowed to vent it - but as it was she was forced into the role of a grieving, worried parent with a lost child. She had contacted law-enforcement and triggered certain shadowy protocols written for similar circumstances. There was no mention of a "One-Eyed Man ", merely vague and confused references to predatory individuals. The story was disseminated in such a way that it was widely believed that I had been found with torn clothing and in a daze, having been attacked and victimized, but these were merely more of my mother's lies.

So in public she played the part of the worried and distraught mother, but I knew that she was secretly upset at the disruption of her carefully structured plans and machinations. She reported to her secret masters every night. When she thought me asleep she crept into her room and made her report to her masters, using a small communications device hidden in the sole of a running shoe.

Soon after the incident with the One-Eyed Man I began to sleep with a knife. I stole a large blade from the kitchen and hid it underneath my pillow, with my sweaty fingers wrapped around the wooden handle. I was still unable to sleep, however, for fear that if I ever truly succumbed to slumber my mother would take the opportunity to harm me further.

But eventually my vigilance paid off. About a month after the One-Eyed Man's visit, and two months total since my father had passed, I caught my mother sneaking into my room in the middle of the night with a hypodermic needle in her hand.

I was aware of her presence from the first moment she entered the room, hearing the door creak as she pushed it aside. Pretending to be asleep, I waited until she stood over me, brandishing her weapon with the intent of injecting me with whatever poisonous concoction her masters had given her.

I sprang up from my bed and swung the knife at her. Before she was totally aware of what had happened, the kitchen knife was plunged halfway through the palm of her hand, and the syringe had fallen to the floor.

She screamed and I ran, away from her and out the back door of the house. It was hot, and I distinctly remember the rush of muggy heat that assaulted me when I opened the door and stepped out from the air-conditioned house and into the yard.

Soon the police and paramedics arrived at my mother's behest. She was taken to the hospital, and would undoubtedly be called before her masters to testify as to how she had failed in her mission of elimination.

The police found me not far from the house, in a gully where I had tripped and fallen. They took me away and treated my scrapes, but I was placed in police custody and taken to a juvenile detention facility.

I knew that any attempt to plead self-defense would be laughable - and that the forces behind my mother would have already succeeded in secreting away any evidence of the attempted murder. I was placed under observation and isolated. Finally, they made the decision to place me in a psychiatric facility. I was twelve. My father was dead and I was alone in the world, unable to depend on the One-Eyed Man for protection from my mother and still bound by the limitations of my age. I served my time in the hospital and returned to the world, my regimen of pacifying mind-control drugs already well underway. It would take me many years to fully break through the layers of conditioning with which they manipulated my teenage years.

And of course, there were also girls. It would be almost impossible to accurately parse where the urge to procreate and the desire for an abatement to gnawing loneliness end and begin in adolescence: the one fuels the other. While both impulses are undoubtedly chimerical, they are no less real for it.

Would that it were possible to make love to every beautiful woman in the world, every comely figure and shapely ankle and rounded bosom. There's so much emptiness, so much drifting impermeable darkness surrounding every nodule of flickering consciousness. In chemistry we learned of the inconceivable scale of microscopic distances, and how there is no real concept of solidity when we are taken into the discrete portions of our atomic framework. There are eons and light years between the lonely molecules, vast gulfs of black space everywhere inside us and all around us.

When I was a child I thought that this loneliness was special and unique, that I was somehow missing out on some crucial part of existence because of some strange inadequacy in my habitual nature. But all children feel alone, when they outgrow their parents and learn to perceive the world through newly disillusioned eyes. Maturation only begins when we realize that this is merely the way it is, and this is always how it has been, and our frustrations at the assumptions of our human birthright are merely the most futile of animal flailings.

19

As Utah plateau gives way to the rising summit of Colorado, the air grows thin and ascetic. Passing through the Rocky Mountains on thin roads carved into the curves of craggy peaks is a breathtaking experience, even as the engine begins to knock and the traffic becomes occasionally severe.

Joanne was a wonderful companion for a road trip. There was so much to learn, so many wonderful things to say and hear about each other, that it became an almost unbearable pleasure to be allowed in her presence. My heart, which had been so heavy since leaving home, grew light and unfettered as we gained altitude.

Perhaps I let my guard down, or perhaps I was merely content to believe that I was being allowed to continue on my journey so long as it proceeded unabated. I believed then, as I believe now, that Joanne was ultimately unaware of any conspiracy, and that whatever involvement she may have had was merely incidental and unknowing. Perhaps she herself had been manipulated into contact with me - I have no way of knowing.

We passed the day in contentment, rising at the border and wending our way through the mountains before eventually beginning our descent to Denver, and the great plains beyond. Highway 40 took us through the high Rockies before settling us down on the slopes of the foothills leading into the flatland, filtering down onto 70, which would take us through the state and into Kansas. Great cities are traditionally built at intersections, be they of land and ocean or of two rivers, and Denver stood at the junction of West and East, between the tumult of geologic uncertainty that characterized the space between Colorado and the Pacific Ocean and the uniform certainty that characterized the Great Plains on their inexorable flight towards the Atlantic.

Swooping down from the hills into the Denver basin, highway 70 multiplies and grows, a two-lane road merging into a four-lane freeway that becomes ten monstrous lanes as it dives toward the city. The incredible elevation of the mountains abates and your ears pop as you are restored to something resembling a normal gravity.

The city is surrounded by layers of suburbs, the seeming prosperity of which increase the further away from the city you travel. Closer to the city proper, the shape and texture of the urban landscape changes into something more determined. The hush of suburban development gives way to the roar of the city.

Joanne had reservations at a large franchise hotel off the freeway about a mile from the city proper. It's usually hard to tell where large cities end and the outlying communities begin, and Denver is no different in this respect, especially considering the city's sprawling nature.

We reached the hotel in the late afternoon, tired and sore from having driven so far but in good spirits regardless. It was no problem to change the reservation to two, and we carried our bags to the room and collapsed on the bed.

Her appointment was set for first in the morning, and she had meetings planned through the early afternoon. The plan was to leave Denver after her last meeting and drive through the evening into Kansas, stopping somewhere in the night and continuing on to Tulsa in the morning.

We took turns with the shower, lounging around the room and watching television. As she bathed I perused a newspaper we had bought in the lobby, secretly looking to see if any references to my travels had made the news. I half expected to be set upon by conventional law enforcement at any time, made a fugitive at the whims of the paranoid conspiracy which I fought.

But much to my relief there was nothing, no references to any manhunt, or to any mysterious explosions in the Utah desert. Not that I expected there to be, really . . . but I had to be wary of any and all outlets through which my foes could reach me.

Instead, and as I should have expected, the news was full of momentous events, strange outbreaks of violence and revolution stretching across the globe. The Vice-President was still missing, and Japan had suffered a massive terrorist attack on their financial sector, sending world economies plummeting.

Joanne emerged from the shower, naked save for a towel wrapped around her head. Her body was strong and bold, muscular in appearance and powerful in reality. She was simply not a meek person, and no part of her appearance broadcast any weakness.

We had passed into comfortable familiarity in a surprisingly short period of time. Although she was older than me, there was a rapport that belied the difference.

As such, I began to wonder why she didn't notice the fact that the television was buzzing. She was sitting on the edge of the bed, drying her hair with a hairdryer, and reading the newspaper, when I began to notice that the rays of the cathode tube were coming down the screen slower and slower, until you could perceive the faces of the actors and personalities being warped and molded by the intense gravitational rays of the electron tube.

I got up off the bed and walked over to the television. There didn't seem to be anything wrong - no smoke or sparks or a frayed cord. I asked Joanne if she noticed anything wrong with the tube - she glanced over for a second and said that she didn't, before returning to her paper.

I tried to put it out of my mind as I climbed into the shower. The water felt good, hot and pure, seeping into the cracks of my skin and washing the dirt and sweat down into the drain. I couldn't hear anything above the white noise of the shower, the splatter and the whine of the pipes, and I closed my eyes and tried to isolate my senses in order to screen out any illicit stimulus. There were traps and illusions everywhere, and I had to retain an impossible focus on my task or I would be distracted and dissuaded.

The humming that I had heard coming from the television set was now everywhere. After I turned the water off it was everywhere, surrounding me and drowning me like fuzzy tinnitus after a rock concert, only amplified and projected from every surface. Everything around me was vibrating in time to the invisible frequency, and I was trapped in the belly of a humongous speaker cone. What did it mean?

Opening the door from the bathroom I saw that Joanne was lying on the bed in her robe, flipping through the channels on the television and still disinterestedly holding that same section of the newspaper she had been looking at when I had entered the shower.

"Do you hear that?" I asked her.

"Hear what?"

"That buzzing, like a low hum, or a million bees."

"No, I don't hear anything like that." She looked rather

strangely at me.

I didn't say anything in reply, merely continued to wipe off my body with the towel and tried to ignore the sound for the moment. I didn't want to scare Joanne if I could help it.

"It might just be some ringing in my ears," I finally said to allay her suspicions. "I used to swim a lot, and I still get tinnitus occasionally."

She didn't say anything. I didn't know whether or not she was satisfied by that answer.

"I'm going to go out in a bit," she said. "I want to scout out where I need to go tomorrow. You want to come along?"

"No, actually, if it's OK, I wouldn't mind taking a nap." I was lying.

"That sounds good, you'd probably just be bored." I couldn't tell what her tone of voice meant: whether she didn't care, or was offended, or perhaps suspicious? "You want me to bring back some dinner?"

"Sure, sure. Sounds good. I'll probably be hungry by then."

"You want anything in particular?"

"No, whatever sounds good to you." I turned away and began to rifle through my bag for clothes. I finally found a clean pair of trousers and a shirt. I needed to do laundry again.

"I might try to find the laundry while you're gone, too. You need something washed?"

"Sure, if you're going." She leaned over to her bag and found an armful of dirty clothes, depositing them in a pile on the floor in front of her bed. "If it's no trouble."

"If I go."

"Yeah, if you go."

She stood up and began to get dressed, moving briskly around the room as she pulled on her clothing.

"I've never liked Colorado," she said. "Something about

it has always seemed off to me, just slightly off-kilter. I can't describe it. If you drive around Denver, you can never find anything to eat . . . it's like people don't eat around here, they just watch Rockies baseball."

"I've never been here before. It seems like an all right kind of place, I suppose." I feigned indifference.

"Stick around for a few days and you see if it doesn't get to you."

I hoped I wouldn't be here for anywhere near that long. She finished dressing and grabbed her pocketbook.

"Is there anything else you need me to do while I'm out?" she asked at the threshold.

"No, I'm good," I replied. I just needed her to leave.

"OK, then I'll be back in a bit, maybe an hour or so. My meeting is in Littleton tomorrow, and that's just a little bit south of here."

"I'll see you when you get back."

She leaned down to kiss me and I replied, investing myself in her presence for so long as she remained. She left, closing the door silently behind her as she went.

As soon as the door shut behind her, the buzzing grew much louder. It was coming from everywhere and nowhere all at once, and the sound made it hard to think. My extremities began to tingle and I was having trouble forming cohesive thoughts.

I lunged towards the bathroom and grabbed a roll of toilet paper. Stuffing little wads of tissue into my ears helped significantly, blocking a large percentage of the noise and allowing me to think. I could still feel the vibrations in the walls and in my arms.

The TV was playing on mute. Waves of distortion washed down the screen, pulsing to an unheard beat. I reached for my bag and found the multi-purpose knife I had taken with me from home. The back of the television set was attached with Phillips head screws to the front, and it was a simple matter to unscrew the plastic casing that surrounded the cathode tube and accompanying electronics.

As I worked the humming all around me grew increasingly intense, to the point where the soporific effects of the noise began to effect me even through the padding in my ears. As the buzzing grew I focused on the beating of blood through my ears, the steady pounding of my heart through the distortion of the static.

Finally the back of the TV fell loose. I pulled it off and placed it on the floor besides the small bureau on which it had been placed.

Inside the TV, where memory served to say that there should have been a large cathode ray tube, there was instead a hideous mutant. Wrapped in a plastic crèche of wires and diodes, there was a small homunculi, the size of an infant child but with the proportions of a man. He was naked save for the various wires and tubes that encircled his body.

His skin was a preternatural white, an unhealthy gray pallor that reminded me of subterranean worms who live and die without ever seeing the light of the surface. His eyes were large and moist, and edged with flakes of disgusting mucus. There was no hair anywhere on the surface of his form.

He was eyeing me with an intense fear, radiating disgust and loathing with every flicker of his elongated calf's eye. As I stared I saw that he was not merely surrounded by wires, he was actually connected to the various mechanisms of the devices, wires and tubes criss-crossing and penetrating the entirety of his body. He was mute, his mouth covered by the aperture of a large black plastic tube which I took to be a feeding device.

As I stared at the tiny abomination I grew more and more confused. The buzzing had ceased the moment I removed the back of the set, but there was something more intense, more invasive at work here: the creature seemed to be staring into me, staring at me and through me so that I could not turn my eyes away.

What was I doing? I didn't understand anything anymore. I couldn't focus my thoughts. Everything seemed to be going so fast, I couldn't catch up to my own perceptions. Memories and recollections flitted through my conscious mind like bullets, I couldn't grab any of them. I was floating in a perpetual state of dread that foreshadowed only doom and despair, and as hard as I tried I was simply overwhelmed by the dark miasma of my own unfocused perceptions.

Why hadn't I been able to focus my thoughts? I tried to scan my mind over the last few days and I found my awareness constantly clouded. One moment I seemed keenly aware of everything around me, filled with the sensation of precise and exacting focus on every facet of my environment . . . and the next I seemed almost asleep, borne aloft by the circumstances of my journey and unconscious of any potential threats.

Why was I confused? Why couldn't I focus anymore? Nothing made sense anymore.

I was still staring down at that thing embedded in the back of the television set. However many minutes had passed, I was oblivious. The thing was gazing up at me intently, seeming almost to communicate with me as I struggled against its disorienting influence.

Stumbling to the bathroom I grabbed a towel from the rack and drenched it in the sink. I wrapped the wet towel around my head and tried to focus my energies: the improvised turban served as a buffer against the disorienting power of the thing in the television set.

Walking slowly and methodically back across the room I grasped the utility knife in my hand. I unfolded the knife blade from its sheathe and stiffened my arm against the task.

The dwarf's eyes grew large as he saw me bearing down on him. I could hear him now, frantic and flaccid, beating his thoughts against the exterior of my mind. He was begging, pleading, screaming for mercy, for me to spare him.

I held my hand in the air, suspending the knife a few inches above his head.

"What are you?" I asked.

The answer came to me in pulses of nauseatingly lucid thought. He was created to control, to read and report back to his masters. He was had been engineered, built and designed to be a voyeur and a puppeteer. Usually his tasks were simple and he executed them with alacrity, but my mind had presented a challenge for him.

From what I gathered from his frantic report, he had never known a life outside of the confines of the television set. He had been born in a lab and only seen the sun through the minds of those whose minds he read and controlled.

He was a pitiful creature, full of anguish and dreadfully afraid of death. He retained the instinct for survival which is, I believe, native in all organisms, but if he had been able to see himself through my eyes I believe he would have desired his own death as fervently as I then desired to destroy him.

After another moment's hesitation I lowered the knife and pierced his skull. It was not firm and hard like a man's skull, but soft and ripe like a piece of fruit. His blood was black and where his brain should have been there was only a soft green pulpy mass, similar in texture and consistency to soggy bran. At the moment of death I heard a great scream that would have deafened me had it been audible, but that quickly faded away to a dull and distant gurgling noise.

After I was certain the creature was dead I pulled its obscene body from the wreckage of the television set and wrapped it in the wet towel that I had coiled around my head. The body couldn't have weighed more than ten pounds, all told. It's limbs were soft and rubbery. I wondered, absent-mindedly, if its skeletal structure was composed purely of cartilage.

I placed the wrapped body on the bureau and speedily replaced the back of the television set. After I replaced the plug in the wall socket it turned back on without any indication that it had been recently opened. The warping lines had gone and the screen looked normal again.

I grabbed my key along with the little bundle and exited the room. No one was in the hallway, so I ran to the stairs and descended to the ground floor. It was early evening, and the hotel was surprisingly empty. I didn't encounter anyone between my room and the bottom floor. There was a small group of travelers off the lobby when I emerged from the stairwell, but if they registered anything they must only have seen a young man with a small bundle of laundry.

Just as I had hoped, there was a small dumpster near the rear entrance to the lobby. I glanced around the parking lot, trying to seem as inconspicuous as possible, and tossed the bundle into the dumpster.

When I reached the room I was sweating copiously. It was coming down my face in sheets and my hands were sticky. I felt hot and cold at the same time, my skin burning but my insides frigid. I tore my shirt off and ran to the air conditioning unit, embracing it on my knees.

When Joanne returned I was lying on the bed, naked again and delirious. I was still sweating and the sheets under my body were soaked.

Her personality flipped in the space of a moment, becoming a placid and reassuring presence at my bedside while leaving the tempestuous lover aside. It was a pleasing sensation, perceiving a new dimension in someone who had already become so naked to me in such a short amount of time.

But there was something else as well, something which

managed to reach me with a startling clarity despite my illness. She sat over me and pressed a cool wet towel to my forehead, giving me sips of ice water when I could manage to sit up. Somehow, despite the fact that my eyes were stinging from the heat, I could see through her, or feel the shape of her thoughts. It's hard to describe. I remembered the dwarf and what it had felt like when his mind had been peering through to mine: like a fine comb being lightly brushed against the grain of my mind. Somehow I was the comb now, and it was if a third invisible arm had been somehow grafted onto my own mind. Without consciously willing anything I felt the intimate shape and content of her thoughts, weighed them for mass and volume, measuring them for length and breadth.

Her thoughts were calm and measured, but with a note of subtle panic underneath. There was honest affection for me, and no hints of the betrayal which I had feared, but there were other, more subtle misgivings lurking underneath. After all, she had known me all of three days, and I had certainly manifested certain odd behaviors. One thought rang loud and clear throughout her mind, like a recurring bass note in a repeated musical phrase: what am I doing? What am I doing? She berated herself, privately, for her impulsiveness, even as she celebrated her spontaneous nature. She feared, more than anything else, the static of inaction. As old as she would soon be, inaction would mean a permanent retirement from those parts of the world which remain perpetually open to the young and courageous. I was not the first young man, even if the feelings were still intense . . .

I felt as if I were about to die, to expire on a hotel bed in Denver as my sweat soaked through to the mattress, but the small part of me that stood above the foggy haze of the sudden illness could feel something happening, something changing and warping deep inside me. The dwarf had left something in my head when he had died, deposited some rare spark in my skull with his own passing. I was burning both inside and out, my body and my mind caught aflame.

20

The fever broke around midnight. Joanne fell asleep atop the bedspread, still in her clothes and curled up near the edge so as to give me my space.

I woke up around six, my body cool and my head swimming in pristine waters. I was cold, the single sheet Joanne had pulled over my body having stuck to the dried sweat from my fever. I was sore all over, and thirsty.

She was huddled in a little ball with a corner of comforter pulled up around her shoulders. I undid her shoes and pulled the rest of the comforter around her body.

Three large glasses of water later I was sated, albeit still weak. I didn't feel like sleeping so I pulled up a chair and sat at the end of the room, facing the large window which stood over the air conditioning unit I had embraced the previous night.

The sun had already begun to rise, thin orange tendrils of light snaking out across the plains of the east and embracing the great mountains of the west. Of course, the sun was always rising somewhere, but it still felt like a magnificently singular event, a locus of possibility.

There were other strange possibilities opening all around me. As I sat in the dim and quiet of the hotel room I became aware of the fact that I could now see the world in added dimensions, reaching out in all directions and perceiving the presence and texture of the minds all around me. There were many sleeping brains, lit by dim fissures of activity, offset by a few waking minds that stood out like glowing beehives. I tried to focus but it was hard: the more I tried to bring my new sense to bear on a specific crevice or corner, the more it spread out across the landscape. I could perceive so many minds, so many thoughts crying and arguing and jostling for space against each other - it grew to terrifyingly vast proportions in no time at all.

As I sat in the growing illumination of the hotel room I began to panic. I couldn't control my new ability, as well as the dark thought that perhaps I would never be able to stand up and move about again for fear of losing all my focus and plunging into madness. Too much stimulation!

But as the tendrils of my new thought spread and encompassed the surrounding geography, I became aware of another landmark in this heretofore unrevealed landscape of the mind. Towards the south and west there was something else entirely, neither a sleeping or waking mind, that radiated calm and serenity in much the same way I imagined my own mind to be projecting anxiety and discontent. I tried to focus my thoughts on this distant spot, seeking to go closer, to separate myself from the thousands and thousands of minds in the intervening distances and to embrace the cooling influence of this new perception. It stood like a dark spire in the heart of a roiling storm, a calming authority in a chaotic world.

Inasmuch as I could "read" anyone's mind, the perceptions of purely psychic communication are limited by our inability to adequately verbalize the mental impulses which we can detect. In much the same way that language is a poor tool with which to describe the realm of advanced mathematics, so to is language utterly incapable of describing the profound dislocation of psychic ability. There are a multitude of dimension which the mind rushes to fill like water in a maze, searching out the hidden canyons that hide beneath stolid appearances.

I resolved, as I tried to focus my thoughts, that I must seek out the strange calming presence I detected, and that I must do so today, before I left Denver. I didn't understand what had happened to me, and I was afraid.

A few hours passed in total silence, without movement

and in absolute concentration. I was unaware of the time that had passed until I heard Joanne stirring on the bed behind me.

"Mmmm," I heard her stretching. "Baby, you OK?"

"Yeah," I tried to answer as nonchalantly as possible. "I'm doing just fine."

"How long you been up?"

"Oh, couple hours."

"You were sick last night."

"I know, I remember a little bit. I remember starting to sweat, and feeling hot . . . and then you came back, and I don't remember much until I woke up."

"Must have been a bug or something . . . food poisoning. I don't know."

"Weird. All this shit in the news must be getting to you." Joanne swung her feet over the side of the bed and rose, tentatively. She looked tired.

"Are you hungry?" she asked.

"Yes," I answered, and I was surprised to find that I actually was. "I guess I missed dinner last night."

"S'OK, you didn't miss anything." She gestured towards a McDonald's bag on the bureau next to the television.

"I guess we need to get out of here." I was concentrating hard on the conversation, trying to stay focused on Joanne and her distinct cerebral outline. She could be my focus, perhaps.

"My appointments aren't for another couple of hours, so we have time. You can shower first. You probably need it after last night."

I agreed. The hot water of the shower felt wonderful on my parched and sweat-dry skin. I stretched I could hear my stiff joints crack as they expanded in the steam.

Everything was much fresher after I was clean, and although I still felt as though I were trying to take a sip of water from a fire hose, I was able to concentrate on singular points of clarity with far less difficulty. Joanne's mind was transparent, a comforting and familiar object despite the lingering undercurrents of dissatisfaction and fear. The pulsating tranquillity was still there as well, lingering on the edges of my perception, calling to me with a siren's song of pity and peace.

We cleared out of the hotel and took breakfast at a Denny's near the freeway. Joanne noticed my distraction, even though I was making every conscious effort to keep from drowning in new sensation. Every step I took in any direction gave me entirely new vistas in which my mind could reach out, seeking to fill the void and explore. Every new face we met was a new brain whose distinctive thumbprint was inexorably burnt onto my memory.

The drive to Littleton was brief, and we soon arrived at our destination. Joanne was scheduled for a series of meetings at an industrial park in the quiet suburb, and we made arrangements for me to explore with the car until her appointments were over at the end of the afternoon. We kissed and I watched her as she entered the building, carrying a large bag of brochures, diagrams and books at her side. She radiated nervous intensity and supreme focus: for the moment, any concerns about me had been forgotten as she entered the building prepared to sell.

I pulled out of the parking lot and allowed the rough outlines of my psychic impressions to lead me to the strange sensations which I felt emanating from across the town. Thankfully, Joanne's appointment was not far from the profoundly placid beacon I was focused on, and after only ten or fifteen minutes of driving along secondary roads and through well-manicured subdivisions I reached my goal.

If the psychic landscape could be envisioned as a three-dimensional grid, the source of the pacific emanations could be represented by a large black sphere floating at the center of an empty field. All mental activity near this spot seemed to have been negated, or at least dimmed.

To my surprise, the exact spot which corresponded to this psychic phenomenon in the real world was a large church. In a morning in the middle of the week it looked to be nearly empty, with only a few cars in the large parking lot.

I parked the car and entered the building. It was a recent construction, with the overwhelming air of bland utility that permeates recent religious institutions. There was a large, dark foyer that led to the large double-doors which, I assumed, opened into the chapel.

As I entered the building, a feeling of implacable contentment swept over me, my brow unfurrowed and the painful concentration began to dissipate. The building was cool and air conditioned.

I pushed aside the large wooden doors and was assailed by a blast of wet air as the pressure between different parts of the building momentarily equalized. The chapel was long and high, with cavernous rafters and long rows of benches placed in rows outward from the pew. It looked very much as you would expect a church to look, from the understated Protestant stained-glass windows to the few intensely devoted weekday worshippers scattered throughout the room. It was hard to recall the last time I had even been in a church, as my family had never worshipped.

Entering this room gave me a feeling of intense relief that washed through my entire body, sweeping through my muscles and sinews with a twinge of electric glee. Whatever had been upset and thrown into panic inside me during the previous night was being soothed and calmed.

I took a seat towards the head of the rows of benches, nearest to the pew and the plain, nondescript wooden cross that stood at the center of the dias. There was a small wooden lectern a few feet in front of the cross. I imagined that delivering oratory in front of such an imposing piece of spiritual furniture must be a harrowing experience.

I sat for a few minutes in total silence, relishing the quiet and calm which the building imposed on my newfound sense of psychic recognizance. After a while a door to the rear of the pew opened and a small man in flowing white robes and soft velvet slippers emerged. Without paying any notice to the rest of the room or the few staggered members of the congregation assembled at such an early hour, be made a beeline to where I was sitting.

He approached me with an easy confidence, an almost beatific poise that translated into unassailable authority.

"You are very punctual," he said as he approached. His voice was clear and lucid, like a forest stream in a cool evening.

"I wasn't aware I was expected."

"You are always expected, my friend," he said to me as he smiled. "Your reputation precedes you."

He motioned me to follow him and led me back across the pew and through the door from which he had emerged. We stepped through a brief hallway and entered another room, a large office set towards the back of the building. Every wall was covered in bookshelves and maps, with luxuriant leather reading chairs placed at the corners.

There was someone else in the room. My new friend preceded me and as I crossed the threshold I caught sight of a familiar face against the far window.

It was my friend, who I had last seen at the party with Trevor. He looked to be in fine form, in an exquisitely tailored dark suit and his fine black hair glossed back with pomade. His tiny horns glinted in the light that came through the window.

"Ah, there you are!" he said as he saw me. "I am glad to see that you have made it so far."

"I didn't expect to see you here," I said. I walked across the room and extended my hand. He accepted my hand but pulled me in closer for a hearty embrace.

"I get around. Of course, your adventures are of the

utmost interest to many of my friends and colleagues."

"It's good to know people are looking out for me," I answered. "I've been through a lot."

"Yes, you certainly had, much more than we could have realistically anticipated." He exchanged an unreadable glance with the pastor as he sat down behind his desk. "You've already seen so much in such a short amount of time. Why, the facility in Berkeley was almost too much to hope for."

"Yeah, I don't think I understood half of that."

"You will. That's a small part of why you're here today, however . . . I hardly want to monopolize the conversation in this regard."

The pastor had seated himself behind the desk and placed his hands in front of him, folded together in the living image of patience.

"Events have been slightly complicated by your encounter with the Receptor last night."

"You mean, that thing in the TV?"

"Yes . . . they are called Receptors. Absolutely beastly creations. It takes a mind of resolute solidity to resist their influence. We did not expect that they would be able to so accurately predict your whereabouts, least of all that they would be able to place a Receptor in your hotel room with such ease."

"Who is 'they'?"

"The same they you have been fighting against since the very beginning, whose pernicious influence we are all dedicated to extinguishing."

"Who are you?" I asked, becoming mildly annoyed by his circuitous answers.

"I am Carter," he answered. "You may have heard my name."

"It rings a bell. I might have heard it."

"It is not important," he replied. "Please, have a seat." He motioned to one of the comfortable leather chairs placed immediately in front of his desk. My friend had taken the opportunity to step to the rear of the room, and pretended to peruse one of the many gilded volumes which lined the walls.

"Sometimes," Carter began, "those who survive an encounter with a Receptor are affected in unforeseen ways. Psychic powers are still very much a mystery to men, and we do not know why some people react in certain ways, and why other men remain unaffected.

"Your encounter with the Receptor awakened something deep inside of your brain, something which now allows you to see the same way they do - into minds and across space, through the pure sphere of mental activity. You are not the first to be so affected, but it is still exceedingly rare."

He paused a moment and reached into his desk, pulling out a black baseball cap emblazoned with the logo of the Colorado Rockies baseball team. He placed it on the desk midway between his seat and mine.

"Put this on."

I reached out for the hat and grabbed it, turning it over in my hands with a puzzled curiosity. After a moment's inspection I placed it on my head.

The sensation of beatific calm which I had perceived through my psychic sense since entering the church faded, as indeed all vestiges of ambient noise in the immediate vicinity. It was still there, but it was distant, muffled and hollow.

"What is this thing?"

"It is a very sophisticated device designed to allow you to harness the energies which you are now able to perceived. The Receptors have been carefully bred and engineered for generations, with the sole purpose of enabling them to control and regulate their interactions on the psychic planes. They are pitiful creatures, really, having been born for one reason, and with no room left in their minds for anything but the execution of their duties. In addition to the ability to carry out their functions, they possess an extremely limited sense of self-preservation, which you undoubtedly experienced last night."

"Yes . . . . it was pitiful. It wanted to live but I don't know why."

"It's hard to breed an animal with no regard for its own survival, which is a problem that many people on all sides of the conflict have devoted many years to solving. Unfortunately, as we have seen, certain parties have had extraordinary success in the field in recent years."

"You mean the labs in Berkeley."

"Yes, they have contributed to the science. Mind control, mind reading, genetic engineering, anti-exhumation - I can't keep up with it all."

"So, what does this hat do?"

"Look in the lining."

I pulled the cap off and poked my finger inside the brim. Sure enough, there was a thin layer of foil all around the interior of the hat.

"What is this, tin foil?"

"No, not foil . . . it looks remarkably similar, but it is actually an incredibly sophisticated weave of microcircuitry designed to jam the frequencies on which psychic information is transmitted. It will not entirely obscure the perception, but it will enable you to survive."

"Survive?"

"Most people do not long survive exposure to unrestricted psychic communication. You have experienced it for - what - six hours? Isn't it an overwhelmingly powerful sensation? Imagine this every hour of every day for the rest of your life. If you wear this hat, you will be protected. There are also . . . other signals, signals which no one has ever been able to isolate. Signals from other planes."

"What do you mean?"

"I don't know. No one does. But you will encounter them

one day - voices and minds from another world, or another universe. They can drive men insane, and have been the sources of inspiration for countless artists throughout the centuries - Blake, for one, Lovecraft for another.

"You must be very careful whenever you take the hat off, because these mysterious voices can assert a ruinous magnetism. You will be drawn to them as Ulysses was drawn to the sirens, but you must resist the temptation, or you will be pulled into a hideous and inescapable insanity."

"But if I keep this hat on most of the time I should be OK?"

"Yes."

I was simultaneously terrified and stimulated. If I had not experienced the powerful and unguessed terror of the preceding hours I would not have been able to believe it.

"In any event," he continued, "your psychic powers are not the reason you have been called here. They are an unforeseen complication, and while we hope they will be able to aid you on your journey, you must take great care not to let them distract you from your purpose.

"You have come a long way and faced many obstacles already. You are almost halfway across the continent and you have already learned more than many people do in an entire lifetime. But your journey is not over yet. Events across the globe are proceeding at an alarming pace, and we must be ready to act. You have never been to Colorado before, have you?"

"No. Never."

"Do you remember the significance of this town?"

"What, Denver?"

"No, not Denver. Littleton. Where we are now."

"Um. Maybe. It might be familiar."

"Perhaps you would recognize the name Columbine."

In an instant new and strange possibilities opened before me and I was seized with a terrible sense of inevitability. I recognized the name.

"On April 20th, 1999, Eric Harris and Dylan Klebold went on a murderous rampage at Columbine high school, killing and wounding dozens of their fellow students and their teachers. The killings became the impetus for a new wave of media scapegoating and precious little actual investigation as to the actual causalities of such an event. The massacre was horrible but, like everything else, it has eventually receded into our collective memories."

"But that is not the real story. Littleton has been long been home to an experimental research lab very similar to the one you saw under People's Park in Berkeley. The killers who were identified as Harris and Klebold were students at Columbine, but they were also the end result of many years of terrible, terrible experiments. Their entire family line was engineered and crafted by the same forces who created the Receptor that you killed last night."

My mind reeled at the possibilities. "So . . . why did they do it? Kill all those people."

"To this day, we have never been able to determine that. The workings of our opponents' organization are opaque to us, just as ours are - hopefully - to them. We have heard rumors to both effects - that the killers were deliberately triggered in a suburban setting in order to gauge their efficiency, and that they were accidentally triggered by unforeseen circumstances. Ultimately, we have never been able to decipher their motivations, and eventually other matters rose to greater prominence."

"You mean September 11th."

"Exactly. These are the matters which we have brought you here to try and avenge. You are, of course, primarily concerned with the death of your father."

"Of course."

"Well, then you need to continue eastward. Head for New York."

"That's where I was headed."

"Good. Good. I sincerely hope you find what you need,

because you hold our fates in your hands, now more than ever."

He stood up, reaching across the desk to shake my hand. His grip was firm and he shook with an exaggerated solemnity. I stood and thanked him for his time before turning to leave. As I approached the door, my friend replaced his book and fell in besides me.

"I will show our young friend to his car," he said as we passed through the portal.

We entered the hallway and he grabbed my arm, motioning me to walk faster.

"What's going on?" I asked him.

He put his finger to his lips, motioning me to be quiet as we exited the church. We walked over to my car and he motioned for me to get in. I unlocked the doors and took my place behind the steering wheel while he sat in the passenger's seat.

I put the key in the ignition and he turned the radio on, pulling the volume dial hard to the right. The car was filled with loud rock and roll.

"I couldn't speak freely in there," he said, yelling over the music. "Carter is an ally for the moment but he serves those who serve our enemies."

"I don't understand," I screamed back over the music.

"It's complicated. He likes to imagine he's a free agent but he's beholden to the same masters that we all are."

"Even me?"

My friend smiled. "No, not you. That's why you are so valuable. You have no masters."

"Is he psychic?" I asked.

"No, he's not. He only knows how to dampen and block the ability, which is what attracted you here this morning. The fact that he is immune enables him to resist the influence of the Receptors and the machines and the other parties who could control him if they wished."

I didn't say anything.

"You can't believe everything he told you," he said after another moment. "Some of what he says is true, other parts are not. He tells you what he wants you to know or believe. Ultimately, he pretends to far more autonomy than he actually enjoys, and he would be appalled to know how much his activities are actually carefully circumscribed by outside forces.

"You can't trust anyone from this point on. I didn't know how fast events had progressed . . . anyone around you could be under their control. Their controls are subtle and varied, so you may not be able to tell who around you is being controlled, even without your hat on. If events have already progressed to an attack on the President . . ."

He made a suggestive gesture to the car we were sitting in, Joanne's car. I tried not to think of the implications of what he was saying.

Finally, he motioned that it was time to leave, before Carter became suspicious. We exchanged pleasantries and he opened his door. Before he exited the car, however, he paused and turned back to ask me one additional question.

"Do you remember where you've heard Carter's name before?" he asked.

I thought for a minute, and realized that I did.

21

I told Joanne that I had been to see Coors' Field while she had been in her meetings, and she didn't inquire further as to why I was wearing a baseball cap. Her meetings had gone surprisingly well, and she was buoyed by the prospect of having exceeded a self-imposed quota for this leg of her trip.

"Almost makes up for the piss-poor reception I've gotten everywhere else."

Leaving Denver to drive east was the most withering part

of the journey to date. Mountains and hills impart security and strength by nature of their ubiquity and scope. As soon as you leave the city limits of Denver and the landscape of outlying industrial parkland falls away, you are surrounded by nothingness, by an encroaching featureless flatness that runs madly towards every horizon. Having been enveloped by mountains and hills and rivers and lakes and oceans my entire life, driving through eastern Colorado felt similar to stepping off a cliff and into freefall above a distant planet, a vast and mysterious expanse uncompromised by any concession to topographic variety. There's just nothing there, a whole lot of nothing spreading for hundreds of miles in any direction.

But at the least it was empty. Even with my new hat, the collective roar of millions of strange minds was a disconcerting presence, a vague but persistent buzzing on the periphery of my awareness. Additionally, the international crisis created an undertow of anxiety and despair that threatened to overwhelm me. Alone, with only Joanne's infinitely familiar psyche to distract me, I was left in comparative solitude. Only the occupants of passing cars and flyspeck towns disturbed the silence.

As much as we had enjoyed the first legs of our trip together, through the beautiful terrain of eastern Utah and western Colorado, the remainder of Colorado and the entirety of Kansas promised to be uniformly dull. Joanne mentioned that much of Oklahoma was similarly blank, but that the northeastern corridor was actually quite beautiful. Not without reason, I was informed, had the region been nicknamed "Green Country".

I said that I had been unaware of that particular appellation. It seemed unlikely, based on my prior associations, namely the Trail of Tears and the Oklahoma City bombing.

Of course I remembered the bombing.

The months after my father died were singularly

eventful, for reasons I have already related. Personal tragedy allows time and space to expand in our perception, until everything in the world around us is connected to our own intimate turmoil. You best remember those events in the greater world which correspond to your own milestones, and said events carry added currency as they become, in your mind, inextricably linked with your own life.

As a child I was still unaware of how much in the world around me actually was tangibly connected to the sources of my own personal despair. The 1995 Oklahoma City bombing, much like the 2001 attacks on New York and Washington, served as a trigger that would enable me to understand the uniquely significant role I was destined to play in the history of the world.

My father had been in the grave for just a few weeks when the Murrah Building exploded, and the synchronicity connecting these two events was a coincidence that even my nascent and untutored skepticism could not ignore. My father had fought in Africa and across the world to prevent tragedies like this from ever coming to pass, and the fact that his death was immediately followed by a massive offensive on the part of his most terrible foes was ample proof that his life had not been spent in vain, and that he had been a good man who lived an important life.

I had never actually connected the dots between the tragedies in New York and Oklahoma City and the Columbine massacre. The shootings had occurred while I was still in my drug-induced stupor, pacified by the machinations of my father's foes and still blind to the web of intricate plans and stratagems that had ensnared my life from the moment of my birth. But the thin strands of fate that connected those April days with September 11th were stronger than I could have imagined, and once I began to break through the barrier of foggy indifference which blanketed my adolescence and teenage years, the junctions revealed themselves.

We left Denver around five and by six we could no longer see the mountains behind us, just undulating flatness for as far as we could perceive in any direction. Dinner was a McDonalds about fifty miles out of town.

As we drove, mostly in silence, I experimented with my hat: taking it off and leaving it on my lap for certain periods of time. I would have to acclimate myself to these new perceptions in some way or another, and it would be necessary for me to learn how best to utilize them as needed.

Joanne's mind was an open book to me, because I understood her reasonably well and had at least an inkling into her thought processes. Every mind functions differently, with different and complex symbologies and recurring metaphors interacting with constantly shifting landscapes of variable dimensions. Its a hard concept to communicate, but a surprisingly intuitive idea to grasp once you become aware.

Was she being manipulated by my enemies? I tried to probe and poke into her thoughts, to see if I could reveal some sort of hint or clue left behind by other agencies. But what would such a clue even look like? I was left somewhat baffled by the fact that I had no way of knowing how to find such tampering, if indeed there was any.

The longer I kept the hat off, the harder it became to concentrate on any specific thing. The taste of burnt tinfoil would creep into the back of my throat and I would begin to lose perspective from my vantage point on the edge of a mental abyss. Psychic vertigo is a very real danger, and the thought of losing my grasp and flying off into an unknowable darkness of melancholy ether filled me with numbing terror.

But terror is the mortar of life, and nowhere is this concept illustrated in a clearer fashion than the great plains. How the settlers must have felt as they pulled their wagons stuffed with their meager belongings across a dark continent, exposed to danger and surrounded on every side by suffocating mystery, I can't imagine.

Around the time the sun began to set behind us I sensed a growing unease in Joanne. She was perturbed, probably, by my quietude and unease, two characteristics she had not known to associate with me in the course of our short acquaintanceship. This also served as another reminder of the true gap that lay between us, despite the superficial intimacy that we shared. Here we were, catapulted across the country together and thrown into each others' arms, for no apparent reason other than that it seemed like a good idea at the time.

I could feel the confusion radiating out of her mind in hoary purple waves of staccato fear, a disconcerting bass note set into a characteristically bright composition. Even with my hat on I heard snatches of thought wafting around the interior of the cabin, whispered fragments of doubt mingled with recrimination but tempered by a strong confidence. She was wound into a tight ball of conflicting impulses and desires, buffeted by fear but bolstered by ambition. Everything inside her mind was so complex, and I desired more than anything at that moment to gain some sort of clean and clear insight into her inner mechanism.

We stopped for the night in a small motel about an hour into Kansas. The land was monotonously flat and uniformly featureless. Kansas was where Superman grew up, and it made perfect sense: this is undoubtedly one of the only places on Earth with the enormity of scale necessary to inculcate a humble god. There is so much insignificance everywhere, surrounding you at every turn.

There was a gas station near the road, and a fast-food restaurant in said gas station was the sole evident source of nourishment anywhere near. It was late and there weren't many people on the road. The motel was only partially full, and the many sleeping minds within registered as no more than quiet nuisances.

We carried our luggage inside and collapsed on the bed. Traveling in a car is a surprisingly exhausting occupation, and after almost a week on the road we were both in need of a good night's rest. A small card near the telephone indicated that the fast-food restaurant delivered to motel customers for a small fee, so we called our order and waited.

In fifteen minutes time there was a prompt knock at the door. Joanne rose, retrieved her purse, and stepped across the room to the doorway. She lifted the door-chain - certainly a formality in such a remote location - and began to open the door.

As soon as the knob was turned the door exploded inward, hitting Joanne's face and sending her sprawling backwards onto the floor. She landed with a dull thud, a slight mewling groan escaping her lips as she reeled. The door swung wide before her and a figure in black strode across the threshold. It was Adam.

I rose and put my hand on my bag. He was holding a gun in his right hand, aiming it squarely at Joanne lying prostrate on the ground. His clothes were uniformly black, with a dark coat and a dark shirt and dark slacks. He looked slightly haggard, with gray half-circles radiating from underneath his eyes and a slightly tousled mop of hair. He was smiling.

My hands were desperately fumbling with my bag, trying to open the zipper and find the hidden guns. Before he said anything Adam saw what I was doing and lifted his gun in my direction.

"Don't," he said. "I've got enough for both of us."

"What the fuck you want?"

"You, of course. I've been following you for a while now. Seemed like a good time to butt in."

Joanne was trying to get up. Her hand was on her face and she was dazed, I don't think she saw the gun in Adam's hand.

"Joanne," I said, "don't move."

She lifted her hand from her face and gazed mutely at the figure poised above her. She opened her mouth and a low wheezing sound passed her lips, it formed crude sibilants against the back of her throat and scraped across her tongue with a soft insistence: "Fu-u-u-u-ck."

"I'll kill your cow right here, my friend, if I have to do this to prove the seriousness of our intent." He lowered the gun from me back to her.

"You're not killing anyone else."

Adam laughed and ran his free hand through his hair, a nervous habit. "You're a tough guy now? The same chickenshit punk who goes around the country asking 'Who are you? What do you know? Have you seen my daddy?' You don't know anything. You're a piece of shit. The whole world is falling apart at the seams but you can't understand how important you are."

I was frozen in place, unable to move for fear of provoking him against Joanne.

His gun was aimed at Joanne but his eyes were on me. This proved to be a mistake when Joanne reached up and punched him in the crotch as hard as she could. He yelped like an animal and dropped his gun to the floor.

I jumped across the gap that separated us and pulled her up off the ground. Her nose was bleeding and a large purple welt had already materialized, ranging from her forehead down to her cheek. She was crying, but she was moving. Adam's face was red and he seemed to be in a lot of pain but he was moving as well, straining across the floor for the gun he had dropped.

Before he reached the gun I kicked him in the face as hard as I could manage. His body went backwards with a violent jerk and the queer motion of his head spattered blood across the near wall. I had probably kicked out a few of his teeth.

I reached down and grabbed his gun, placing it in my back pocket. I grabbed my duffel bag and motioned Joanne towards the open door.

Someone had slashed our tires. To make matters worse, the parking lot which had been half-full of trucks and passenger cars not twenty minutes ago was suddenly empty. There wasn't a soul anywhere to be seen.

Joanne was beginning to blubber, her tears coming fast and mixing with the blood streaming down her chin. I grabbed her hand and we ran as fast as we could. The gas station sat in the distance, maybe two hundred yards down the road, and beyond that lay the interstate. Behind us, I heard Adam thrashing in the hotel room, rising from where I had left him sprawled, and evacuating his lungs with a great moaning roar.

We ran down the road, our shoes slapping on the hot asphalt. The sun had been and gone, but the heat of the day lingered. We were breathing hard and sweating when we reached the gas station.

The building was empty. The convenience store with the sandwich shop to one side was locked and closed. There were no cars at the self-serve gasoline pumps.

I debated whether or not I dared to risk a call on a public telephone. I knew they were watching me, and that some agency had isolated Joanne and I on this lonely stretch of road in the middle of Kansas, but whether or not they had foreseen every possible vector of the operation was unknown.

In the two seconds during which I debated the merits of calling, I decided to risk the possibility of compromising my position further and call 911. The receiver was cold on my face as I pushed the three buttons and waited for the connection. Without ringing, the phone picked up and I began to speak.

"Hello, I'm being -"

"Don't waste your time," the voice on the other end of

the receiver spoke. "You should know better." There was a click and a hiss, and the line was dead.

I turned around and Joanne was gone. The darkness was pressing inward, and the light from distant streetlamps stood like hazy flashlights against grim velvet atmosphere. The cars roared along the freeway, some few hundred yards further away, but I couldn't hear them.

I grabbed for my baseball cap, pulling it off my head with a wild motion before stuffing it into my back pocket. Immediately the surrounding mental landscape sprang into clear focus. I could see - feel, perceive - Joanne's distinctive mind running, hobbling away just a few dozen yards in the opposite direction of the interstate. There was another mind, however, black and malefic, a singularly opaque density running after her.

I turned and ran in the direction of Joanne's thoughts, my legs taking me into the night. As soon as I left the pavement of the gas station's parking lot, the darkness enveloped me and I was on uneven ground.

From the safety of a speeding car Kansas seems to be as flat as a board, but on foot the countryside reveals surprising contours. Joanne was running as fast as she could in the opposite direction of the freeway, filled with panic and dread and fear. Her emotions were yellow and red, tremulous and corrosive. She was half out of her mind from the shock of the injury, and she was running for her life.

Adam, meanwhile, was also running surprisingly fast in Joanne's direction, making a beeline from the hotel through the fields in hopes of intersecting her path. I don't know how he could see in this pervasive darkness, but he seemed to be able to see exactly where Joanne was heading even though I could barely see three feet in front of my face. Their minds bobbed above the physical realm, removed from the three-dimensional topography of the region and set on an empty blue grid.

But the land wasn't flat. There was gullies and ravines all across the fields, with streams and pathways jutting at obscure angles from distant landmarks. I tripped and stumbled a number of times, and soon my hands and knees were covered with bloody scrapes. I was still hauling my duffel bag and it swung dumbly behind me as I ran.

I stumbled onto a clearing in the field, a large half-acre of flat paved concrete laid into the landscape many years ago and abandoned. There was a pile of construction debris set off to one side, heaps of stone and masonry, jagged metal poles sticking out at odd angles. Tall weeds lay all across the surface, pointing upwards out of tiny cracks in the stone. Whatever was being built here, it had been abandoned many years ago.

Joanne had stopped running and had fallen on the distant edge of the platform. Her body heaved, and her hoarse breathing echoed through the clear and fetid night.

"Joanne!" I called.

"I'm here," she replied, weakly. "I'm scared."

I ran to her and knelt at her side. She had tripped on a stone and she was sprawled on her stomach. Her face was covered in sweat, tears and blood, her hair matted from sudden exertion and her eyes raw and squinted.

"What's happening? Who is that?" she whispered.

I didn't answer her. Adam emerged on the opposite side of the concrete, stumbling slightly but still imposing. He saw us on the ground in the distance and smiled. I could see him quite clearly - the darkness was strong but the white field of concrete reflected what moonlight there was. His figure was wreathed in black, melting into the night, but his face stood out.

"You can't run," he yelled. "We're coming to get you wherever you go. This shit is going to stop - no more unexpected detours." His voice whistled when his tongue passed over the soft hiss of the letter "s" - the sound of missing teeth.

He walked to the pile of debris and pulled out a length of rusted rebar attached to a football-sized chunk of crumbling concrete. It was about four feet long and the rough dimensions of the kind of hammer you toss in track events. Swinging the weapon at his side, he approached us.

I stood up and reached into my back pocket. Adam's gun was still there. I pulled out the weapon and aimed it.

"You've never fired a gun in your life, boy."

"It can't be that hard."

He continued to walk, nonplused. The distance between us shrank from thirty feet to twenty feet.

"You can't kill me. Your father couldn't kill me."

I cocked the hammer with my thumb and pulled the trigger. The gun exploded and sent a shockwave through my arm. There was a yell and a thump as Adam fell to the ground.

"You motherfucker." He was lying on his back, with a small pool of blood already visible under him against the bright white concrete. His right leg was curled up under him. It looked as if I had hit him on that leg, somewhere above his knee.

I walked the last few feet between us and lifted the gun again. My hand and wrist were still smarting from the blast, so I steadied the gun with my other hand as I took aim. I tried to focus on his face as my hands clenched the weapon.

Before I could pull the trigger, Adam swung his hammer low and wide, catching the back of my legs. I crumpled to the ground like a doll, tumbling backwards and hitting my head on the stone floor.

Consciousness left me for a fleeting moment. I woke in a daze, with everything moving in slow motion. Adam had pulled himself to his feet and was slowly shuffling the last few yards to where Joanne lay passed out on the ground. I tried to open my mouth, to yell out a warning or to scream or cry, but my body was strangely unresponsive. I became aware of a loud buzzing in the distance.

I watched, helpless and strangely remote, as Adam raised his hammer and brought it down on Joanne with a terrible sickening finality. The sound of her skull breaking seemed to remind me of broken pottery and wet melons. I could feel her mind, crying out in a pulse of red and yellow and orange terror and confusion, a pink and vulnerable organism suddenly exposed to the atmosphere and filled with a fleeting rush of impending mortality.

The landscape receded until the only thing I saw or felt was Joanne, her mind and soul ebbing away just a few feet distant. Her psychic essence was malleable and soft, a spinning ghost in the darkness, sending out progressive waves of purple and blue and violet and indigo regret, regret and fear mingled with the gray fabric of the night, creeping tendrils of panic slowly receding as the mind faded into an imperceptible pinpoint.

In the end there's nothing left but a light, a swiftly spinning light in the distant darkness, a neutron star blinking out of existence in gradual throbs. She was bleeding all across the ground, her brain crushed with shards of broken skull sticking to bloody hair follicles, and all I could see or feel was the last quiet desperate moments of her soul as it flickered like a candle flame. The light went dark red and finally dissipated, passing out and into itself as if it had never been.

There was a hole in the sky where Joanne had been, a gaping wound in the fabric of the cosmos where her mind had imploded and left a hollow, broken shell. I felt the terrible gravity of this implosion, the almost irresistible pull of the final dissolution, as a dying star collapses on itself so too does the human soul submit to the terrible grip of gravitational distress and fall inwards - to emerge never again.

I was crying, the tears flowing out of my eyes like water. Vaguely, as if in a dream, I saw a helicopter come down from the sky to retrieve Adam, leaving me here alone with

Joanne's body as I stared at the indigo maw in the heart of the universe where her mind had flown.

After a time I regained my composure enough to pull my hat back on my head. I ceased to perceive Joanne's death, and in fact the entire world grew fuzzy and soft as I lay and stared at the high moon. It was yellow and distant, a half-circle of illumination that floated just above the earth and yet unimaginably distant. In a moment I dreamed that I flew between the worlds and set sail across the void for distant suns. In time I slept, with Joanne's lifeless body ten feet from my head and my duffel bag still safely slung around my shoulder.

22

I awoke with moonlight still raining on my body. In the long feverish moment when my eyes first opened I fought to recall, to recollect my circumstances. Remembrance of the tragic night and Joanne's grisly death filled me with nausea.

My head ached and my entire body was sore, filled with weakness from my enervating rest. It was an effort to lift my body up and into a seated position, and it was furthermore an effort to avoid seeing Joanne's decaying corpse, which still lay to the side of the clearing. Just a glance, at this point, would probably have been more than I could bear.

There was a faint breeze and the thin stalks of prairie grass were swaying contentedly beneath the sky. I rose on unsteady feet and began the long walk back towards the road, in hopes of putting this debacle behind me.

Too many people had already died, and I was no closer to understanding the true nature of my quest. However many parties there were assembled against me or for me, who wished to manipulate me or to destroy me, I was determined to make my way across the country and find my answers before being killed myself.

So far, at least, they had shown a remarkable willingness to let me live. I was important, and my knowledge was valuable. But they had had the opportunity to steal my bag many times, and with it my notebooks - did they already have my research? Why did they need me alive if they had access to my information? Why was I so important?

There wasn't enough information for me to properly assess my situation. If I had been dangerous, they could have probably killed me long ago. If I had been necessary, they could simply have captured me and used me. For some reason my autonomy in this matter is valuable.

Nothing was making sense anymore. Joanne was dead, Morris was dead, my dad was dead - all dead in an attempt to steer me somewhere, to protect or to manipulate me. The bodies were beginning to pile up and I hadn't even begun to understand the real purpose of the ineffable tragedies which defined our lives.

The motel was still empty. Joanne's car was still the only car in the lot. I found a bundle of cash in Joanne's suitcase and placed it in my pocket. The rest of her stuff would remain until someone found it, or until it was retrieved.

I bought some aspirin out of the motel vending machine and swallowed a paper cup full of water in an attempt to stifle my raging headache. I had a feeling that I would be hurting for a few days.

The walk from the motel back to the interstate was longer than I expected. Distances traversed by automobile are always underestimated on foot. The gas station was likewise abandoned, the lonely streetlamps still glaring across the torpid midnight.

There were no shortage of trucks moving across the interstate. I walked up the embankment and presented my thumb to the road, and it was no longer than ten or twenty minutes before a truck pulled up and opened the door.

His name was Glenn and he was hauling frozen turkeys to Topeka. He was friendly and amiable, as eager for conversation as Morris had been. I tried not to fall asleep but the temptation to lean my head against the seat and doze was too much. I woke up at a truck stop outside of Topeka. Glenn shook me awake and I thanked him for the ride.

The sun had been up for an hour or so, and the heat of the day had not yet begun to sting. I tumbled out of the truck cabin and into the diner, ordering myself a cup of coffee and a plate of pancakes.

After I ate my breakfast I sat, finishing my coffee and trying to organize my next move. After a while another trucker came up and inquired if I needed a ride.

"How could you tell?"

"Well, you got the look about you. You look like you been down twelve miles of bad road. I'll bet you're interesting conversation."

His name was Henry and he hauled loads for department stores. He wasn't supposed to take riders, but he still did it anyway. I had to shimmy over to the passenger side through the driver's door so as not to trip the tattler installed by the company.

Henry had been driving for about five years and had hopes of one day becoming an independent operator. He was ambitious, with mutual funds and an MBA - he had drifted into trucking only because the hours suited his temperament, and remained a businessman at heart.

I told him I was heading east and he was as well, south and then east through Oklahoma and into Arkansas. Four hours later we hit Tulsa just as the sun was rising into its highest position of the day. Talk radio was on continuously, a steady hum of news in those days of portent. The President had declared an emergency meeting of the UN Security Council to try and stem the tide of rising violence that obeyed no national borders.

Henry's route was fairly well proscribed - he dropped his trailer at one department store and picked up an empty trailer to take back to the distribution center. It was fairly low-impact work, as far as trucking went, but it was money in the bank.

This is essentially how I came to be stranded at a Kohl's department store in the town of Owasso, Oklahoma, about ten minutes north of Tulsa. Henry left the truck for lunch and I was left to my own devices. I had no intention of following him on his entire route back up through Kansas, so I resolved to find a ride into Tulsa and from Tulsa on eastward.

If the heat in Kansas had been dry and inexorable, like the steady heat from a distant blast furnace, Oklahoma was wet and sticky like the inside of God's mouth. Residents seem nonplused, but within five minutes my shirt was soaked to the skin.

I entered the Kohl's with the intention of buying a package of socks and maybe a T-shirt, but I soon realized that I had no desire to leave the store's protective cocoon of air conditioning. It was not hard to see that there was something intolerable in the red and implacable horror of an Oklahoma summer.

The aisles were narrow and made narrower by the heaps of merchandise stacked at every corner. There were bright white sales signs on every open service, along with large blown-up photographs of happy multiracial couples enjoying their Kohl's purchases. The incessant soft-rock muzak being piped into the store via the overhead speakers was almost enough to offset the pleasure of the air conditioning.

I was mindlessly browsing, with a package of tube socks and two black T-shirts in my hand when I came across the One-Eyed Man. He was pretending to study a rack of cheap suits as I saw him, and he indicated with a very subtle nod of his head that he had seen me as well.

Immediately I took my purchases to the front of the store and paid. The One-Eyed Man stopped pretending to price Dockers and exited the store. I took my purchases and left the store as well.

Once again the heat battered me down. There was a group of surly-looking Kohl's employees assembled a few dozen yards down the sidewalk, smoking cigarettes and seemingly unfazed by what appeared to me to be an inconceivable temperature. This was the heartland of America, and even as the world grew smaller and smaller, beset by tragedy and terror, Americans remained steadfastly insouciant.

The One-Eyed Man was smoking a cigarette himself, sitting next to a black car in the back of the parking lot. I approached the car and he motioned me to the passenger seat, throwing his cigarette to the asphalt and grinding it with the tow of his boot.

I threw my bags in the back seat of the car and took my seat. It was a large automobile, luxuriant and new. It occurred to me that the One-Eyed Man was not without resources if this was his car.

He turned the ignition and the cabin filled with blessedly frigid air. The sweat cooled and dried on my face, and my body began to feel vaguely distorted.

"I'm glad to see you," I finally said, after he had began driving and turned on to the freeway.

"Well, yes. You've had an exciting trip so far, I gather."

Highway 169 poured downhill from a slight grade, a lie to the assumption that the state was flat. There were undulations and hills all across the region, albeit nowhere near as extreme as you would find in California or Colorado. As in Kansas, the feeling of all-engulfing vulnerability still pervaded the geography. It was a feeling not unlike that of being an insect on a petri dish, exposed and unable to protect yourself from the power of an unkind God. This was tornado country.

Almost all the cars on the road had NASCAR stickers affixed to their bumpers.

"You could say it's been interesting, I guess," I finally said after a long and pregnant pause. "I'm trying to make my way."

"You're not doing a very good job of it." I was surprised by the finality in his voice. "You've almost been dead how many times now? And are you paying any attention to the news?"

"I don't have a clue what I'm doing." The words came out in painful clumps. "I can't seem to follow the threads . . . every time I think I know where I'm going, something happens to throw me off the track."

"You've got to shape up. If you can't get yourself together between here and New York, you're doomed. You have to be ready."

"For what?" I began to raise my voice. "What the hell is waiting for me there? Everyone seems to know more than I do."

He didn't say anything, guiding the car down the road. We had been driving for about ten minutes when we came into Tulsa. You can see the stunted spires of the downtown business district from Owasso on a clear day, but as you neared the city they disappeared. Everything was too flat.

Oklahoma is situated at almost the exact midpoint between the two coasts, and as such any trend that starts on either coast reaches here last, after it has already crept across the vast regions in-between and exhausted itself in the intermediacy. So it was with economics: Tulsa had been among the last cities to feel the effects of the post-September 11th economic malaise, but once it had arrived it had devastated the area. There were tens of thousands of feet of empty and unused office space in the downtown.

The sun seemed strangely weak in the atmosphere, despite the heat. Colors were washed out and sodden, almost as if the life had been wrung out from the landscape.

Green things grew in abundance, but I am certain that the countryside becomes grim in July and August, as the summer plants wilt in the perpetual sun and the vague stink of rot begins to pervade the countryside.

"You have seen many things but you still comprehend little of the big picture. The events which have led you inexorably down this road, no matter how seemingly random or unrelated, have all occurred as set forth in methodical detail many decades ago."

"Where are we going?" I asked.

"We're going to get ice cream."

Sure enough we were. We had entered Tulsa proper and pulled off the freeway, down the 31st street offramp and into the parking lot of a Braum's ice cream parlor. He parked the car in silence and together we entered the store.

It was blessedly cool inside. It seemed to be an odd mixture of restaurant and supermarket, with half the room devoted to tables and chairs and the other half to freezer cases containing paper cartons of ice cream.

We ordered our food and retired to a distant corner of the restaurant, he with his cone and I with a sundae. Although it seemed uncharacteristically odd, it was definitely a welcome turn of events.

"How's your sundae?" he asked after we had sat in silence for a few minutes.

"Good. Hit the right spot."

"I had a feeling it would."

"So. Why are you here?"

"Things have come to a head."

"Things. Things. I don't understand anything anymore."

"No, of course not. You're not supposed to. It's frustrating, I know. There are . . . accommodations that must be observed. I am not an independent operator in this matter, much as I wish it were otherwise."

"You take your orders from someone, then."

"Yes. I take my orders just like everyone else. I always

have. I am not supposed to - I can't tell you everything you want to know. Everything that you have seen has been arranged for your education in just such a way that it will all make sense when you can perceive the capstone. Your maturity has been very carefully controlled."

"So - everything that has happened . . ."

"Not everything. There have been anomalies."

The sense of safety and confidence I had been conditioned to feel in presence of my supposed protector began to wane. He seemed nervous, deeply agitated.

The restaurant was fairly crowded - it was a hot day and the ice cream was very cold. Still, I decided to take the risk, and lifted my hat off my head.

Immediately the psychic field sprang into my perception, emerging from the back of my mind where it had receded into a dull roar and into crystalline focus at the forefront of my mind. I kept my eyes on those of my companion and continued to listen as he continued to talk. I focused all my energies on his words and the mind that lay behind them.

"It won't do you any good," he said in a weary voice. "I've been proofed against that kind of probe for a very long time."

It was true - his mind registered as nothing more than an opaque mass, "visible" with the eye of my mind but totally illegible. After studying it for another vain moment I replaced my hat.

"That is something that wasn't supposed to happen," he gestured towards my head. "Only a very small percentage of the population reacts to Receptors like that. There was no way of knowing you'd be one of them."

"You set it on me?"

"No . . . no, we would never have done that. But there are others. There are other groups who we do not control. That's why I'm here today. They are growing impatient -"

"What are they waiting for? I'm going to New York, aren't I?" My voice rose despite my best efforts. I imagined my frustration registering as peaks and valleys of pink and purple energy coruscating outwards from my mind.

"It's not that simple." He was obviously conflicted - his words were slow and deliberate. He had finished his ice cream cone and placed the paper wrapper on the table before him.

"Well, why isn't it? Why can't you tell me who is doing this, who's trying to kill me, who's trying to 'help' me, I can't make sense of any of it."

"Be patient. It will make sense, that's all I can tell you."

"Did Joanne have to die?"

His eyes narrowed and his mouth pursed until his lips were ghostly white. He struggled for words.

"No. That was . . . collateral damage. She was in the way. We couldn't save her."

"She didn't need to die!" My voice was rising now and he grew more and more anxious with every word. His eyes scanned the room behind me.

"You need to be quiet. You can't speak freely in public." His teeth were clenched now, his words barely a whisper.

"She loved me, she didn't have to be killed like that. I don't know what kind of monsters are running after me -"

"It's time to go." He stood up peremptorily and grabbed the ice cream wrapper in his hand. I followed, disposing my trash and returning to the car.

He turned on the engine and we felt the blast of warm air from the air conditioning, rapidly plunging to cool in the space of a few seconds. He turned on the radio - it was set to a college station playing something weird - and turned it up loud.

Leaning across the seat towards me he yelled in my ear:

"I couldn't do this at any other time. They can hear us everywhere."

I nodded my assent.

"I'm sorry this has to happen. There are too many people involved, too many interests. You'll understand why soon enough."

I nodded again.

"Just remember, I've protected you from a lot of things that you will never even know. I've been there for years, even when you couldn't see me. You're alive today because your father told me to protect you. I can't . . ."

He seemed unsure, almost melancholy.

"I can't protect you any more. I've done all I can do. You probably won't see me again."

He turned the radio off again and pulled the car out of the parking lot. He turned left down the road and drove for a block until we reached Mingo St. Mingo is a wide boulevard that runs from one side of Tulsa to the other, bisecting the eastern portion of the town in a south-east direction. The car turned left and right after that pulled into a long parking lot in front of an unassuming strip mall.

It didn't seem to be a bad neighborhood, merely quiet and poor, the kind of business district that sits on the edge of lower-middle class residential districts and neither rots nor grows, merely sits and waits. This particular strip mall had a Mexican restaurant, a tortilla store, a dance studio and a comic book store, lined up in narrow storefronts one after the other.

He parked the car at the far north side of the lot. There weren't a lot of other cars there, but there was a shiny black van parked at the opposite end of the lot. There were a handful of figures in black suits standing around the van smoking cigarettes.

The One-Eyed Man stopped the car and pulled the keys out of the ignition.

"I'm sorry, but this is the best way. Remember . . ." He hesitated, emotion at the edge of his voice. "Don't listen to them. I never touched you."

He opened the door and got out, motioning for me to follow. It was a patently suspicious situation but I didn't say anything. I opened my bag and fished out one of the guns I had accumulated, sliding it into my back pocket as I exited the car.

He was already halfway across the parking lot, walking briskly and without hesitation. Whatever was happening, he seemed willing to face it without any further deliberation.

Two of the suited figures met him at the center of the parking lot. They exchanged a few words that I couldn't hear, and then they retreated to their van as I came up besides the one-eyed man.

"Who are they?" I asked.

"They're your new handlers."

"Handlers. I don't need a handler."

He turned and leveled a withering look at me.

"You'd have been dead years ago without one. You're very valuable . . ."

His words trailed off as both of our heads turned and saw the figure approaching us from the black van. He was wearing a black suit and tie just like his companions, but he seemed to be the leader. He was wearing a white-neck brace and his face, bruised purple and swollen, was covered in bandages. He was limping on crutches, his right leg in a full cast. He looked at me and smiled, a handful of missing teeth showing black in the bright afternoon daylight. It was Adam.

"What the fuck . . ." My hand went to the gun my back pocket.

"You're mine," Adam said with a delirious smile. "I had to pull in a few favors but you're mine now. I'm in a lot of pain - you have no idea how much pain I'm in right now - but it was worth it to see you here, now."

"Go back to the car." The One-Eyed Man said it quietly and softly.

"What?" My hand clenched over the gun in my pocket.

"Just go." He turned and looked at me for a second before I moved.

"Don't go anywhere -" Before Adam could finish the

sentence the One-Eyed Man had pulled a gun out from a holster on his back and shot him in the head. The shot fell like a stone in the muggy afternoon air, echoing across the parking lot and against the nearby buildings. Adam's underlings looked at each other, looked at us, and reached for their weapons.

"Go!" He pulled the keys to his car out of his pocket and tossed them back to me with one hand while he unloaded the rest of his clip into the two attendants who flanked Adam's strangely folded and silent body. They fell next to their boss, screams curdled in their mouths. Their bodies hit the ground with wet slaps.

I was already to the car, throwing open the door and tossing my bag in the passenger seat by the time the last of his bullets had hit their mark. I threw the car in reverse and the tires squealed as my foot hit the accelerator. Craning my neck backwards I turned the wheel and aimed for where the One-Eyed Man was standing. I slammed on the breaks and he opened the back door to enter.

In the moment before he was able to throw his body along the backseat I saw a number of things. With my head craned over the seat I saw two more goons approaching the car from where they had been sitting in the black van. They ran towards us and stopped, aiming their guns and shooting.

As I twisted my head around to face forward I caught a glimpse of the storefronts. A handful of people had assembled along the walkway running along the storefronts - I saw two men looking out from the door to the comic book store, a middle-aged gentleman with glasses, his mouth standing agape at the spectacle, and another, younger man in a hooded sweatshirt, his face obscured. It looked hot.

Then my eyes were on the road in front of us and he had landed in the backseat and I pulled the gearshift into first and pushed as hard as I could on the accelerator. The back door shut as we surged forward and I heard the last couple goons shooting after us as we peeled out of the parking lot and onto the boulevard. There were a couple of loud pops as their bullets found the trunk of the car, but they missed the windows and the tires.

I was racing as fast as I could down the street, weaving in and out of traffic and trying not to get us killed. We were four blocks away, hurtling down 31st street when I asked him if he could see anyone following us down the street.

"No . . . I can't see anyone."

His voice was a croak, hoarse and rough. I slowed the car down and adjusted the mirror until I could see him. He was lying sideways on the back seat, his face white and blanketed with sweat. His hands were clutching at his tummy, dark crimson blood spilling through and onto the seat.

"We have to get you to the hospital." Immediately my throat began to constrict, I didn't know what was going on or what I was doing. I was lost in the middle of a strange city.

I pulled the car over and into a supermarket parking lot. I reached into my bag to find a shirt or towel to staunch the flow of blood.

"Don't bother," he gasped. "I'm dead. I can feel it. I've been in too many fights . . . no one walks away from this."

"What do I do?"

"I was so . . . stupid. I should never have trusted him. He's not the man I knew. Remember that."

"Remember what? Who are you talking about?"

He seemed to be staring at a space just above where my head was, his pupils shrinking and his face losing every hint of color.

"You have to go to New York . . . it's waiting for you. Just like you planned. No detours anymore. Get on a bus and go there. You'll see . . . you'll see . . ."

"I'll see what? Tell me!"

His head began to shake, bobbing from side to side on his neck. It looked as if her were having trouble staying conscious, almost as if her were falling asleep.

"Remember . . . your father . . ."

He leaned forward as if he was trying to whisper something to me. His eyes were wide and his expression intense. And then it appeared as if he forgot his train of thought. He leaned back against the seat and closed his eyes. It was over. His hands fell away from his stomach and a jumble of blood and shredded tissue poured forth from the wound. He couldn't have survived a shot like that under any circumstances. A bubble of red blood expanded out of his mouth as the final breath escaped his body, a slight rattling from deep in his chest that echoed through the car.

I opened the car door and grabbed my bag. I locked the car and left his body sitting in the parking lot of that supermarket. I inquired directions inside the supermarket, bought a bottle of water and set off across town. His last ominous words were floating in my head as I began the walk to the bus station.

23

It took a few hours to reach the bus station. Tulsa is only a medium-sized city but it covers a lot of ground. I hitched a couple rides down the boulevards but mostly I walked in that oppressive afternoon heat.

Much to my surprise I was harassed no further that day. I think I saw a few cars following me at various times, but after what had happened in front of the comic book store it seemed slightly odd that whomever gave Adam his orders wasn't still intent on poaching me. Perhaps there were still more layers of complication of which I was unaware, or perhaps Adam had become a rogue agent. It occurred to me that the experiments he had overseen in Berkeley may well have driven him mad.

The money I still had from the beginning of my trip, combined with Joanne's bankroll and what I was able to find in the one-eyed man's car, had grown into a sizable stash. I bought a ticket to New York, with as few stops as possible on the way. The bus left around sunset, hitting the road for Memphis and points east.

I had a few hours in downtown Tulsa before the bus left. Downtown Tulsa is particularly bereft of interest, a small concentration of large corporate towers surrounded by industrial and residential sprawl. Dinner was a Subway sandwich.

The bus was empty when it rolled up to the station, and I was one of the first on board. I made a beeline for the back of the bus, staking out territory next to the small port-a-john at the rear. The bus idled in the station for about a half-hour before we were ready to leave. It was only about half-full by the time it came to leave.

Right before the bus driver closed the double doors at the head of the vehicle, one more passenger ran out of the terminal and up the stairs. I was staring out the window, looking at the sun setting over northern Tulsa, as the last passenger crept up the aisle and sat down next to me.

There were many open seats scattered throughout the bus. Anyone who's ridden a bus knows the uniquely uncomfortable sensation of having your space invaded by strangers. In this instance it was doubly uncomfortable because there was something indefinably familiar about my new companion.

The bus pulled out of the depot and my seatmate was quiet. He was wearing a large hooded sweatshirt pulled tight around his face, obscuring his features. For a moment he seemed content to sit in quiet, but after we had merged onto the freeway I felt a sharp prick under my ribs.

"Don't move a muscle, don't say a word."

I turned my head towards my assailant. He pulled the hood down from around his face and I saw that it was John, the strange man who had saved my life in Berkeley and then tried to kill me in Truckee. He was holding a small knife at my abdomen, and I didn't doubt his willingness to use it.

"You are a fool to leave your trail so blatant. You have blazed a path across this country."

"I've been told that," I said quietly. "You're not the only one who's been following me."

"I'm certain of that," he said. "I've seen them. I've followed them, too."

"You tried to kill me."

"No. I didn't. You merely ventured into a certain . . . experiment of mine. If I had known at the time just who you were and what you meant, I would never have attempted to rope you into my control group."

"Control group."

"Yes, that is what I called them. I was on the verge of a breakthrough, with that group, before you interfered. After you took our van and left they tried to kill me. But they were weak and eventually they devolved into infighting over the last remaining heroin. It was a shame, considering all the work I had done, for them to end up as common junkies."

"You wanted to make me a junkie."

"No, no. I wanted to enlist your help in the service of mankind against our implacable enemies."

I didn't say anything to this. I began to suspect that my foe was not in his right mind - his words were feverish and dangerously lucid.

"You and I, we are very much alike," he began again.

"Really. I don't see how."

"No, you wouldn't . . . but I know more than you. I know about your quest, now, and about your father. You are after knowledge, knowledge which will enable you to finally avenge your father's death. This knowledge awaits you in New York."

"Do you know what is waiting for me?"

"No, no one does. The underground is buzzing, but there are only fragments, here and there, of anything useful. People know you're important. They know that rival groups are competing to either destroy or subvert you. They know that there are also powerful factors invested in the eventual success of your quest. But aside from that . . . no one I have spoken to understands more than that."

"That's essentially what I know, what I've known all along. Since I left home a week ago I haven't learned a single concrete thing, I've just been driven further and further into confusion." I was growing increasingly frustrated. His blade was still pressing into my ribs but I felt confident that he would not allow me to die, at least for the moment.

"Perhaps you would learn something from my story." He didn't seem to be leaving me much choice.

"What are you going to do? Are you going to hold that knife on me until the bus stops?"

He didn't say anything for a moment, and then slowly pulled the knife back. He held it on his lap as we rode, but after a while we both forgot it was there.

"I'm coming with you," he finally said. "I now know that your quest is the fulfillment of my desires as well. We are after the very same things, you and I. Although I didn't know it when we first met, it was no coincidence that we did.

"On April 19th, 1993, the federal government lay siege to the Branch Davidian compound in Waco, Texas. I don't know if you are old enough to remember, but the images from the siege were broadcast all across the world. The official story was that the government had isolated a group of religious separatists who were stockpiling weapons in anticipation of an ordained judgment day foretold by David

Koresh.

"That was bullshit. The Clinton Justice Department was told that Koresh had been stockpiling weapons, yes, but in the end they were no more than catspaws. The Waco assault was merely the first in a series of very public maneuvers in a long-standing secret war. The very same war -"

"The same war that my father fought."

"Yes. The same war that your father fought, and which had been fought in the shadows for the whole of the twentieth century, as well as a good part of the nineteenth and eighteenth. There were as many sides as their were interests, all overlapping and interacting in an elaborate series of crosses and double-crosses. You've heard all sorts of names - the Trilateral Commission, the Illuminati, the Military Industrial Complex, the Freemasons - all of them specifically inaccurate while still managing to evoke a shade of the actual truth. These are old, old . . . ancient interests at war. There are secrets at the heart of this war older than humanity itself.

"The first two World Wars were both fought for reasons other than those we learned in high school. Certainly, Hitler and Stalin and Roosevelt existed, but the reasons for the conflicts between the nations were nothing like they told the public. All the wars of the last 150 have been fought over resources, pure and simple, and those who stand to profit from the distribution of resources have pulled the strings that pull the triggers.

"But by resources I don't simply mean oil and coal and metal - there are many more important resources on our planet than those.

"In any event, the Cold War that followed World War Two was actually a very hot war for those who followed the secret conflicts of the underground. Many things were at stake besides merely the futile questions of Communism and Democracy. But the multiple parties who composed the shifting alliances, the same parties who had coalesced into final alliances during the first five decades of the last century, were also assured of perpetual stalemate by the relatively even distribution and strength of their forces.

"But then everything changed. And the centuries-old conflict suddenly drew to a surprising and unexpected climax. The catalyst for this crucial endgame was your father."

Without realizing it I made a loud intake of breath. I didn't know how much - if any - of this I could believe, but if even a fraction was true . . .

"As you probably know, your father fought in Vietnam. It was during that war that he was secretly drafted into the CIA. After being indoctrinated into the secrets of that organization, he served for a time under their auspices.

"But your father was a very smart man. After a time he learned more of the secrets which lay at the heart of the intelligence apparatus that Truman and Eisenhower had constructed. The CIA was merely the very public face of another agency, which even the President of the United States did not know existed. He penetrated this agency and was indoctrinated into the heart of the most secret conspiracy in the history of the world.

"He spent the majority of the next two decades working his way through the ranks, fighting in the boiling jungles of Africa and Asia, leading men and killing. Eventually he came to a position of no small authority in the ranks of his organization, and learned a few more things which made him one of the half-dozen most dangerous men on the planet."

He stopped for a moment, lifting his head and scanning the bus. No one appeared to be paying us any attention, but that was a foolish hope. It was best merely to assume that we were under surveillance at all times.

"We're being watched," he whispered.

"Of course," I replied. "I'm sure half of these people are

plants. They don't know which ones are real passengers and which ones are agents or counter agents or whatever. I've been dealing with this since I left California."

"Well, it's too late to stop now. We're going to have to make it to New York."

Of course I didn't say anything, but I felt certain that if I did make it to New York it would be unaccompanied by him.

"If I had known that you were his son, I would never have . . . I mean, I knew something, I had heard whispers. But I didn't know that you were really him, or . . . or I probably wouldn't have had anything to do with you. I thought you were probably just another agent, on his trail, but no, you're actually him.

"The Soviet Union didn't fall because of economic instability or political revolution. It fell for the very simple reason that the United States space shuttle Challenger exploded in 1986.

"Not even the President of the United States or the Premiere of the Soviet Union knew the real reason behind the space program. The space program as we know it was initially conceived by the Nazis during World War Two for a very simple reason: to establish permanent diplomatic contact with beings from beyond our sphere.

"What Hitler didn't know was that this diplomatic contact had already been established decades before he was born. There are creatures beyond our ken, living in our galaxy, who have long-standing interests in the continued evolution of our planet. Neither the Axis nor the Allies understood that the rocket programs they were both rushing to develop were essentially mooted by the psychic communication that the underground agencies had established in the years leading up to war.

As he spoke my thoughts were unaccountably drawn to the rumors I had already heard echoing through the distant psychic ether, the faint rumblings of madmen who yet remained on the periphery of my awareness.

"Your father learned the significance of the space program, and was able to act accordingly. The astronauts who died in the Challenger were, from his point of view, regrettable collateral damage - only one in any given space flight crew will ever know the real nature of a given mission. They all had to die to ensure that the message would be properly received.

"And the message was certainly received, loud and clear. Just a few years later the international instability wreaked by the shuttle explosion resulted in the collapse of the Soviet Union. As the conflicts which had shaped the Cold War drew to a close, the ostensible cover for the conflicts faded as well.

"There is much that we - those of us who dwell on the outside of the underground - will probably never understand. We do not know, for instance, just why the aliens cannot materialize physically on our planet. We do not know what tangible assets they demand from our planet in return for their continued cooperation - or, as some would term it, their continued policy of benign neglect. Whatever it was, the momentary disruption caused by the destruction of the Challenger was enough to send massive disturbances through the fabric of the competing organizations. Enough so that by the middle of the 90s they had all essentially abandoned their operations overseas in favor of concentrating their forces on an all-out war for domination of American resources. The vacuum that the end of the conflict created was more than enough to destabilize volatile regions like Rwanda, which had previously been held intact by the torsion of conflicting forces.

"Alien technology is pervasive throughout society, but the real choice bits have been kept from the public and applied selectively. The entire edifice of psychiatry has been co-opted in order that the Powers That Be can exercise their power on those few individuals who gain insight into their organization. I think we've both been victimized by their harmful mind-control drugs."

I remembered the sticky worms who lived in the pill capsules and hid in my body, and how they dulled my senses and made me prone to harmful suggestion.

"But the collapse of the Eastern bloc has caused a shift not only in the strategies but in the very goals of the organizations. The technological support enjoyed by multiple sides of the conflict has steadily dwindled, which has caused many to believe that a rapprochement with the extraterrestrials is coming, perhaps within a generation. Accordingly, the research and development infrastructures of these organizations has blossomed, in an attempt to deconstruct and synthesize the alien technologies. There are certain advanced applications to which the creatures who created the technologies could never have imagined . . . certain cultural and physical difference which we have been busy developing ourselves for the preceding decade."

"Mind control," I said.

"Yes, exactly. That is why we were both in Berkeley that night, and that was the nature of my experiments as well. Tell me, did you actually see the laboratory?"

"Yes I did. It was horrible."

"Some of their scientists have gone quite mad, or so I hear. But sadism has always played an important role in the secret sciences.

"The Branch Davidian compound in Waco, Texas was the front for another, far more intricate underground laboratory. The Davidians actually believed themselves to be a persecuted religious group, but they were in actuality merely the first of many test subjects manipulated to induce a state of severe suggestibility.

"Did Clinton know about the lab? No one has been able to prove conclusively. Even if Clinton was a catspaw, there is a faction who believes that he at least had an inkling as to the secret machinations behind his office - he was perhaps the shrewdest man to hold the Presidency since Truman.

"In any event, the first real test of these experiments would be held exactly two years after the incident in Waco, Texas. I was a student at the University of Oklahoma in Norman, on a short trip up the road to Oklahoma City."

"The bombing."

"Yes, the bombing. I was there. I was actually inside St. Joseph's church at the time, just adjacent to the Murrah Building. I was lucky enough to have been in the cellar of the church, and when the building was nearly razed by the blast I was protected by the 100-year old earth walls. The Church is still there - slightly amended. There's a big statue of Jesus out front, facing the memorial.

"I didn't know it at the time but I had seen the makings of the tragedy. I was trapped under the rubble of the church for almost a full day, waiting to be rescued, and in that time my thoughts constantly replayed the events of the explosion.

"I know for a fact that Timothy McVeigh was a patsy. His story was constructed nearly from a whole cloth. A bit of ironic poetic license was used to tie his story in with Waco and the ostensible cover used by the government to explain the Branch Davidian incident. He was a cipher, kidnapped and brainwashed for the express purpose of providing a cover for the real events of April 19th, 1995.

"The organizations have perfected the use of synthetic opiate compounds in mind control, and it was these substances which controlled the real Oklahoma City bombers. I know because I saw them, in the hours leading directly to the bombing. They were normal people, men and women just like you and me, but they were absolutely in the thrall of the commander who controlled their supply of the opiate. Remember at the campsite, when I told you about how opiates affect addicts?"

"Yes."

"Well, after investigating the matter on my own for a considerable amount of time I was able to discover the secret of their technique. They've created an opiate that affects the addiction centers of the brain almost exclusively, without ever impacting the pleasure centers - creating the massive dependency without any of the pleasure. Using the compound enables those with a proprietary interest in controlling a captive army of suicidal drones to practically rewrite the brains of their vassals to suit their mission - inculcating such a high degree of suggestibility as to render them impotent lemmings, incapable of independent thought in any capacity whatsoever.

"After the bombing I switched my major to chemistry in hopes of understanding the process. When I encountered you I had come as close as I ever had to synthesizing the correct dosage, but my companions still retained enough of their independence to assert their will in the absence of a strong control. Which is why they revolted at the first opportunity."

"That was what you had in mind for me?"

"Well, I had no idea at the time who you actually were. Had I known, the thought would never had crossed my mind."

"Cold comfort, I suppose."

"Yes, well. In any event, the techniques were modeled on what I saw immediately prior to the bombing - which was, a group of half-a-dozen men and women under the direct supervision of the man who controlled their dosages. They were all situated very near to the blast, so no evidence remained to cause suspicion among government authorities. All the fingers pointed logically to McVeigh, so any conflicting reports were dismissed out of hand.

"But I saw them. They received their last dosage in the basement of St. Joseph's, and I saw everything. The building was supposed to be empty that day at that time -

my presence was unanticipated, and so they took few precautions. I saw them shoot up, mindless zombies controlled by the lure of the chemicals in their arms. They were wearing black, and the color matched their lack of vigor.

"After the bombing I didn't see any reports on what I had seen, and what couldn't have gone ignored . . . I have indirect proof that those few living witnesses who testified to seeing the group in the moments before the blast were purposefully silenced. I escaped merely through my discretion, but even given that it was something of a miracle.

"Of course, in just a few years there would be additional corroboration for my theories . . . the Columbine massacre, quite interestingly staged just one day after the fourth anniversary of the Oklahoma City bombing, seemed to correspond perfectly with what I understood of the mind-control techniques used by the organizations. As we both know, there are also laboratories hidden underneath Littleton. There are some who maintain that, in any event, the Columbine murders were actually a mistake, the result of an injudicious training regimen that produced a premature massacre. There are others who claimed that it was planned.

"The architects of these incidents construct their plans with the utmost attention to detail. The general public can be controlled most accurately through sharp shocks to the system, and it is perfectly conceivable that the Columbine massacre was a dry-run for the massive sociological experiment that would begin on September 11th, 2001.

"There's so much we don't know. We know that the groups exist, and we see the consequences of their actions, but we are almost totally ignorant of the actual composition of their organization or their membership. We know that in the years following the Challenger explosion there was a consolidation of multiple groups under two distinct umbrellas. This is where your father became important - he was one of the first to broach the idea of gradual reintegration among the many disparate groups. Perhaps he foresaw a time when the resources of multiple groups would be necessary to leverage against the future of humanity."

"But how is it," I asked, "that if so little is known about these organizations and their goals, you know so much about my father's life and career?"

"Your father's death sent shockwaves throughout the underworld. Even outside of the immediate sphere of his organization, he was known and respected. As such, his death commanded the attention of a few far-flung individuals on the outskirts of the intelligence field - individuals with contacts in the world of conspiracy research, such as myself."

"So the timing of the Oklahoma City bombing was no coincidence, coming so close on the heels of my father's passing?"

"No. Nothing is a coincidence anymore. Even the date of McVeigh's execution - June, 11 2001. Write the date numerically: 6/11/01. Flip that date upside down and you have 9/11/01. These things are important. Competing organizations use these kinds of appellations to communicate intentions across continents. Just three months after one group's patsy was killed, another group delivered the most shocking blow yet."

"But," I asked, "how do you know that we're dealing with different groups? Who's to say they haven't already been consolidated, and everything else is just created to maintain the illusion of schism? What if one group already won and no one else knows about it, and all their seemingly counterproductive actions are really being coordinated from on high?"

"Those are very good questions, which no one has an answer to. But . . . we will soon."

He suddenly looked at me, across the seat, with a satisfied grin on his face.

"You're going to follow me."

"All the way to New York. Whatever the reason is for your trip, something vitally important is going to happen once you reach the east coast. Something is waiting. You've already seen, just in the course of this past week, more than most of us who have been following these machinations for decades. Someone is watching you, controlling your perambulations and ensuring that you remain safe and secure. I am certain as well . . ." he paused a moment and lowered his voice, "that we are being watched and our conversations monitored even as we speak. But that is to be expected. I don't know anything they don't, so I am relatively confident that I haven't given nay irrecoverable secrets. But you do - or you wouldn't have been so quiet through our conversation."

I didn't say a word. My companion was obviously deranged - he knew a great deal that I did not but much of what he said carried the distinct whiff of overheated hysteria. Where his information and mine overlapped I could be reasonably certain of corroboration, but his attempts at clarification only led me further down the route of obfuscation. I resisted the temptation to take his storytelling at literal face value. His answers only asked more questions.

"I saw you at the comic book store," he said after a moment's awkward pause. "I was inside shopping and you were outside fighting those men. I saw from the doorway."

I remembered seeing him, now, his face obscured by his hooded sweatshirt, standing alongside the bespectacled owner.

"Of course, there are no coincidences. Synchronicity is everywhere. Do you remember the poster on the ceiling of my van?"

"'The New Universe Sold Here'?"

"Yes, yes! Do you know what that means?"

"No . . . I didn't."

"The New Universe was ostensibly a comic book line introduced by Marvel in the late 80s - unsuccessful, faded from sight after only a few years. But in reality, we have come to understand that the New U was actually a massive syntactic incubator for radical precognitive social engineering."

"I don't understand what you're talking about."

"The New Universe was created by the Powers That Be in order to create a laboratory in which strange ideas could be incubated and tested."

He reached into his knapsack and pulled out a small bag of comics.

"No one knows this but maybe a handful of people in the United States. The experiment was conducted through so many layers of redundant management that no one had any idea where the actual ideas originated . . . and many of the ideas originated in the minds of the ruling councils of the most powerful agencies in the world. If you know what to look for, these books are written in a kind of code, a subliminal dialect designed to be understood by only a chosen few. The men and women who wrote and drew these books didn't even know what they were doing at the time - and certainly, some of that strange disconnect comes through in terms of the books' tone.

"The man who sold me these books in Tulsa didn't think they were worth anything - he had half a complete run of 'Star Brand' sitting in a quarter box, dusty and forgotten. He was happy to be rid of them. No one understands how important these books were. Anyone reading them could have stumbled upon the secrets of the last two decades . . ."

He handed one of the books to me. It was prematurely old, with wrinkles across the cover and the bottom corners of the pages turned up. There was a super-hero on the cover, a blond man without a mask clothed in a red leather jumpsuit, some terrible 80s fashion. He was floating above the Earth, unsupported in the vacuum with an arm outstretched towards the reader.

Arkansas was an uneventful state to drive through in the dark. There was really nothing to see - just endless darkness leading over rolling green foothills. The occasional city enlightened the darkness, but soon it was hard to resist the lure of sleep.

We spoke for a bit longer but for the most part John's expertise - such that it was - had been exhausted. He was tired both physically and mentally, and retired to the seat opposite mine across the aisle, curling up against the window and sleeping. I don't think he was worried that I was going anywhere, not anymore and not after our long conversation. He seemed certain that we were within the range of each other's confidence. He was a fool.

The state slowly passed beneath the wheels of the bus and within a few more hours we were within sight of Memphis. The city is bright, lit up at night and reflected against the Mississippi river. As you approach the city on the Arkansas side of the river there's nothing, but urban Memphis reaches out to grab you as soon as the bridge terminates in Tennessee.

John had slept peacefully for the last couple hours, and even as the bus slowed down to navigate the tight Memphis streets he was undisturbed. He had moved during the ride so that his head lay on the seat near the aisle, his body curled up against the wall under the window.

Perhaps I would be able to dodge him when the bus came to a stop? I didn't know. His knife was still sitting on his lap, covered up to the hilt by a fold of his shirt. Anyone walking by to use the bathroom would simply see a young man sleeping, and pay no heed to the small object obscured in his lap.

We rolled into the bus stop in the small hours of the morning, before the sun had begun to rise over the horizon.

There were many passengers continuing on through the next stop, but everyone who wasn't comfortably sleeping disembarked in order to stretch their legs.

I looked over at John sleeping on the seat and ran through my options. I had been planning on riding the bus at least through Nashville, but I needed to find a way to lose John permanently.

The bus was empty. I leaned over the seat and pulled the knife off his lap as gently as I could. With as little deliberation as possible I buried the knife to the hilt in his temple as he slept. His body jerked for a moment, a slight gurgle escaping his lips, and then he fell still and silent. I pulled the knife out and his wound began to bleed.

I stanched the flow of blood with a folded handkerchief and pulled the hood of his sweatshirt over his head. Anyone who passed him on the bus would assume he was merely sleeping. Of course, he would eventually be found, but by that time I would probably be far away. I had given another fake name to the bus company when I bought my ticket with cash - "Hans Castorp" - but the ticket lady hadn't gotten the joke, which served as proof positive of the inefficiency of our secondary schools.

I threw the wet knife into my duffel bag, as well as the bag of comic books from his knapsack. I reasoned that I might well have need of something to read before the journey was over. Stepping off the bus in the clear and muggy darkness of the Memphis morning, I felt a slight twinge of sympathy for John, but considering the fact that he had tried to kill me twice it was only very slight.

There had to be another bus leaving the station. I was confident that the forces which had protected me up to now would continue to protect me until I reached the proscribed end of my journey.

After studying the departures board I went to the restroom, in desperate need of a piss. I walked through the doorway and found that the restroom was dark. I stumbled for a moment in the darkness, trying to find a light switch - and then there was something hard and sharp on the back of my head. I fell against the tiled floor in the darkness and in those last few moments before I lost consciousness I registered the distinct but curiously distant sensation of my pants filling with urine.

24

I woke up in a dark room. It was hot and sticky, the floor and the walls were metal and there didn't seem to be any air circulating. I could smell the dried piss on my pants. My duffel bag was gone, and someone had taken my hat.

How long had I been out? There was something sore on the back of my head, a soft spot covered with dried blood. If there had been a window or a doorway I could have seen the sun, but as it was I had no idea if I had been unconscious for two hours or two days.

I was trapped. The dimensions of my prison appeared to be roughly four paces by eight paces, with an indeterminate height above me (I tried to touch the ceiling but it was beyond the range of my tallest jump). The room hung in perpetual blackness, without the slightest hint of light from any aperture or crease in the walls.

Exploring all the walls of my prison I found that one of the smaller walls - the furthest end of the rectangular box from where I awoke - seemed to be composed of a slightly different material than the other walls. There were seams at regular intervals, perhaps at every foot. Was it a door of some sort?

After pondering the mystery for an indeterminate period, I heard a great rumbling noise and the floor began to shake. I lost my balance and fell to the floor amid the tumult. Was I moving? It seemed as if I was - and then it occurred to me. My prison was almost exactly the shape and size of a truck trailer.

The box was lightproofed, soundproofed and almost airtight (there had to have been some vent or I would have died), but it couldn't mask the movement of the truck. I was being taken somewhere. Curling up on the floor of the truck, I tried to sleep.

It didn't take long before the sensory deprivation began to affect me. One strange property of the box could be seen in the fact that despite the loss of my hat I was unable to detect anything of the psychic landscape outside of my prison. I surmised that the trailer must have been coated with the same substance which lined the interior of my hat, the blocking agent that protected me from hearing the thoughts of others unbidden.

But the shielding was not perfect. Although I could not perceive another human mind anywhere in my proximity, I could hear the faint trillings of strange voices from unimaginable distances. These were the voices I had heard from afar as whispers, the terrible secretive presences who dwelt on far planes. Usually, they were distant enough to be ignored, but now, with no other psyches to compete for attention, they stood at the forefront of my attention.

I tried to think about something else, anything else than the possibility of being forced to confront those insane, inhuman voices which I heard. I remembered John, who I had killed, and cast my mind back over his story. Much of it didn't make any sense, but there were parts that matched what I knew, or believed that I knew. There was no doubt that he was mad, but there was also a high probability that his madness had been spurred by an unfortunate encounter with those same forces which control our world and shape our destinies.

Obviously, the most pressing question in his story would have been: why were you in the basement of St. Joseph's in the first place? Does St. Joseph's even have a basement? In the midst of his seeming full disclosure there were odd omissions that cast a revealing light on his narrative.

He was unable to define anything specific regarding the nature and shape of the organizations which conducted these secret wars, other than the vaguest hints of institutional upheaval. I knew more about the multiple agencies than John had - based on my own research and personal experience with the one-eyed man. John's conclusions were very much akin to those of a scientist attempting to deduce the complex mating habits of an elephant from a few stray footprints left in the sand.

But my secrets were in jeopardy. Whoever had my duffel bag had my notebooks, and with them the blueprints of a lifetime's research, save for the most damning clues which I retained in my own mind. Perhaps whoever had taken me already knew everything. If they were one of the organizations which my father had served, they would already knew anything his son did.

All roads lead back to the enigma of my father. I still didn't know who had killed him, or why he had died. The forces he had dedicated his life to destroying were quantitatively little different from the forces which he had marshaled. What were the goals of these shadowy secret armies? From whence did they spring?

I was tired, exhausted from my travels and the endless unnerving mysteries which surrounded me. Nothing made sense, nothing added up to any sort of discernible pattern.

New York was the answer. I knew that if I reached Manhattan I would have the opportunity to place everything in proper contcxt. September 11th was the keystone to everything wrong and strange in my life, and if I could decipher the meaning behind that, then all the other enigmas would cease swirling and finally coalesce.

Without any external gauge of time, I drifted in and out of consciousness without warning. I slept and dreamt and opened my eyes in perpetual darkness, believing myself still asleep. My dreams were wild and bright, informed by the voices which I tried to ignore but which I could no longer restrain. They came to me in my sleep and told me things that I wished never to learn. I cannot know where these fervid, febrile rantings ended and my own dreams began.

There are other worlds, where the sky dawns pink and purple, and the waters ripple in a queasy approximation of our own oceans, under the influence of a strange gravity and alien tidal forces. The creatures who count their days under this strange sky can communicate vast distances with the powers of their minds. Over the last few centuries they have guided the progression of our civilization, but despite their best efforts a rift has developed in the ranks of the secret society that regulates our commerce with the extra-terrestrials.

One side believes very fervently that mankind's destiny is too valuable to be compromised by the unknowable agendas of mysterious aliens, and has set its not-inconsiderable resources to synthesizing the alien technology for use in the defense of Earth. The ideological rift has widened to open warfare, with every group choosing a side and staking out a claim for the future of humanity.

But on which side did my father align himself with? On this question the voices were mysteriously silent.

I saw images of nebulae and galaxy, distant interstellar architecture on a scale far grander than the human mind can comprehend. These are the distances which no temporal body can overcome, and which can only be surpassed and mastered by mind. I felt the agony of oblivion, the cold aching supremacy of scale on a supra-rational scope.

I tossed and turned in my sleep, screaming into the silent night. How long was I imprisoned? I felt that certainly days had passed, long days of captivity and deprivation. I had been given no food or water, and the pangs of hunger were hard upon my body. The heat never abated, and I began to fear dehydration.

Sleep came unbidden. I feared the voices as I feared the grave, hard and unyielding reminders of intoxicating madness. Certainly a part of me desired to dismiss the voices as mere insanity, the product of a delusional mind, but to do so would ultimately have been to call into question every component of my quest to date. I was unprepared to take that final step, not after I had already lost so much to come so far.

Visions of Joanne appeared before me, and Constance and Lauren as well. All women I had loved, in my way, although I had come to loathe the latter and mourn the former. But love was beyond me, as I stood on the precipice of monumental discovery. I knew that ultimately I had chosen a life of danger, and those near me had already suffered. My father had taken great risks in siring me, and I was unwilling to perpetuate those risks on another generation.

I dreamt of death, and the pervasive stink of mortality filled my senses.

A small child clutching a stuffed rabbit is escorted to a waiting car. The car is connected to a series of pulleys and levers, which when activated send the car hurtling into a specially-erected concrete wall. The child is instantly killed, her bones liquefied by the force of the impact.

I'm a Jewish man in Poland, 1944, pale skin hanging from brittle bones held together by sinews and spite. I'm in a camp and I feel tired and hungry every hour of the day. I sit down for one moment to catch my breath and I wake up in a crematory, the intense flame eating into my body and melting my emaciated tissues. I die and disperse, a thousand particulates of ash in the cold October night.

I am sealed in a coffin, dead and decaying . . . I pound the lid and scratch at the wood until my fingers are raw and bleeding. I scream until my lungs are raw, and I fall in and out of consciousness. My fingers are covered in blood, and

I don't know where the dream ends and reality begins.

I'm trapped in the mental asylum again, my body restored to childhood dimensions and my mind not yet inured to the perpetual instability of chronic mental illness. I'm running through the halls and the nurses are following me and trying to restrain me from hurting myself but I don't want to have anything to do with the because I'm afraid of them and I don't want to be sick anymore.

I'm in a laboratory just like the one in Berkeley - maybe it is in Berkeley. There are bits and pieces of meat scattered around the room, pieces of men cut and spliced in haphazard fashion. The floor is dull gray tile, just like a shower stall. There is a very slight slant to floor, and I realize that the incline carries down to a drain in the center of the room. That is where the blood flows, and the scientists hose the floor every night.

The scientists are covered in white linen uniforms, stained and spattered with the blood of their victims. They've been working for months, trying all this time to piece together the architecture of their perfect vessel.

I look down at the table at one of the half-formed bodies and I see familiar faces staring back at me. Mohamed Atta is half-complete, with his familiar, placid disdain already firmly cemented. His arms are still misshapen, with rough stitching still in place to attach ligaments and musculature. He's waiting for his legs to be completed and attached.

They've also got Ahmed al Ghamdi and Nawaf al Hazmi in various stages of construction on the tables. There are bodies everywhere, dismembered and organized by shape and size, chunks of flesh sewn together and discarded in large bins at the corners of the room. This is the Devil's workshop, and these are his instruments.

When the bodies are finished they will insert warm and supple brains that have been carefully conditioned for maximum subservience. These drones won't have a long shelf life, but that will hardly matter. They will exist in a state of perpetual ecstasy, buoyed by the artificial opiates coursing through their systems from the moment of their creation. The pain centers of their brain will have been deactivated, ensuring that their patchwork bodies will feel no discomfort. The massive amount of antibiotics required to prevent total systems failure and physical disintegration would prove toxic for anyone else, but these specimens won't live long enough to suffer the effects of a ravaged liver.

The scene shifts and I'm floating in the air above Colorado. People are running and screaming across the rolling fields and green hillocks surrounding Columbine high school. This is the universal perspective, the scene as seen from the helicopter circling above, broadcasting the image to television screens across the country. The incident will spark a redundant debate on gun safety and violent media, while the true causes will be ignored due to the invisible hand of clandestine conspiracy. No doctor will ever be allowed to examine the bodies and find the impossible chemical compounds in the gunmen's bodies, the strange, otherworldly compounds with only a vague resemblance to any known opiates.

Nothing else can explain the inexplicable. The inhumanity of violence, the moral repugnance of fanaticism and hatred - these are not ideas that can be easily reconciled. They can't explain the fundamental connections and invisible perceptions that undergird the tragic events in our lives. There has to be a connection, there has to be a revelation - or nothing makes sense.

I'm a cloud over Oklahoma in late April - drifting through the impossibly high skies and looking down on the incredible destruction wrought by one bomb on one building. Acres and acres of rubble and wreckage in every direction, ruined homes and shuttered businesses.

There are people everywhere, crawling across the wreckage, looking desperately for survivors and bodies and evidence, men with dogs, specialized search & rescue teams assembled from across the country. There are volunteers, hundreds of them, from nearby military bases and businesses, policemen and firemen doing their duties, civilians. There is more food than a thousand workmen could ever eat, an incredible, futile gesture of palliation. The volunteers accept with gratitude, even if their entire world has been shaken to the core by the events of the preceding week. They are covered in dust and dirt and blood, the brave and eager dogs' paws are broken and cut from the wreckage. The volunteers are helpless, they can never be consoled. They cannot resurrect the dead, they cannot make the madness less real, the madness will haunt them until they die.

I can't remember anything after a certain point. The visions become too intense, the associations too painful. The darkness inside my eyelids is brighter than the darkness in my prison. I could have been trapped for a week or a month, the only way I knew I was still alive was the fact that I still felt pain - the pain of incessant hunger, the pain of bleeding hands as I railed against the walls of my prison in an unformed stupor. Nothing else made any sense, but the beating of my heart and the pulse of electric pain in my extremities gave me a way to record the passage of time, second by second slipping away out of my fingers and into the darkness.

More than anything I wanted to shut out the voices I heard from afar, the strange demonic presences who broadcast their grim and ghastly imagery directly into my mind. There was nothing I could do to save myself from falling into the gravity of these obscene disclosures. I didn't care whether the voices were real or imagined, I just wanted them to stop.

But before they stopped, there was one more thing for me to see.

25

The morning was bright and clear. Summer still hung in the air, despite a slight beckoning breeze that hinted towards the onset of fall. The leaves had yet to turn in New England. The faded greens and yellows of the spring and summer would shift almost overnight into lush browns and reds and sepias. Of course, every leaf that fell would eventually need to be raked, but that was a thought for another day.

He woke with the dawn, boiled a pot of coffee in the kitchen and ate a bagel. He didn't have time for an elaborate breakfast, and he knew he'd be hungry before lunchtime.

His wife was still sleeping, smiling contentedly as she nestled between the sheets. He crept into the bedroom and kissed her on the cheek without waking her as she slept - a neat trick, he always thought.

His small suitcase had been packed the previous night, deposited next to the front door along with his briefcase. The man was getting to be an old hand at this kind of travel, and repeated jaunts had taken the edge off what had been a jittery and nervous pre-flight ritual. When you rarely fly, he thought, it can be an exciting and nerve-wracking event - but when you fly twice a week, it gets old.

The commute into Boston is always a bear. There's a small bit of guilt in the back of his brain, bewailing the fact that he has never had the strength of convictions necessary to submit to the rigors of public or semi-public transportation. But, of course it's easy to ignore white guilt when you've worked hard and can afford a nice car.

He parks his car and boards the shuttle to the terminal. It's a long ride in through the vast network of roads and pathways surrounding the terminals at Logan, but eventually he is deposited at the American pavilion. A glance at his watch and the white-and-gold face tells him that it's 6:50, meaning that he is right on time.

There's a small line at the counter which he gets to skip, in favor of the first-class ticket agent - one of the few luxuries afforded the business traveler in this misbegotten age. He remembered just a few years ago when they predicted that no one would ever have to take another business trip after the digital revolution had its way with us. But here we are, and it seems like he's traveling now more than ever. The personal touch must be more important than most of the efficiency experts had imagined. He knew that these trips were probably the lease effective use of his time possible, so there had to be some sort of rationalization for them. They certainly weren't very fun.

The suitcase is tagged and taken at the gate, and he's got his boarding pass in the breast pocket of his dark, off-the-rack Brooks Brothers suitcoat. Still only 7:05, there's still time to grab a donut before the flight.

He boards flight 11 for Los Angeles at 7:20, after eating a large cinnamon bun and drinking another cup of coffee. He is feeling slightly depressed despite the relative uneventfulness of his morning, a twinge of anxiety cutting through the fugue of airport purgatorium. Morning travel just doesn't agree with him. He had a seat near the front of the plane, with only two rows standing between him and the cockpit area.

He had purchased two magazines at the terminal newsstand, an issue of "The New Yorker" and an issue of "Playboy" wrapped in shiny cellophane - the latter of which he did not intend to open until he had landed in California and checked in to his hotel room. It was a small and petty luxury, another of those perks he accorded himself while traveling.

In the twenty minutes or so until the plane takes off he

busies himself studying the entertainment listings that occupy the first twenty pages of "The New Yorker". He was always on the lookout for something that his wife would find interesting. They weren't together lately as often as he would like, and small trips to see Broadway shows or rock concerts were really the least he could do in exchange for her patience.

The plane is sealed and the captain speaks over the intercom - the same boilerplate speech every time. The plane begins to move and he replaces the magazine in his briefcase. He wouldn't be able to concentrate on anything until they were in the air - the massive, involuntary movement of take-off made him slightly nauseous, to tell the truth.

In just a few moments the plane moves across the great swaths of concrete that mark the airport runways and has already begun the run up to take-off. Absent-mindedly he watches the ground recede and the plane gain altitude over the distant city, growing ever smaller in the forced perspective of their incredibly fast ascent. It always made his heart skip a beat, which he realized was due to the pressures exerted by additional Gs during acceleration, but which was a breathtakingly majestic association nonetheless.

The plane has rose almost to its cruising altitude when he reaches down to find his briefcase. He is distracted, however, by a strange jostling in the next rows up. Two men who had been seated in the second row - right in front of him - rise from their seats and walk to the front of the plane. There were two stewardesses seated towards the front of the plane, near the cockpit, in the small pantry stocked with sodas and juice. The two men lunge into the pantry and there are noises of a vain and brief struggle - banging and a muffled scream.

The man rises in his seat in order to get a better view of what is happening. There's not a lot of room to maneuver -

even in first class he could do no more than crouch under the overhanging baggage compartments. First class bought legroom, not headroom. He sees the two stewardesses sprawled on the floor, clutching their sides as if they had been stabbed, gasping for breath and too scared to scream. One of the men who had stabbed them is standing over them, oblivious to their suffering, rifling through their pockets looking for something.

He turns his head and sees two men rising from their seats in business class, just behind first. They both produce weapons to match those of their compatriots - box cutting knives, like the kind used in warehouses - and run up the aisle towards where their fellows have incapacitated the first two flight attendants. The plane isn't full, and there aren't many people in first class who could present much of a challenge to the imposing men with the makeshift knives. In addition to the man there were a few other business passengers, older and obviously terrified by the brief struggle.

Another man who had been seated in business rose to follow the two men with knives. But this one was different - the four men with the knives had the dark, olive-skinned complexion of Middle Easterners, but this other man was fair. He rose up from his seat and lunged forward at the two men in the aisle.

It was cramped quarters. The two men turned slowly to face the third right at the moment he reached them, striking with his fist against the nearest of the attackers. The man he struck - the side of his fist, flat on the side of the head - fell sideways across a seat as the other man brandished his knife towards the interloper.

But it was over before it began. A fifth assailant appears from behind the interloper. The man, who had been situated a row or two behind the action in business, sneaks up behind him and grabs his head. In the moment it takes for the interloper to register the presence of another attacker, the new attacker has pulled the blade of his small knife across the man's throat. The blood spurts across the inside of the cabin, a robust geyser. The would-be hero's limp and twitching body is thrown across an empty seat.

The three from business class join their fellows at the front of the plane. The first two pull a key-ring from the pocket of one of the stabbed stewardesses. They open the door to the cockpit and three of the hijackers enter silently.

All this had occurred in less than thirty seconds - a well-planned and executed coup, executed seamlessly but for the brief intervention of an unexpected Samaritan, now dead. There are muffled yells from the cabin as the captains are assaulted - the door is closed. No one sees whether the men die valiantly or are ambushed. However the captains are dispatched, it is quick and decisive. The hijackers have control of the plane.

The two hijackers who had stayed outside of the cabin begin yelling at those passengers who remain in first class and business to get up and move backwards in the plane, in broken English and excited Arabic, using the force of their convictions to carry their sentiment. One of the older men rises and moves towards the hijackers, some sort of action in his mind, but both hijackers produce cans of mace and spray it indiscriminately around the first class cabin. The man begins to cough and his eyes are watering.

There is are a few isolated English phrases scattered through the exhortions - "Move back," "Get back", "Motherfuckers". Those remaining in first class and business cover their faces and stream back to coach. The man who had been closest to the action pulls one of the stewardesses up from the ground and drags her out of first class - she has lost a lot of blood and was now coughing from the mace in the air. The other stewardess rose on her own power. She didn't seem to have been injured as severely.

The partition that separated coach from business and first

class had effectively screened the conflict from the rest of the plane. The handful of passengers who had been in the upper sections and seen the conflict streamed back in confusion, a few of them coughing and crying from the mace. Nothing anyone said seemed to make any sense.

The man lifts the bleeding stewardess into an empty seat near the front of coach. He reaches over to the next seat and finds a blanket, which he folds and presses against the wound on her abdomen. She has already lost a great deal of blood and is very pale, with sweat pouring down her face.

One of the stewardesses from the back of the plane sees him and makes her way to the seat where he was attending to the wounded girl. They exchange a look of grim disbelief. He leans over to the new stewardess and whispered in her ear, very softly:

"I think we're being hijacked."

The stewardess nods her assent. She reaches up and pulls down one of the oxygen masks that are ever ready to fall down in the case of an emergency and straps it to the wounded stewardesses face. She is in and out of consciousness.

The man wonders why there isn't more panic. Certainly, there was an uproar when the passengers had escaped to coach from first class - but the stewardesses were quick to assess the situation and circulate the cabin reassuring the passengers that there is a routine medical emergency at the front of the plane, and stress that the situation is under control. A few of the flight attendants busy themselves with medical supplies.

It doesn't take long for the passengers to realize that something outside the purview of a medical emergency is happening. This is evident from the way the plane is bobbing and weaving in the air. The man glances down at his watch and sees that it is 8:26.

There are frantic whispers throughout the cabin, to the effect that a bomb has been smuggled onboard and that they have been hijacked. The flight attendants are valiantly trying to stem the rising tide of panic as the plane continued to pitch from side to side. Is there a doctor onboard, they ask?

The man keeps the blanket pressed against the stewardess' wound, but the blanket is small and it is soon soaked. His fingers are red and sticky. Her breathing has become shallow and faint. She is dying.

All the man can think of is a movie he had seen on television once, a made-for-TV movie about one of those hijackings that had happened during the 80s. The plane had been hijacked by terrorists in hopes that certain demands would be met, the passengers held hostage by the terrorists as bargaining chips. Some of the passengers were released, he thought, but maybe some of them had been killed in the crossfire. The United States never negotiates with terrorists - he had seen that in a movie too, and wonders whether or not it is true.

Invariably these things ended badly. Either they would be used as collateral to gain the release of a political prisoner, or against the withdrawal of Israel from certain territories, or they would be held captive in Iran or Syria or any number of countries with unfriendly diplomatic ties to the United States.

After the initial waves of panic recede, the cabin is quiet. Some passengers begin to cry, softly - children blubbering into their mothers' arms and young girls staring out the portholes with bewilderment. The plane continues to bank and weave, and it seems as if they are losing altitude as well. They are going a lot faster than they were supposed to be.

The hijackers are still situated at the front of the plane, holding their knives in front of them and rocking on the balls of their feet. They haven't ventured back into the coach section, they are content to protect the cockpit doors. They are crying as well, from what the man can see through the curtain that separates the sections, probably from the mace particles still floating around the cabin.

He looks at his watch - it was 8:43.

One of the flight attendants who has been circulating the cabin stops at the front of coach, near where the man and the dying stewardess are situated. She has loosened her necktie and she is sweating. The cabin pressure was odd, everyone was starting to sweat. She was speaking on a cellular phone.

"Something is wrong," she says. "We're in a rapid descent." Her voice remains calm and quiet despite the circumstances. She was fielding information to a third party, who knows where . . . what could they do? How could they help them?

The thought crosses his mind for the very first time that perhaps this is not going to be the hostage crisis that he has imagined. Perhaps he should have done something before it was too late. Perhaps he had underestimated the situation. Perhaps they had no intention of selling us as bargaining chips to free some Palestinian political prisoner.

"We are flying low," she says. She rises and leans over to one of the windows. "We are flying very, very low. We are flying way too low."

The man looks out the window and sees New York City looming below them. It is a beautiful sight, despite the circumstances, with the sun low on the Atlantic horizon and the steel buildings glimmering in the sunlight. Everywhere below him he could see the city, thousands and millions of residents going about their business, driving and walking to work across concrete streets. Wasn't there an election today? He seemed to recall having heard something about a municipal election in New York.

He regretted that he hadn't woken his wife to say good-bye. He regretted that they had never had children, that they had never traveled as widely as they wanted, that they had never been to Paris.

He regretted that he had cheated on her last summer at that company retreat, and that most likely she would never know, or if she did that it would be broached in an unbelievably unpleasant way. He regretted that he hadn't spoken to his brother in five years. He regretted the laundry he had left unfolded in a basket on the living room couch.

The stewardess is standing over him, in the aisle. All the blood has drained out of her face as she looks out the window at the city speeding up towards them. The wounded stewardess is unconscious, barely breathing, almost dead. The man is still holding the towel against her abdomen with his right hand, but he realizes that it's really not necessary anymore.

"Oh my God we are way too low."

She spoke these last words and lowered the phone. The man reached up and clutched at her free hand, squeezing it tightly with his clean left hand. She looked down on him and smiled weakly - despite the circumstances, she was beautiful.

In an oddly distant fashion, the man reflected that he might be able to take in a show after all -

26

I wake up in a dumpster, reclined on bags of slop from a restaurant kitchen with my head pillowed by a soggy cardboard box. My stomach aches and I feel dizzy. I am so thirsty my throat cannot produce sound.

Lifting myself out of the dumpster I fall to the ground, my legs weak and unable to stand. My fingers are raw and covered in dried blood. But to my amazement my fingers are clenched around my duffel bag, and a quick examination proves that the contents are intact - my notebooks, my guns and my bankroll untouched. The bag of John's comic books is there as well. The Colorado

Rockies hat that is lined with the magic tinfoil to ward off the voices from the other realm is back upon my head.

The sounds of the city surround me, and I am engulfed in urban drama before I am aware of where I am. I stumble out of the alleyway where I awoke and onto the street. Passersby recoil at my appearance.

There is a hot-dog stand fifty feet down the street. I stumble along the sidewalk until I reach it, peeling a ten-dollar note from my bankroll and gesturing towards the bottled water. He hands me a cool plastic bottle and I am pouring the liquid down my throat as fast as I can tear the lid off. I am so hungry but I know I can't eat anything until I am hydrated again, and even then I will have to be careful.

If I am dehydrated, the thought occurs to me, I should probably go to the hospital. But then again, whomever is trying to get me would undoubtedly be able to find me if I checked into the hospital. I shall have to take it easy.

I down three bottles of water in just a few minutes. The liquid lubricates my throat, until I am able to forces a few ragged syllables through the cavity.

"Where -" I cough a few times. The hot dog vendor is simultaneously appalled by and curious at my spectacle. He seems to be implying that I'm warding off other customers, but I don't care. "Where am I?"

"Where are you? What do you mean?"

"I mean - where the fuck am I?"

"You're on Broadway. See the theaters?" He gestured outwards to the street, and sure enough, there were theaters, broad shiny marquees and huge billboards elevated across the surface of the buildings' exteriors.

"Broad - you mean, this is New York?"

The hot-dog man looks at me as if I was mad, which, it occurs to me, is probably a safe assumption from his point of view. I turned my head upwards and the buildings rose up to pierce the sky, tall and massive and powerful chunks of institutional granite hewn by the ancestors of our race.

"I . . . I didn't know where I was, is all."

I turn away, trying not to mutter loudly. If I was in New York, I had been cooped up for over a thousand miles of driving . . . it had to have been longer than that. It felt like forever.

Standing in the middle of the street and talking to myself, I realized that I made quite a spectacle. My hair was wild, I hadn't shaved in a week and a half, there was a bloody sore on the back of my head, I smelled of garbage, I had pissed my pants recently, and I was wearing a Colorado Rockies hat with what appeared to be ripped tin-foil peaking out from under the brim. If I had seen me, I would have been suitably unimpressed.

But there would be time enough for a shower and a shave later. I had come three thousand miles across the country and my goal was now only a few hundred yards away.

The World Trade Center was situated at the far end of Manhattan island. I knew that I just had to keep walking south on Broadway and I would come to it - the street bisected the island. I didn't anticipate any trouble finding the ruins. "All roads lead to Rome".

There's a newspaper stand on the sidewalk. The headline of the New York Times reads "MID-EAST RECONSTRUCTION BEGINS". I glance at the photo there's a picture of refugees, huddled on the shores of the Galilee - women with black scarves wrapped tightly around their heads, holding starving children and staring into the camera. There's a smaller headline underneath that reads: "CONGRESS VOTES ON BURMESE WITHDRAWL".

The crowds of tourists and businessmen and delivery persons steered clear of me. I was a shambling mess, but I walked with a purpose that belied my absolute dishevellment. I keep my head down, trying very hard not to be distracted by any impressive landmarks. It all recedes behind me.

It didn't take very long at all. I don't know what I had been expecting, but it certainly wasn't an easy stroll down the street. There were no cars following me, no double agents hidden behind newsstands, no low-flying helicopter chases. I walked the half-dozen blocks to Vesey St, turned right and followed the street until it stopped at the intersection with Church. I crossed the road and I was there.

I put my hands up and grabbed onto the chain-link fence which surrounded the site. Steeling myself, I opened my eyes once again and stared down into the abyss.

But there was nothing there. What was I expecting? I don't know - a giant red "X" written on the ground, the mark of buried treasure? There was nothing there. It was a hole in the ground, filled with the temporary edifices of construction companies, teeming with bulldozers and pickup trucks and tiny workers rushing across like ants in the summer heat. There was nothing left, nothing at all to signify what had been.

There would be a memorial, later. But nothing from the actual event remained, no momento to stand as requiem. There were flowers placed at random points along the fence, poking through the holes, sometimes attached to homemade cards. But the significance of these small curios was as unmistakable as it was intimate. The survivors made their own memorials, the dead could not be consoled. The meaning we gave to these rituals was only ever what we provided ourselves, and I felt nothing.

"Something of a disappointment?"

I turned towards the voice. A man was standing on the sidewalk only five feet away. He had come up while I was lost in reverie, sliding softly behind me. He was wearing a white suit and a white shirt, open to the collar. He was an older man, with a few small scars on his face and his thinning hair slicked back. He carried the air of one who is accustomed to money and the trappings of money.

When I was younger there was a photograph on my bureau of a young man with almond eyes and dark brown hair, a slightly rakish grin and a muscular torso heaving underneath a thin T-shirt. He's hugging my mother and I can't quite understand the mixture of emotion on his face, even after all these years - joy was undoubtedly there, but mixed and tempered with a distance, regret and sadness. I don't remember ever loving my mother but this man in the photo did, once. This man in the photo, whose face I had almost forgotten, stood before me now - a couple decades older, but amazingly preserved.

"Dad." The syllable left my mouth before I was aware, escaping the lips before the thought had even managed to coalesce. It was a fearful and portentous word, and suddenly everything changed.

"You're alive."

He smiled. "You noticed! I'm glad."

"But . . . how -"

"Don't. Just - don't. I know you must have a million questions, but if you think about it, everything should make sense. I'm glad you made it."

"I almost didn't."

"That is doubtful. Every step of your trip was very carefully monitored to prevent any unexpected meddling - of course, we couldn't prevent everything, as you saw. But you handled yourself well."

The traffic whizzed by on Church, oblivious to the drama on the sidewalk. I wondered where my father had come from.

"You've been . . . pulling strings?"

Again, he laughed. It wasn't the happy sound I remembered, there was something harsh and ascetic in the noise.

"Pulling strings? No, no . . . I haven't been pulling strings. I tell the people who pull the strings which way to make the dolls move. I pay the puppeteers, if you want to use such a clumsy metaphor. Only a dozen people on the face of the planet know who I am, and only half of those know that I'm still alive. You are the seventh, I think."

"But why?"

"Because I had to be dead. The last decade has been very busy for me: things are beginning to come together that have been in the planning stages since before my grandfather was born. It just happens that I'm the one who happens to be alive to see these plans come to fruition - this last week has been incredibly busy. Those plans left little room for maneuvering, so unfortunately my little hideaway vacation life with your mother and you had to be terminated as quietly as possible. If my enemies thought me dead, they would have had little reason to try to learn if I had any children lying around. I think I did a pretty good job of keeping it all under my hat, actually - although I did have some friends."

"The one-eyed man."

"Who? Oh, yes - Werner. He never told you his name? His name was Werner Louis. I met him in Egypt in 1978. He was perhaps my best friend in the world - I will miss him."

"Could you have saved him?"

"Saved him? No, unfortunately - he didn't have an eye for the big picture, you could say. When he understood what his role was to be in the endgame, he balked, and you saw the unfortunate results of that. If it makes you feel better, he thought he was trying to protect you."

"But - he saved my life. Adam was trying to kill me."

"Yes, it looked like that, I suppose - Adam was overzealous. He was somewhat driven. He'd been involved in the experiments too long to simply just slide back into field work, and I should have recognized that. But he was essentially a good man -"

"He killed Joanne."

He blinked, didn't say anything. After a moment seemed to remember.

"Oh yes, her . . . nothing for it, I'm afraid. You can do better than that. That's why we spent all those years promoting Constance - don't you prefer her? Aren't you eager to marry her? She really is perfect for you."

I turned and stared at the pit again, trying to discern some meaning in the mass of construction tents which I had missed, some secret that would help me navigate these betrayals.

"Anyway," he said after a long, slightly uncomfortable pause, "I'm glad you're here. I couldn't come to you directly, you understand that. I knew that if I wanted my son I would have to wait for you, lay out the clues and see if you were clever enough to find them. You would have to want to fine me. But - you did and you have. You're here. We can be together again. You're my son, and now I can train you to follow in my footsteps. Everything is coming together. I can't tell you how happy -"

"Why did they all have to die?" I spun around, gesturing wildly and yelling. I realized after another moment that I was crying.

"Who? Who died now?"

"Them!" I pointed down into the pit, where the twin towers of the World Trade Center had once stood.

"Oh . . . them. Well, I don't suppose there's anything I can say that could put it into context for you now. But it was for the best - it had to happen. Once you're with me and learn the ropes you'll understand just why that is, I can't just explain it to you in a moment -"

"Then don't bother." I looked at him for a moment, tears streaming down my face. "I don't want to hear it - I can't believe it."

"I'm sorry, but that's the truth. We're almost to the end. We've won - we've got the bastards on the run. Everything is coming together. It looks ugly now, but when you put it all together in the aggregate it is going to blossom into something so wonderful -"

"No, you're lying. There's nothing worth this, nothing that explains or justifies this. I thought . . . I grew up thinking you were a hero, that you died fighting to save the world - but that was just a lie. You're nothing. I want nothing to do with you."

His eyes narrowed and his lips pursed. He was angry, but retained the self control necessary to keep his composure.

"If you go now, you will never see me again. I will never contact you, I will be dead to you again, and there will be no second chances."

"Did you do this?" I turned and waved at the hole again. "Did you send those monsters to do this?"

He looked hurt, and slightly bemused, as if he were not in the habit of having to explain himself.

"Yes," he said, simply.

"Then I am not your son, not any longer."

"Fine." He drew in a deep breath, and exhaled. "I'm sorry this had to happen, especially after you've worked so hard. But I suppose we all must live with ourselves. I sleep just fine, in case you were wondering." A bold hauteur had crept into his voice.

As he spoke, a white limousine rolled up to the curb. A chauffeur emerged from the cabin, walking around the car and opening the door for my father to re-enter.

"When I die, providing you are still alive, you will receive a small disbursement from my estate. Do not try to find me again."

He entered the limousine, but before he closed the door he called after me.

"One more thing. An associate requested I pass this package on to you - he suspected that you would decide as you have. He wanted me to give this to you either way . . . he said you would understand."

He held out a small unmarked package wrapped in

brown paper and bundled together with string. I took it and he left, the limo pulling into traffic and disappearing into Manhattan.

I threw the bundle into my duffel bag and set off down the street. I was going home, but first I had to find a hotel.

There had been a nice one just a block or so up from the site, but they didn't want to let me enter looking as I did. I peeled off a hundred dollars for the doorman and they arranged to have me enter through the service door. I paid in cash and arranged to have a fresh change of clothes sent up to my room.

I stripped and threw my clothes into a pile near the door - I would have to throw them out. I crawled into the shower and the filth poured off my skin in massive waves. I had sweat, bled, pissed and cried enough in the past week for a platoon, and all this effluvia came off my body and threatened to clog the drain. I shaved as well, ridding myself of the week-old beard I had accumulated. Bathing was a difficult proposition, as it mandated the removal of my hat for limited periods of time - but the sensory stimulation of water and soap on my body enabled me to focus on keeping my bearings.

After I had showered I drank more water, as I was still weak, and ordered a hamburger and french fries from room service. I tried to eat just a few fries at first, but greed overcame me and in no time at all I ate the whole burger. This was a mistake, as I soon threw up most of the lunch. But, it had at least been momentarily satisfying.

After I had fumigated my mouth with antiseptic rinse and breath mints, I collapsed into the bed. The curtains were pulled shut, and with no lights on the room approximated a natural moonless twilight. I fell instantly into a deep and hearty slumber, with the taste of pomegranate - lingering from the mouth wash - faintly but distinctly on my lips.

27

I rose after eighteen hours of dreamless sleep, showered again and pulled on a fresh pair of slacks and a clean white shirt. My old clothes were bound for the incinerator.

Stopping in the lobby for a haircut, I was forced to take off my hat. Standing in the middle of New York is a profoundly unpleasant experience for a psychic, especially one unable to protect himself - just the twenty minutes required to trim my hair was almost too much for my fragile focus.

Before I boarded the shuttle to the airport, I had the foresight to place the guns I had accumulated in a small cardboard Federal Express box, unloaded and padded with newspaper. They would probably reach home before I did.

Once I reached the airport I bought a seat on the quickest flight home I could find. As I imagined, airport security were suspicious regarding the fact that I wished to pay in cash for an immediate flight, but I acquiesced to every security measure they introduced. In the end they could produce no satisfactory reason disallowing me to board the flight I desired.

Before leaving the airport I sent a telegram to my mother, instructing her to pick me up at the airport. I had no desire to hear her voice again before it was absolutely necessary.

The flight was long and boring. This vast country, which had taken the sum of my perambulations for the preceding weeks, passed under my feet in the course of a brief eight-hour plane ride. Our flight had to detour around eastern Pennsylvania airspace, for vague reasons relating to events which had occurred during my imprisonment.

I pulled John's comic books out of my duffel, as I had neglected to buy anything else for the flight. The package from my father sat menacingly in my bag, but I hadn't any desire to open it anytime soon.

"The Star Brand" was certainly one of the odder books I had ever read. The plot of the series concerned a young man, Ken Connell, who gains god-like powers seemingly at random, at the whim of a strange and mysterious old man. The problem is that Connell doesn't know what to do with his powers: he doesn't live in a world with superheroes and villains, he is merely a normal guy living in 1980s Pittsburgh.

Most superhero comic books are filled with action: fighting and interpersonal conflict. These books carried a peculiar weight because the narrative focus was inaction and stasis, as Connell spent his days wrestling with the moral and ethical issues implicit in being the most powerful person on Earth. It sounds more sophisticated in explication than execution, but the books still managed to carry a compelling naturalistic heft due to the unambitious, strikingly mediocre nature of their protagonist. Over the course of about a dozen issues he tries everything his limited imagination can conceive in order to wield the power wisely, finally attempting to rid himself of it - and this last act of irresponsible abdication destroys Pittsburgh and kills millions of people.

I have to admit that despite the ad-hoc nature of the books - these were obviously not top-sellers from the way the creative teams varied every issue - they were still memorable. Superman and Spider-Man never fail, not really, and seeing someone fail so horribly and irrevocably when faced with the responsibility of great power served as a sobering conclusion to a decidedly downbeat series.

I dozed in my seat and my dreams were black and inky, full of water and marked by panic. The ocean is rising around me and I am drowning, the sun is gone and the stars are distant.

On the second leg of the journey, from Salt Lake City in a quick jaunt to Sacramento, I am stuck next to a boorish bachelor who insists on picking my brain about the Kennedy assassination. He's got a dog-eared paperback filled with conspiracy theories and conflicting accounts of malfeasance. Of course, it is in my interests not to appear as strikingly disinterested in the subject as I actually am. I merely reply that I trust implicitly the results of the Warren Report investigations and inquire as to whether or not he has read the report's official findings on the matter, which, as I say, "should be sufficient to clear up any lingering confusion in the matter".

The plane lands in California - Sacramento - and my mother meets me at the gate. She doesn't say anything as I approach, merely begins to cry, putting her arm around me and rocking slowly back and forth, feigning the appropriate rituals of love and relief.

I don't have any luggage. Her car is waiting outside the terminal. We drive in silence for a while before either of us says a word. After a while, when she has allowed the rhythmic monotony of the long drive up Highway 5 to exert an appropriately calming influence on her nerves, she finally speaks:

"Are you OK?"

"Yes," I say, in as bland and noncommittal a tone as I can muster.

"You - you were in Denver?" She motions towards my hat.

"Ah - yes. I passed through Denver."

"How much do you remember?"

I thought for a minute, trying to pick the right words to adequately convey my level of distress.

"More than I wish."

"When did you stop taking your pills?"

"Before I left college, mom."

I can tell she's started to cry. She has this act down well, I think as she wipes the tears away. She must be relieved to see me back, though not for the reasons she pretends - I wonder, how did her overlords explain my absence?

"Do . . . do you want to go back to the hospital?"

"Yes, I think I do. I just have a few things to take care of."

I'm not lying. I fully intend to sign myself back into the institution, and eagerly await the fugue state which the alien mind-control medicine will bring me. My senses have been sharp and keen for so long that I pine for the insincerity of chemical neurasthenia.

"Well, I'm just glad - so relieved - that you are safe and sound. I was so worried."

She's crying again - trying not to seem desperately relieved, or pretending to try to not feel emotions she pretended at.

We arrived in town after a dull five hours, pulling into the driveway in the dead of night. I had been a long day for me - made longer by having gained three hours on the plane - and I was tired.

There was a package leaning against the door of the house. The guns, which I had sent overnight express, had indeed arrived before me.

"What's in the box?" my mother asked as she handed the package to me.

"Something I couldn't carry on the plane."

I felt confident that I could sleep undisturbed. I had already passed through the crucible and emerged on the other side, having failed in my appointed task and returned, relatively unmolested, to the appearance of a banal life. I was of no use to the organizations that wanted my father - or those which my father controlled. I could not discern any difference, if there actually was one - I was out of it all. I would be content to consign myself to a banal and boring existence, shorn of any complicity with the shadow world of my father, save for one more thing.

The day after we arrived home I visited Constance at her home. It was assumed that the wedding was to be discussed no more. The secrets of my past institutionalizations had come out following my disappearance, and although Connie had known of the "problem" and assumed it safely in my past, the full weight of my "problems" made it impossible for her to continue as my fiancé. This gave me no small relief to hear.

But her manner and tone were unnecessarily condescending. I suddenly felt myself as they perceived me to be, or wished me to feel perceived as - a bird egg, fragile and small, ready to be broken at a moment's notice. We made small talk and she grew increasingly uncomfortable as the conversation proceeded. Finally I could avoid it no longer, and brought up the final matter which I had come to discuss with her.

"Connie," I said, in a low and reassuring tone, "I forgive you."

She blanched a moment, blinking twice and feigning befuddlement.

"What are you talking about, honey?"

"You don't have to call me honey. It's OK. I'm glad we've got everything out in the open. I'm going away and all of this will be in the past, or at least we can pretend that it is. For what it's worth, though, I do forgive you."

"Forgive me for what?" She was never one for jewelry but there was a silver bracelet on her wrist - new.

"Don't be coy, it's resolutely unattractive. You don't have to dissemble. I understand what has happened, and I fully declare my defeat. I am going away."

Her face clouded, her words growing strained and particular. She feigned confusion well, although it rankled me to see the denial.

"I . . . I don't understand what you're talking about. I think maybe you need to leave."

"Connie. I am happy to leave, to put you and my mother and all of this in my past, and take your space bugs down my gullet every day and forget I ever knew all about you.

But I would just appreciate - if you could - a little acknowledgment. Just give me the satisfaction of seeing your other face."

She rose in her seat. She was wringing her hands.

"I really think you should leave."

"Come on, just admit it. I just want to see the satisfaction in your smile, you bitch, just give me that much. I'm over, done. I admit it. I just want some admission, which is more than I asked from anyone else."

"You're really scaring me." She shrunk away from me, tears falling on her cheeks as a pitiful quaver snuck so subtly into her voice. I admit I may have raised my voice.

"Just tell me, Connie. Did you ever talk to my dad? Do you get your orders from him?"

"Your dad's dead, he's been dead for ten years. I saw him in the ground. Why are you talking like this?" She was blubbering now, she was really doing a good job. Of course, the more she denied her temerity the angrier I grew.

"No he's not, and you know it. Does he pay you? Or do you get your orders from someone else? My mother? Or was it Werner?"

"Werner? I don't know who Werner is . . . please, just leave me alone, please God I'm sorry."

She's crouching in the corner of her hallway, blubbering like a baby and holding up her hands to protect herself. She's lying and I can't fucking stand it anymore. I reach into my back pocket and pull out the gun I had taken from Adam in Kansas - there are three bullets left in the clip.

"Just tell me, just admit it. Admit and I'll leave, I'll be gone and you'll never see me again. Admit it. Admit it." My voice had risen, I was screaming and hoarse.

"Admit what? I don't know, oh God I don't know what you want -"

I pulled the trigger and emptied the clip into her lying face. Her head exploded backwards, blood and brains and skull splattering across the pristine light pink wallpaper of the Gooding's living room. I stepped backwards and sat on the sofa. I didn't smoke but I felt that this might be an appropriate time to do so.

28

They found me sitting calmly on the living room sofa, holding the gun in my lap. Since there was no reason to pretend that I hadn't done it, I freely admitted that I had.

Things proceeded, as I would have expected, fairly swiftly from that moment. I was taken into custody with minimum fuss. There was no interrogation at first because I made no attempts to deny that I had shot her. When they asked me why I had done it I merely said that she had been lying - I was confident that the appropriate people would understand. As they took me into custody they removed my hat but I was able to have it restored after I informed them that without it I would be driven mad by the unending cacophony of voices in my head.

I asked for newspapers, telling them I wished to catch up on the last two weeks of news. They complied. I was somewhat shocked to find no references to the catastrophic events which had occupied the news for the preceding weeks of my travels. The headlines involved budget disputes and banal crimes - no massive geopolitical upheaval.

Unfortunately, matters were further complicated by a chain of events which I could not control. After I had been in police custody for a few days, they came and questioned me regarding the murders of Morris Singer, Joanne Janesczi and John Long. Of course, I had murdered John, but I could not admit that I had, lest they implicate me in the murders of the other two as well. I knew for a fact that Morris and Joanne had been killed by the same sinister agencies that had pursued me across America.

But they said they had evidence - fingerprints, murder weapons (a bloody knife in my duffel bag) and even witnesses. They drew a picture of my cross-country trip that resembled nothing so much as a drunken binge of terror, full of death and dismemberment and murder and whoring - yes, they even knew about the whore.

As they laid their evidence before me I realized that I was very much screwed. Of course I laughed, I laughed and laughed and laughed because I knew that the Powers That Be - motivated, no doubt, by my father - had tightened the noose around me in such a methodical fashion that even if I had not killed Connie (undoubtedly a happy coincidence for them in terms of tying up loose ends) I would still have been effectively incapacitated. I was going away for a very long time, one way or another.

My mother visited me in the jail a few times but she soon dropped all pretense of maternal affection. Of course, she feigned worry and concern and shame and all those good emotions, but mostly I suspect my imprisonment and impending institutionalization filled her with relief more than anything else. Her assignment was over, and I am sure that whichever agency provided her remuneration had arranged a fat retirement package in return for her having handled me so skillfully.

The only other visitor I received was my friend. He came in his customary spotless suit and tie, dressed impeccably despite the surroundings. His red face seemed pale under the harsh fluorescent lights, but his little horns still twinkled gaily.

"Well," he said, pulling up a chair and sitting in front of the bars, "this is quite the pickle you've gotten yourself into."

"Yeah, isn't it."

"See, my boy, I can't say I'm disappointed in you, because I know that to the very end you followed your heart. I know that you tried your best and you did what you knew to be right - and ultimately you did what you had to do. I respect you so much for that, even if I can't deny that it's a shame to see you end up like this."

"I know you had such high hopes for me. In the end, I know you're the only one who I could ever trust."

"Thank you, my boy . . . that means a great deal to me. I know you resent the machinations of your elders, but I want you to know - for my part - that I never tried to hurt you. Almost everyone else you've ever met has wanted to manipulate you, to push you this way or that, but I only ever tried to give you good advice, and to help you navigate the difficult path life had thrown before you. But . . . my powers are inevitably constrained by circumstances."

"Yeah." I sighed deeply.

"Now, as much as it pains me to say so, I am afraid that this may be the last time you ever see me."

I looked up at my friend, and although I try at all times to keep a tight rein on emotions, I must have broadcast my disappoint rather plainly.

"Unfortunately, you know why this is so. My powers are limited, my abilities circumscribed by context. They've got you back on those damned pills again, and they'll make me invisible to you. As much as I wish it were otherwise."

I mumbled an apology.

"What was that? I didn't hear that . . ."

"I said, I wanted to take the pills."

He looked startled.

"I'm sorry to hear that."

"I'm just sick of it all. I'm sick of being paranoid. I'm sick of feeling so much responsibility, of knowing how the world works and being unable to do anything but watch from a tiny corner. I want the voices to go away, because I just can't deal with them anymore. I am . . . I am eager to be able to regard all of this, all my life to date, as a delusion. I want to be able take my hat off. I'm prepared to sleep for the rest of my life."

"An understandable impulse. It may be for the best . . . really, there's no choice in the matter. I hate to have to say good-bye to you, but I am afraid that you know I must."

He rose and extended his hand to me through the bars. The guard, positioned at the end of the hallway, motioned him to take his hand back. He blanched, and tried to smile. He waved as he walked back down the long hallway. I have never seen him again, although I do not strictly exclude the possibility.

My one hope was that during the arraignment I would be allowed to present my carefully compiled journals to the court - perhaps they would not excuse what I knew myself to have done, but they would at least have offered an explanation, perhaps mitigating circumstances that the judge would look upon favorably.

Before the trial they arranged for me to meet with a psychiatrist. She was, all things considered, a nice lady who honestly seemed to want the best for me despite what she knew and suspected me of being. We spoke at length and I conducted a series of tests at her requests.

I asked to be provided with my journals but when they were presented to me in the presence of the court psychiatrist they were not the same. Oh, they looked identical to the notebooks I had spent years and years filling with the secret minutiae of the grand conspiracy, but when I opened them up and flipped through the pages my neat, tightly-packed handwriting had been replaced by page after page after page of manic scribbling, obscene drawings and nonsensical ramblings.

I explained this to her and she neither seemed surprised or curious - she merely took notes in her book and asked me to elaborate on the contents of my missing notebooks. I also asked her, later, why the news in the newspapers I had been provided had changed, and why the catastrophic events of the preceding weeks had been erased from their pages. Again, she merely wrote in her book and made bland observations.

As I expected, these meetings came to haunt me in court, when the psychiatrist testified that I was clearly insane. To this effect my notebooks, or rather the fake notebooks which had been provided in place of my notebooks, were introduced to the court. Although I testified that they were not mine, I could feel the weight of evidence hanging heavy over my head, as the machinery of the state and all the darker forces above were mobilized to render me invisible and impotent. I was trapped, an un-person, a psychotic madman.

They produced another exhibit in court. The package my father had given me in New York - the paper bundle tied together with string and left unmarked - had been opened by the investigating detectives. They found a pile of "YOUNG MEAT" magazines, accompanied by a fake invoice. The issues in hand were particularly odious, featuring ten and twelve-year-olds in sexual congress with multiple men and women, in addition to various barnyard animals. There was a lot of blood, and one of the detectives said in an editorial aside that he regarded these magazines as the most depraved and violent child pornography he had ever had the misfortune of viewing. It even looked, on close examination, as if one of the magazine's pictorials depicted the death of a young blonde girl about the age of Princess, death by vivisection, graphic sexualized disembowelment. It could have been produced by a computer, but experts differed as to the magazine's actual origins.

I asked the judge why the newspapers made no reference to the kidnapping of the Vice-President or to the nuclear war in Israel, and was answered with stony silence.

My mother made a token appearance to plead with the court for its understanding in light of difficult circumstances. She had lied with skill and verve throughout my entire life, but never before with such willful deprecation of the truth. She wove a complex and emotional story of a scarred and troubled boy, affected by the death of his father and beset by unfortunate mental illness from a young age. She related that even after I had been "stabilized", I still remained unhealthily fixated on disasters such as Oklahoma City and September 11th. She cried before the judge, and her tears would have melted the hardest of hearts - but this was no theater, it was a Grand Guignol. Her tears made me ill.

In light of such evidence as this, it didn't take very long for the judge to decide my case to the detriment of my mental faculties and sign me into a high-security mental institution. Hopefully, he said, successful treatment would allow me to one day feel remorse for my heinous crimes. I told him with all sincerity that I dearly wished for that day to arrive as soon as possible. Once I was declared incompetent my appointed attorney arranged for a plea deal which I would have readily assented to had I been allowed.

I was led out of the courthouse in shackles. A sizable crowd had assembled to see me off. Not a lot happens in small towns, and this was certainly the biggest thing to happen in ours for quite a while. There were many people who had known and loved Connie, who had wondered as to how our relationship had survived in the face of my continuing intransigence. Grimly, they had been vindicated by the turn of events.

There were reporters from the bigger papers, all the way from San Francisco and Portland. It had grown into a three-ring media circus, which did not surprise me in the least. There were flashbulbs and video cameras in my face, and I imagined my face beamed across the country as a small news item from Reuters or the Associated Press - a concise tale of murder, communicated through the enduring prurient interests of the hoi polloi.

As I was escorted to the police cruiser which was to facilitate my departure, I espied two small figures sitting on the opposite side of the street from the courthouse, smoking cigars and waving gaily. It was Mr. Stanford, whom I am certain had arranged for the pornography to be given me, and Adam. Of course, Adam was dead, his brains scattered across a comic book store parking lot in Tulsa, Oklahoma. A large Dixieland band struck up a song behind them, "When The Saints Go Marching In" exploding with the sudden violence of a thunderclap in the clear afternoon.

I threw my head back and laughed, laughed and laughed until I screamed and my voice became hoarse from screaming.

29

When I was young the sun was bright and warm. I walked through fields of flowers and green grass. The breeze rose in the morning and carried pollen down the river, curving slightly towards the sea.

Once I carried rod and reel, fishing in the streams and standing on the riverbanks. There were days, and many more, for field and river in abundance.

Sloping mountain meadows in the crisp clean air, filled with weeds and dandelions swaying in the wind. There are stones and pebbles in the pathway, grinding underfoot.

I could not hold a rod or ford a stream, the palsy in my hand has grown too strong. My dreams are numb and faded, momentos of a scattered time. Trapped by fragile meat and bone, this body serves as prison for my mind and memories.

When I close my eyes I feel that I am young again, and wicked days are yet to come. My feet and legs are small and quick, my hands reach for rocks and climb the tallest trees. The sticky sap of naked pine clings across my hand, the smell of wood and loamy earth around me everywhere. Ants crawl across my forearm in the afternoon, they reek of mint and salt.

Earth and soil, the aroma of age and rot, the weight of ages past and future, pulling me from where I stand and stretching me across the seas of time. The sun is cold and days are short while I remember splendors past.

I am trapped in fog and night, and images fail to coalesce against the backdrop of gray evening. I am weary of confusion, an endless limbo of ever-present now. Causality has escaped my grasp and moments cannot accrue or congeal.

I have in the past spoken words which I now regret, and I have see things which cannot be unseen. The enemy still lurks, crouched in the dusk of perpetual night, waiting for me to stumble. I do not wish to be alone, I cannot face the days ahead.

I feel that I have lost something, that something vital has been replaced by something soft and yielding. I try to read and the pages fade in memory until I am lost, wandering a labyrinth that offers no solution. The intricacies of my life are lost in distant shadows.

They put me in a car and drive me away. Adrift in windless seas I wash ashore and stumble awkwardly, I am lost in distant lands. My hands are bound and my feet are tied, I am drugged and left for dead. The weight of my head is too much for me to bear, I slump against the window and stare across the open plains.

We are driving fast across gently sloping hill and dale, the road is smooth and precise. I see mountains in the distance, and trees clumped against the feet of the mountains, naked in the wind.

There are fields and pastures where the cows can eat and rest, the calves are small and tender and they romp throughout the morning. Fields of flowing golden wheat sway gently in the breeze, I am held and captivated by the simple virtues of this land.

While driving through a forest we are overcome by

darkness, the sun disappearing behind a canopy of green and yellow leaves. I close my eyes and I am asleep, held by the rocking rhythm of the car driving slowly up and down the countryside.

But the forest eventually gives way to scattered copses. The car emerges from the thick midday twilight and the sun, high in the afternoon arc, streams down through the leaves as we speed by. The light playing against my eyelids wakes me gently and I am engulfed in light, shining down in a thousand shades of cascading color.

Greens and browns and yellows, auburn and ochre and gold, splintered through a thousand tiny softly swinging prisms as the light from a distant star reflects across the afternoon. I cannot see anything but the light shaking and shining across my face, a kaleidoscope of light and dark that covers me with sweet kisses. I am warm and at peace, and the sun is in the sky.

THE END

timoneil5000@hotmail.com

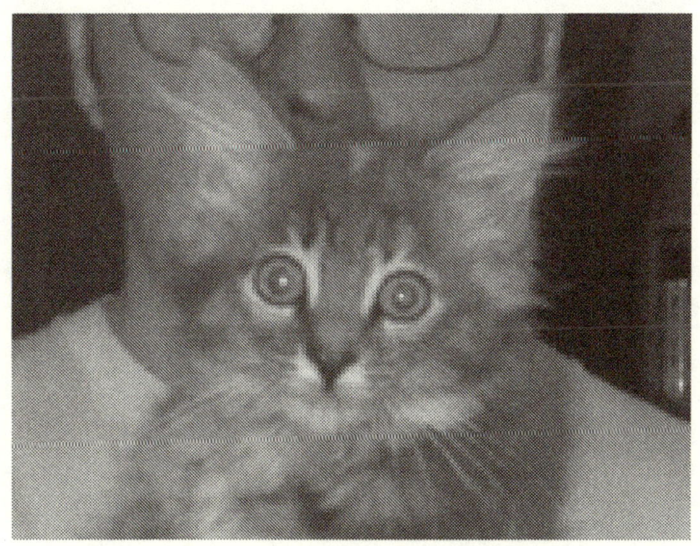

www.ingramcontent.com/pod-product-compliance
Lightning Source LLC
LaVergne TN
LVHW091039080826
845145LV00002B/548

* 9 7 8 0 6 1 5 1 7 7 9 4 6 *